Also by **Rick Mofina**

SIX SECONDS

Coming soon
EVERY FEAR

THE DYING HOUR

RICK MOFINA

MIRA

Published in Great Britain 2009.
MIRA Books, Eton House, 18-24 Paradise Road,
Richmond, Surrey, TW9 1SR

© Rick Mofina 2005

ISBN 978 0 7783 0309 1

58-0909

Printed and bound in Spain
by Litografia Rosés S.A., Barcelona

This book is for Wendy Dudley

He who learns must suffer. And even in our sleep pain that cannot forget falls drop by drop upon our heart, and in our own despair, against our will, comes wisdom to us by the awful grace of God.

—Aeschylus
(525–456 BC),
Agamemnon

1

Karen Harding had to get away.

She was alone, driving from Seattle north on Interstate 5, wipers slapping at the rain as she tried to understand why her fiancé was suddenly forcing her to make a life-changing decision.

Karen brushed her tears away.

Why was he doing this? Luke's change of heart had staggered her. She needed to leave for a few days. To think. After they had spoken she threw some things into a bag, tossed it into her Toyota, and set off to see her big sister, Marlene, who lived in Vancouver. Karen didn't bother calling ahead. This was an emergency. Besides, Marlene would be home. She and her husband rarely left town because of their two kids and their jobs.

The air horn of a Freightliner yanked Karen's attention back to the highway. Her windshield was a watery curtain. Lights from oncoming traffic stabbed at her from the darkness. Big rigs trailed blinding spray as they passed, their wakes nearly swamping her.

Time for a break.

She exited at a truck stop outside Bellingham. A massive map of Washington and British Columbia covered the lobby wall. Below it, a corkboard papered with ads for trucks, bonding agents, and driving jobs. Faces of missing children, women, and fugitive men stared at her from posters. Video games beeped and ponged next to the soda and snack machines.

She was hungry.

In the restaurant, country music mingled with the aroma of deep-fried food and coffee and the clink of cutlery. Amid the murmur of weary men in ball-caps, plaid shirts, and jeans, Karen searched for a seat.

She walked by a woman and a young girl laughing over ice cream, a white-haired couple sharing soft conversation over soup, then a bearded man who wore dark glasses and the white collar of a reverend. He was sitting alone reading a book and sipping coffee. She found a booth by the window and ordered a chicken sandwich.

Wind-driven rain bled against the glass. The truck stop's electrical power surged; the lights flickered. Karen glanced around the diner. The reverend was watching her. He offered a warm smile. Karen tried smiling but looked away.

She ached to talk to her sister, to someone who might offer guidance. Maybe the reverend being there was a sign. Perhaps she could talk to him. Could she confide her dilemma to a stranger? She looked to his booth but he was gone.

Karen noticed the tip left by his coffee cup as the din in the diner grew louder. Those who were on cell phones began alerting others to trouble arising from the storm, a wreck at the border crossing near Blaine.

"A reefer and a loaded tanker," one of them said. "Going to push your wait time way, way back. A couple of hours."

Not good.

Karen needed to reach her sister tonight. She looked at her folded map for an alternative entry into Canada. She'd always crossed at Blaine. She examined the web of roads in Washington's northwest corner. Lynden looked easy enough. Exit northbound on Route 539 at the north end of Bellingham, straight shot to the border. If Lynden was choked, she'd try Sumas.

The storm was unrelenting.

Karen couldn't see much. Gusts rattled her Toyota. She tightened her grip, questioned her sanity, and considered returning to her apartment in Seattle. Or at least finding a motel for the night.

No.

She estimated that she could be at Marlene's home in less than two hours if she was cautious.

But this route made her uneasy. She saw fewer towns, buildings, houses, lights. She pressed on, unable to see the streams, the forested foothills, or the slopes of the Cascade Mountains. But they were out there. Veiled by darkness. As she drove deeper into it, Karen felt alone. Vulnerable. As if she were being swallowed. She switched on her radio to find a jazz station to help her relax.

A warning light began blinking. The low-fuel indicator.

How could that be? It made no sense. She had filled up at the truck stop. Maybe it was faulty? All right. She'd stop at the next gas station. Just to be safe. But there was nothing out there except the wind, the rain, and the night. She kept driving. After a few more miles, more warning lights began flashing. Engine. Oil. Her car began vibrating. The motor sputtered, then began bucking. Karen was jolted.

"Dear Lord."

She pulled over, switched off the ignition, and took a deep breath. *Be calm. Wait ten minutes, start the car, and drive slowly to the nearest gas station.* Ten minutes passed. Karen turned the key. Nothing.

She tried again.

Nothing.

Take it easy. She fished through her bag for her cell phone and address book. She'd call the auto club. But the familiar silver shape of her phone failed to emerge. It had to be there. Karen dumped the contents of her bag on the passenger seat, feeling her stomach tighten. In her hurry to leave Seattle she had forgotten her phone. It was in her apartment. Charging on her kitchen counter.

She closed her eyes. Inhaled, then exhaled slowly. Rain hammered on her car as the wind rocked it. She tried starting it again. Nothing. She reached for the manual and flipped through it, knowing it was futile. She knew nothing about cars.

Karen had no choice, she had to try something. She reached for the hood release. She found her penlight and umbrella. Maybe the trouble was obvious. She got out and a violent gust snapped her umbrella, tearing the cloth, exposing the frame's prongs, like the ribs of an eviscerated animal.

Karen managed to raise the hood. Her tiny light came to life and she probed an alien world of wires, metal, rubber, hoses, and plastic reservoirs with colored fluids. Maybe something had come loose. Right. How would she know? As she reached into the engine to test a cable the road began glowing in intense white light. The hissing rain yielded to a growing roar as a line of several big trucks thundered by, throwing waves of spray that drenched her.

Furious, Karen retreated into her car.

She tossed her twisted umbrella into the backseat, then grabbed the wheel to steady herself. Soaked to her bones, she began shivering. *Don't panic. Think of a plan. Stay in the car. Change into dry clothes.* Maybe a patrol car or Samaritan would stop and call a tow truck or something. If not, she could spend the night in her Toyota. It wasn't too cold. She had a blanket. In the morning, she'd start walking. The next town couldn't be far.

She reached for her clothes bag and stopped. Two white circles blossomed in her rearview mirror. A vehicle had pulled onto the shoulder and was approaching. The lights grew brighter as it crept closer, coming to a stop a few yards behind her. It looked like an RV.

Someone was going to help her.

A door opened on the RV's passenger side and a figure stepped out. A man. Wearing a long overcoat and a hat. He stood at the rear bumper of Karen's car, silhouetted in the glare of his high beams and the curtain of rain. Hope fluttered in her stomach. She wiped her hands across her face and smoothed her wet hair as his shadow crossed the light.

The first thing she noticed at her door was a white collar, and then she recognized the beard and ball cap of the reverend from the truck stop. Relieved, she lowered her window about ten inches.

"Your car giving you trouble, miss?"

Karen hesitated. She couldn't see his face. His voice was grating, a rough whisper.

"Yes, it quit and won't start."

"Is anyone coming to help you?"

"No."

"Let me take a look."

The reverend switched on a flashlight and walked to the front. The hood was still raised. Karen felt him pulling and tapping as he inspected the motor.

"Try starting it now!"

She turned the key. Nothing happened. The front end dipped as he pressed hard on something.

"Again."

Nothing. He closed the hood, returned to the window.

"Smells like something's burned out on you. Could be anything. I've got a phone in my motor home. I can call a service truck for you, if you like."

"Yes, please. Oh, wait." She turned to the passenger seat, sifted through the contents emptied from her bag. "I'm a member of the auto club. Here's their card with the toll-free line."

"Goodness." He swept his flashlight from the card to Karen. "You're sopping wet."

"I tried fixing it myself."

"I can see that. You shouldn't sit here and risk catching cold. You're welcome to wait in the RV until they come."

Karen weighed his offer. He seemed kind. He was a clergyman. She had considered approaching him at the truck stop to talk. Rain poured from his hat as he waited.

"You're a Christian, aren't you, Karen?"

She caught her breath.

"How did you know that, and my name?"

The hat tipped to her club card.

"Your name's on your card here and I noticed you have an *Ichthus* bumper sticker, the fish symbol for Jesus."

"Oh, right." She nodded. "Of course."

"I saw you in the restaurant near Bellingham. You looked troubled."

Karen was half smiling in amazement as she reflected on everything that had happened to her today. She had prayed for help. Was this a sign? A reverend finding her adrift in her personal storm? Was it all part of a master plan?

She collected her things, then followed the reverend

to his vehicle. He opened the door. A few small papers swirled from the RV and fluttered into the night before Karen stepped inside.

2

Len Tolba, a deputy sheriff with Sawridge County, took another hit of coffee and looked toward the morning sun washing over the mountains as he rolled his four-by-four past Laurel, northbound on 539.

Hell of a storm last night.

Top of his shift and he was heading for Lynden to investigate a complaint of local teens who had spray-painted obscenities at the Pioneer Museum.

Tolba shrugged off his frustration.

He was twenty-nine years old and had put in five years with the highway patrol. Not that there was anything wrong with what he was doing. No, sir. Not at all. He enjoyed it and was grateful to serve. But he had more to offer.

Tolba wanted to make detective.

He'd taken courses, studied, saved his comp time to take more classes, and attend seminars out of state. He was ready. On his passenger seat was a well-thumbed copy of the latest homicide investigators' textbook. He'd read it so many times he could damn near recite entire chapters. Still, he knew the only way to be good at a thing was to do it.

Now, rumors were going around that council was going to approve the department's budget to expand the detective division. Tolba figured this would be his chance.

Major crimes happened around here. They got their share of homicides, sex crimes, and arsons, that's for sure. The population was under two hundred and fifty thousand, but a lot of traffic moved through the county. Sawridge was located in Washington's northwest corner, covering 2,120 square miles stretching from Okanagan County in the east, to the Strait of Georgia in the west. From Skagit County on the south, to the Canadian border on the north. It also encompassed some of the most remote regions in America.

Some of it still wild.

Tolba took another sip of coffee and his radio crackled with a call.

"What's your twenty, Len?"

"North on 539, about three or four clicks north of Laurel."

"Got a report of a breakdown or abandoned vehicle. Toyota. Blue. Washington registration. Ready to copy?"

His dispatcher recited the plate number, then put it on his computer.

"Trucker out of Bellingham said he saw it there last night and this morning. He puts it seven miles north of Laurel."

"Likely a breakdown from the storm. I should be coming up on it. There. I see it."

The Toyota sat on a lonely stretch of road that sliced through rolling forests of cedar, hemlock, and Douglas fir. He turned on his emergency lights as he eased up on it.

First things first.

Tolba began typing on his computer keyboard, requesting checks for warrants, theft reports, and information on the owner. His query came back showing nothing outstanding. The car was registered to Karen Katherine Harding of Seattle. Twenty-four years old, according to her date of birth. White female. Brown hair. Blue eyes. Five feet three inches. One hundred ten pounds.

The computer beeped. Karen's driver's license picture appeared on Tolba's screen. Pretty, he thought, peering at her face for a moment before grabbing his clipboard. He checked to ensure that he had an impound notice before getting out to tag the Toyota.

As Tolba closed his door he saw an enormous crow approaching from a treetop. Gliding so near above him as it did, he heard the beat of its wings, the silky whoosh of its black feathers, saw its beak open to release a *squawk-caw* before it vanished somewhere over the forest. Tolba pulled his attention back to the Toyota.

Let's check it out first, test your detective powers of observation, he kidded himself. He noticed the Jesus fish bumper sticker. The student parking sticker for a Seattle college. The car appeared to be well kept and in good condition. No flat tires. Nothing leaking. The rear seat had a travel bag and an umbrella.

Tolba paused to consider the umbrella.

It was in bad shape, like it had been destroyed in last night's storm, then tossed in the back. His attention moved from the back to the front seat. Now this was strange.

The keys were still in the ignition.

The door was unlocked.

He checked the highway's shoulder, walking thirty, maybe forty yards in each direction.

Nothing.

He went back to his four-by-four and reached for his radio.

3

Just over a hundred miles south in Seattle, Trudy Moore heard activity in the apartment above hers.

Sounded like Karen was back, she thought, glancing at the time while getting ready to put in a morning shift at the coffee shop a few blocks away. This was Trudy's busy day because she had three afternoon classes.

After washing her breakfast dishes and tidying up, she filled a watering can to tend to her plants, reminding herself how lucky she was to live in this gorgeous building in Capitol Hill.

It was a classic stone apartment house built around 1910. Her place was a second-story one bedroom with hardwood floors and bay windows overlooking downtown, the Space Needle and the Olympic Mountains to the west. She had managed to get a terrific sublet deal through a friend.

A door slammed overhead, startling her.

Strange.

Trudy's apartment was identical to the one above her where Karen Harding lived. Both of them had been tenants for close to a year and had become attuned to each other's living rhythms. Karen was as quiet as a church mouse, which was Trudy's nickname for her because Karen went to church every Sunday morning.

Karen would certainly never slam a door. Maybe the door handle slipped. Trudy resumed checking over her lecture notes, tapping her pen against her pages, until she heard footfalls. Heavier than she was used to. The floor creaked as though someone was walking throughout the entire apartment. Walking, *urgently*. Doors opening and closing.

What was going on? That didn't sound like Karen.

Trudy remembered hearing her leave last night. Heard her descend the stairs. From the window she'd seen Karen hurrying to her car and driving off in the rain. Afterward Karen's phone rang at least six times. Come to think of it, it started ringing again earlier this morning and went unanswered.

Trudy waved it all off. None of her business.

She glanced at the time, calculating how much she had to study before collecting her books, getting on her bike, and riding to the coffee shop.

Karen's phone started ringing again.

This time someone upstairs picked it up and Trudy heard the faint sound of someone talking. More footsteps, a door opened, thudded closed. Then the hall stairs creaked as someone quickly descended them.

Trudy heard the rush of a person passing by her door. A big person.

That is definitely not Karen.

Trudy was absolutely certain because she was staring at Karen's parking space and her car was still not there.

4

The vague feeling that something was wrong nagged at Marlene Clark throughout much of her morning.

She couldn't pinpoint the source.

It had nothing to do with her job as a nurse at Vancouver General Hospital. In fact, the surgery to remove the enlarged spleen of a sixty-year-old woman had gone well. Marlene had suppressed the twinge of puzzling unease at the back of her mind, concentrating on passing sponges and instruments from the tray to the surgeon.

After the operation, worry began niggling at her again. What was it? She didn't know. She was sure it had nothing to do with work, with the kids, or her husband. Just a cloudy sensation that something wasn't right.

She glanced at her watch and started for recovery. On the way she called her house to check with her sitter, Wanda, who was watching Timothy and Rachel.

"Everything's fine, Marlene. All quiet here. Want to talk to the kids?"

A few seconds of chatting with Timothy and Rachel

relieved her. She went to post-op where she reviewed the spleen patient's chart. Later, she found an empty staff room and began eating a late lunch as she checked her schedule for the next day's surgery.

A twenty-year-old woman was having her gall bladder removed. Given the patient's age, Marlene would double-check for any body jewelry that might have to be taken out before the operation. Studs in tongues were popular, she thought as Anita from the desk poked her head into the room.

"There you are. Telephone call for you, Mar."

Marlene glanced at the extension number of the line in the room.

"Can you put it through here?"

"No problem."

In the moment she waited, she thought of Bill. He'd mentioned something about going out to dinner. The line rang and she picked it up.

"Hello, this is Marlene."

"Hi, Marlene, it's Luke. Luke Terrell, Karen's boy friend."

Luke? Why was he calling her here? Was he in town?

"Hi, Luke."

"I'm sorry to be bothering you, but, um—"

The tone of his voice was weird.

"What is it?"

"Is Karen in Vancouver visiting you? Or has she called?"

"No. Why? What's going on?"

"Please don't get worried. Please, but the police just called me—"

"Police!"

"They found Karen's car off the highway, 539, near Laurel—"

As Luke explained the little he knew, a hollow sickening feeling seeped into Marlene's stomach. Ears pounding, she seized upon bits of his account...Karen left her apartment with a bag...left without her cell phone...there was a storm...car abandoned...missing...

Luke was scaring her, stirring her mysterious fear, twisting it all horribly into focus.

It was about the dream she'd had last night.

A nightmare about Karen.

She was screaming and screaming.

5

"*She died?*"

Jason Wade, a rookie police reporter at the *Seattle Mirror*, pressed the phone to his head to hear over the newsroom's scanners. He needed to be certain of what the cop was telling him.

"She died in the hospital an hour ago," the lieutenant said.

First edition deadline was looming. Jason jabbed the night editor's extension.

"Beale."

"Got an update on the I-405 traffic accident in Bellevue. State Patrol confirmed the woman just died of her injuries."

"One hundred max."

One hundred words. Gladys Chambers deserved more than that, Jason thought. She was seventy-two, driving home from a seniors' club where she played the organ when a tire blew and her car rolled.

"I can give you a little profile, she's a retired Boeing worker."

"We're tight. One hundred."

One hundred words didn't even warrant a byline. It was as if Gladys Chambers was somehow being cheated in death. Jason wanted to write more about her life but followed orders.

The night editors ruled his world.

Embittered veterans who had boiled his job down to a few commandments. Never turn off the police scanners. Never let the *Seattle Times* or *Post-Intelligencer* beat you. Write exactly to the length we tell you. Never take criticism of your writing personally. Everybody produces crap and the day side knows jack.

Obey and learn.

Jason knocked out exactly one hundred words, then sent his story to the copy desk.

Behold the lot of a cub reporter on the police beat of a major metro.

Discarded sections of the *Mirror*, the *L.A. Times,* and *USA Today* were splayed on his desk. He considered them along with the used-up notebooks, junk food wrappers, outdated press releases, and his future.

He was failing.

He was a month into the paper's legendary soul-destroying six-month internship program and all he had to show for it were eight bylines. He had to get his name in print more often. This was his shot at a job with the best damn newspaper in the Pacific Northwest, a kick-ass operation.

He couldn't afford to fail.

Jason called up the wires, scrolling through them for anything breaking. Little had moved since he last looked. He checked regional Web sites for press releases, then made more checks going down the tattered list of numbers for police, fire, paramedics, and port people throughout the Sea-Tac area. Call after call yielded nothing new.

Except for the organ lady's death, it was an uneventful night.

Jason went to see Vic Beale, the night editor, typing before a large flat-screen monitor.

"Instead of searching the wires, I'm going to call around the state, see if I can dig something up."

Beale, a craggy-faced man with wispy gray hair, peered over his glasses. His attention paused at the silver stud earring in Jason's left lobe, then the few days' growth of whiskers that suggested a Vandyke.

"We're jammed for space. If you get anything, it'd better be good."

"I've got nothing to lose."

"Knock yourself out."

At his keyboard, Jason summoned the *Mirror*'s universal call list, a massive file of names, numbers, and contact information for anything and everything. He decided to start with the border and work his way south.

He called the Blaine crossing.

"Hi, Jason Wade from the *Seattle Mirror*. Anything shaking up your way tonight? Any arrests, seizures? Any oddball incidents?"

The duty officer gave him an officious brush-off. "You guys know you're supposed to call the press office."

"Yeah, but those people don't know as much as you. And I bet they don't work as hard."

"You got that right."

"So between you and me, did anything happen for you tonight, anything worth pursuing?"

"Naw. Try Sumas. I heard there was something out that way."

"Thanks."

The woman who answered the line at Sumas was cheery.

"Nothing going on here, dear. I'd try Lynden."

The number for the Lynden border crossing rang and rang. Jason was hanging up when the line clicked, and he pulled the phone back to his ear.

"No, nothing here." The Lynden man's name was Jenkins. "Sorry, you got a bad tip."

"Well, I'm just poking around."

"That thing's got nothing to do with us."

That thing? What thing?

"Excuse me?" Jason sat up.

"You want the Sawridge County Sheriff."

"Why, what's going on?"

"Likely nothing, but they found an abandoned car on 539 about ten miles south of us."

"Abandoned car? What about it?"

"I guess they're trying to find the owner, a young Seattle woman."

"Why? Is there foul play or something?"

"I've got no idea. Call the county, but you didn't get it from us."

Jason persisted with several calls to Sawridge County until he connected with Detective Hank Stralla. The cop listened patiently, then told him they had concerns over a car abandoned on 539.

"We're attempting to locate the owner to be sure she's unharmed."

"Why concerns about a car? I mean that sort of thing happens all the time, right?"

"We're going to wait until tomorrow before releasing anything."

"That suggests you have something. What's happening tomorrow? Do you suspect foul play?"

Stralla let a moment of silence pass between them.

"Until we locate the owner, we really can't say much."

Something in Stralla's tone triggered Jason's instincts—this was the precise moment to push.

"Would you consider releasing a few details now? A story in tomorrow's *Mirror* might help. You know our circulation is statewide. Goes right to the border."

Stralla considered the proposal.

"Tell you what. Let me make a few calls. I'll get right back to you either way. What's your number?"

Jason gave Stralla his number, telling him he had about an hour before the paper's next deadline.

"I'll get back to you as soon as I can," Stralla said.

Jason hung up.

Maybe he was on to something here. He glanced at Beale and the editors. Should he alert them? Alert them to what? He hadn't nailed anything down. He'd forgot-

ten another commandment. Never oversell a story.
Besides, this could be nothing.

Better sit tight.

6

Jason stared at the clock.

No word yet from Detective Stralla. He watched the second hand sweeping time away, downed the last of his cold coffee, tossed the Styro cup in the trash, got up, and paced the desolate newsroom.

He was the only metro reporter on night duty.

The small crew at the copy desk worked with subdued intensity on the first edition, oblivious to the police radio chatter. Keeping an ear tuned to the scanner and his phone, Jason went to the newsroom bulletin board and browsed the administrative memos and staff notes offering items for sale. Like a Starcraft with a 45 Merc, or Mariners tickets and discounts on Hawaiian getaways.

Then he saw his own picture under the banner: MEET OUR INTERNS.

Jason's face and bio were up there among the six junior reporters hired for the *Mirror*'s internship program. *The lucky ones,* Neena Swain, the assistant managing editor, had told them when they had first arrived.

"You have a golden opportunity to prove yourself

to us. You won't be coddled here. School's out. This is the real world. We're paying you a full-time reporter's rate and we have expectations."

She adjusted her glasses with cool precision, then locked eyes with each intern at the boardroom table.

"On every story you'll go up against the *Seattle Times* and the *Post-Intelligencer*. So you'd better make damn sure that you're the first reporter on it, and the last one to leave. You get the best quotes and you get it right. Every damn time." Neena Swain brought her fist down on the table. "The *Seattle Mirror* has won nine goddamned Pulitzer Prizes and *we will not* tolerate anything less than excellence. At the end of six months one of you, and only one of you, will be hired full-time."

The rest would be gone.

That was the deal. A do-or-die competition. All of the interns had impressive resumes with experience at the *New York Times,* the *Chicago Tribune, Newsweek,* the *Los Angeles Times*, and the *Wall Street Journal.* All of them came from big-name schools like Columbia, Northwestern, Missouri, Arizona State, and UCLA.

All of them but Jason Wade.

He had worked as a forklift driver at Pacific Peaks Brewery near the airport to put himself through community college. And he'd put in part-time shifts as a reporter at a now-defunct Seattle weekly, while selling freelance pieces wherever he could, including one to the *Mirror.*

It was a crime feature on beat cops that had caught the eye of Ron Nestor, the Mirror's metro editor, who gave Wade the last spot in the intern program after another candidate dropped out at the last minute.

Jason got in by the skin of his teeth.

It was likely why he was assigned to the most loathed position at any newspaper, the night police beat.

"Looks like you drew the short straw," Ben Randolf said. He was a tall good-looking guy from Columbia who'd worked at the *Chicago Tribune*. His parents were New York investment bankers. "Best of luck, buddy." He winked at Astrid Grant, standing with them.

"It's a good situation for you, Jason." Astrid Grant had worked at *Newsweek*. Her father was an exec at a big studio in Los Angeles and she had graduated from UCLA. "Personally, I detest police, but it's a good fit for you, what with your background, don't you think?"

Later, Ron Nestor gave Jason a pep talk.

"The police desk is vital, Jason. Don't sell it short. The crime beat is the front line of news. The radio scanner is our lifeline to stories that will stop the heart of Seattle, or break it."

It was a mean, brutal business and Jason yearned to be part of it. But here they were, a month into the program, and each of the others had nailed front-page stories and long showcased features. All he had managed so far were eight small, forgettable, inside hits.

He walked away from the bulletin board.

The *Mirror* was at Harrison and Fourth, a few blocks north of downtown. The newsroom was on the seventh floor, its west wall made of glass. He gazed into the night. It was clear after yesterday's storm. He watched the running lights of the boats cutting across Elliott Bay, trying hard not to think about the brewery and what awaited him if he failed to get a job with the *Mirror*.

He was twenty-five and had already lost too much. Like Valerie. She just up and left him. *No. Admit it. You drove her away.* How many months had it been? It still hurt. *Get over it, loser, you blew it with her.*

Jason's phone rang. He trotted back to his desk. It was Stralla.

"We're prepared to release a few details to you."

He glanced at the clock. Forty minutes until deadline for the *Mirror*'s second edition, which was the largest.

"Are you releasing this to everyone?"

"Just you tonight. It's all yours. No one else has called."

Jason hunched forward in his chair, his pulse kicking up as he squeezed his pen and wrote down every detail Stralla gave him in the case of Karen Katherine Harding. Then he told Vic Beale what he had.

"You're sure it's exclusive?"

"Got it confirmed from the detective on the case."

"And you got a picture?"

"Yup."

"Get moving. I'll talk to Mack about taking it for page one. You've got thirty-five minutes to get it to me. Move it."

Fingers poised over his keys, Jason concentrated and began working on his lead. Thirty minutes later he was done and proofreading his story.

By JASON WADE
Seattle Mirror

Police are baffled as to the whereabouts of a Seattle college student after her car was found abandoned near the Canadian border.

Sawridge County Sheriff's deputies have little evidence to help them explain what happened to Karen Katherine Harding.

A deputy on patrol found her 1998 Blue Toyota Corolla parked on the northbound shoulder of State Route 539, some 10 miles from the Lynden border crossing into Canada. The car's keys were in the ignition. The doors were unlocked. Investigators found no signs of violence or a struggle among her belongings, which included an overnight bag.

"On the face of it, it's strange. We're attempting to locate Ms. Harding. Until then we cannot rule out the possibility of foul play," Det. Hank Stralla told the Mirror last night.

It's believed Harding may have had car trouble while driving in an intense storm after leaving her Capitol Hill apartment Tuesday evening. Stralla said Harding has a sister who lives in Vancouver, British Columbia, and suspects she may have been on her way there for a visit. Harding informed no one of her destination, he said, declining to discuss further details about her disappearance.

Harding is 24 years old, 5 feet 3 inches tall, 110 pounds, with brown hair and blue eyes.

Anyone who has information concerning her whereabouts should contact the Sawridge County Sheriff's Office.

Jason hit the Send button, delivering the story to the night desk for editing, then he began kneading the tension in his neck, when Beale called him.

"Front's taking your story below the fold. Nice work."

"Thanks."

Jason left his desk for the internal viewing window at the far end of the newsroom and looked down two stories at the massive German-built presses. The smells of ink, hydraulic fluid, and newsprint were heavy in the air. The pressmen were busy replating and making adjustments for the next edition. Soon bells rang and the building trembled as the presses began to roll.

Later Jason wandered back into the news section, to Beale, who was watching Letterman on the big-screen TV on the high shelf.

"What do you think? Is she dead?" Jason asked.

"She could surface. It happens. But who knows? Pretty college girl all alone on a stormy night. I'll tell you one thing." Beale switched off the set, collected his jacket and bag to leave. "Readers will eat this up. People love a mystery."

7

A seagull shrieked from the waterfront as Jason Wade walked to the parking lot. Gentle breezes skipped along the bay, carrying the smell of brine and the long, mournful sound of a tug.

He stopped to watch the *Mirror*'s delivery trucks rumble from the docks, laden with bundles of the edition carrying his story. His first front-page story. On its way to a metropolitan area of three and a half million people. To every doorstep in every neighborhood, to every street and corner store where the *Mirror* battled the *Times* and the *P-I* for readers.

Beat you both.

He stared at his byline for what must've been the tenth time tonight, drawn again to Karen Harding's picture.

He hoped she was still alive. He didn't wish for anything bad to happen to her just so he could get a good story. Although he needed one. No matter what had happened to her, this one was his and he wasn't going to let it go.

He rolled up the paper and unlocked his car, a 1969

red Ford Falcon. Spotted with primer, it had sat for years in the garage of a firefighter's widow on Mercer Island. She had placed a for-sale ad online. Jason was the first to respond. It needed some work but ran good. Six hundred bucks. The Falcon might not be pretty, but it had never let him down.

He headed for Denny Way. As he wheeled toward Broad Street the Space Needle ascended before him. To the south, the skyline glittered with its tallest buildings, the Bank of America Tower, Two Union Square, and Washington Mutual. Not far from them was Pike Place Market.

Jason marveled at Seattle. Jet City. The Emerald City.

At this time of night, it was all his.

Northbound on Aurora Avenue, he thought that maybe he should mark the evening with a little celebration. He'd earned it. Temptation beckoned from the back of his throat and he drew his hand across his mouth.

No. Forget that and get home.

To the east he saw Gas Works Park as he approached the Aurora Avenue Bridge, which spanned Lake Union. On lazy, sunny days he'd come here to watch the sailboats, or the ships navigating the Ballard Locks and the Lake Washington Ship Canal on their way to the ocean. He also knew the darker history of the bridge. Everyone did. Since its construction, a lot of people had jumped from it to their deaths.

After he entered the eastern edge of Fremont, he

stopped for Chinese takeout from Johnny Pearl's.
Thirty minutes later he was home.

His neighborhood was on the fringes of Fremont
and Wallingford, a peaceful enclave of quiet family
homes. His building was a large, nineteenth-century
house that had been divided into apartments.

He had moved here halfway through college to put
some distance between him, his old man, and the brewery. The stairs creaked as he climbed them to the third
floor and unlocked his door.

He kept the lights low. It relaxed him. His living
room had oak floors and two secondhand, dark green
leather sofas he'd picked up for free from a dentist
who was closing his office. The sofas faced each other
before the fireplace, which was bordered by built-in
bookcases. A low-standing coffee table smothered with
newspapers rose between them.

At the opposite end of the room, Washington-born
Jimi Hendrix, Jason's beloved god of rock, was frozen in a giant poster above his thirty-gallon aquarium.
Aware of the hour and not wanting to disturb his
neighbor below, he carefully lifted a chair from the
kitchen. Without a sound he placed it before the tank,
which made the room glow in soft blue light. The tiny
tropical fish gliding among the coral, the sunken ship,
the diver, and the bubbles soothed him. A little sign
near the diver warned FISH WILL ATTACK ON COMMAND.

Jason cut a lonely figure, sitting there eating his
chicken fried rice and ginger beef, his newspaper on
the floor below him as he looked at his story for the
thousandth time.

A dream realized.

As far back as he could remember, all he wanted to be was a writer. And ever since he began reading people like Crane, Steinbeck, and Hemingway, he figured being a reporter was the best training, a ticket to the greatest story on earth: life.

He studied its daily dramas every morning on his first job in the business, delivering the *Seattle Mirror*. Reading the news took his mind off of his own troubles, like when his mother walked out on him and his old man.

She had worked alongside his father on the bottling line at the brewery. But she was drowning, she had written in her note, and was leaving to survive. Her desertion crushed Jason.

"We have to keep going, Jay," his father said one night while they were watching a game on TV. "She'll come back, you'll see."

But she didn't.

Later on, as Jason tried to comprehend how his mother could just leave, his grades plunged, his college dream slipped away, and his father got him a job at the brewery.

They would rise before the sun, get into his father's pickup, and drive to the dreary concentration of dirty brick buildings, smoke-plumed stacks, and the overpowering smell of hops. For Jason, it was a gate to hell and he understood why the thermos in his old man's lunch bucket was spiked with bourbon.

Jason's bucket always carried a book.

He vowed to pull himself out of that place. Between loading trailers with pallets of beer, he read classic literature, saved his money, went to night school, improved his grades, enrolled in college, worked weekends at the brewery. He also drank a bit. All right, more than a bit. Hell, name a writer who didn't. He moved into the apartment, wrote for the campus paper, and freelanced stories while working part-time at a Seattle weekly.

Then he met Valerie.

She was a graphic artist from Olympia. Her parents had died in a car accident years ago and she had no other family. A loner like him. They fell in love, talked about living together, marriage, kids, the whole thing. What they had going was deep and good.

Until he destroyed it.

He'd stopped off at a bar after working late, forgetting how a week earlier he had stood her up for a movie by doing the same thing. Only on this night, the anniversary of the day his mother had walked out, he'd forgotten about Valerie's company's awards banquet. He arrived underdressed, late, and drunk.

"How could you do this, Jason? Don't you have any self-respect?" Valerie's voice broke in the cab. He never forgot the hurt clouding her eyes a few days later. "We need time apart," she told him. "There's a short-term job I'm taking in Los Angeles. I'm driving down next week. Alone."

That was that.

Man, that was that. Jason blinked at the beaded

bracelet on his wrist and almost smiled. A gift from Valerie. The bracelets were popular at Pike Place Market where she'd bought an identical pair when they first began dating. "One for you, one for me." She had laughed, slipping it on him. "We're handcuffed together. Forever."

Jason had tried to reach her in Los Angeles, but it was futile. She never called or e-mailed him. He didn't know the company in L.A. All he could do was hope she would come back so he could make things right. But it dawned on him that he was like his father, that he had lost the woman in his life and, like his old man, drank to ease the pain.

That was several months ago.

In the aftermath, Jason painstakingly regained control. He quit drinking and clung to the only dream he had left, becoming a reporter. He was so close now, he thought, staring at the front page of the *Seattle Mirror*.

He finished eating, then went to his fridge, opened the door, and stared at the lone bottle of beer. He kept it there to prove to himself he didn't need it anymore. That he was not like his father. Right, but he deserved to celebrate. Just tonight.

No.

He reached for a bottled water, shut the door, picked up his fresh copy of the *Mirror* from the floor, headed down the hall. After brushing his teeth, he fell into bed, exhausted. He removed the bracelet, capped it on his bedpost, then folded the paper so he could study his piece.

Karen Harding stared at him from the newsprint.
He could not take his eyes from hers.
It was as if she were pleading for him to help her.

8

Karen Harding was surfacing.

Eyes closed.

Dreaming, still dreaming, she was rising slowly to consciousness as her senses awakened. Her head throbbed with the noise. A drone. Deafening against her ears. Something rolling, circulating at high speed like a power tool. Like a buzz saw.

Her entire body bounced gently as if on a spring. Swaying. Floating. Moving as she grappled to keep dreaming of her sister. Marlene. She was talking to Marlene. She needed to see Marlene. Calling out to her. And Luke. She was no longer upset with Luke. She needed them. Desperately. Why didn't they hear? Why didn't they come to her?

Her ears were pounding. Was that her heart beating? *Closer now. Almost there.*

Her dreams faded and she could feel her blood pulsating in her ears. Then a sickening feeling slithered in her stomach. Something has happened. *You're not dreaming.*

Don't open your eyes.

Her heart began to hammer. She shuddered. Instinct told her to feign unconsciousness. Assess everything. She tried to swallow, but it was difficult to breathe. Her jaw ached. Her teeth biting on something foreign wedged in her mouth. Her tongue timidly probed the object. It was large, circular, fabric and twisted like a cord, which went completely around her head.

She was gagged.

Her mouth was filled with a terrible bitter taste. Breathing was hard. Swallowing air hurt. Her cheeks were wet with drool.

Don't open your eyes.

There was pressure near her hands. Karen strained her fingers, feeling the coils of rope binding her wrists. She drew short quick breaths. Her ankles. She felt pressure at her ankles and ordered her muscles to move her feet apart. Nothing happened. Her feet were bound. She was on her back.

What was happening to her?

God. Please help.

Keeping her eyes closed, she clawed at her memory. *Go back. Think.* She'd been driving. Upset with Luke, she had left Seattle to see Marlene in Vancouver. Her car had broken down in the storm and someone stopped.

The reverend.

So kind.

She had stepped into his RV. It had a strange odor. Newspapers, maps, files, and other assorted items were strewn about the front. A bad feeling overwhelmed her. She wanted to return to her car but didn't want to appear ungrateful. He'd been so good to stop and help, and then everything went dark.

Then she remembered feeling as if someone was carrying her....

Her heart slammed against her rib cage.

Oh God!

Karen swallowed. She was fully conscious. She knew she was moving. Traveling. She opened her eyes to darkness. She tried to lift her head but struck it against something hard, knocking her back. She manipulated her hands to the right and felt a hard wall.

Gooseflesh rose on her entire body.

Oh, dear God!

Karen was terrified. She tried to scream but couldn't. She tried to kick but couldn't. She tried to pound her fists against all sides of her tomb but couldn't. She began to sob but it only made her choke and gasp.

She forced herself to be calm.

Oh God. What's happening?

Be calm. Be calm. Be calm.

She had to stay calm and think. She had no sense of how long she'd been here. Or if it was real. Was it real? Or was it just some sort of joke? A sick college rite of passage? One of Luke's stupid friends? Trying to scare her? It wasn't funny.

It wasn't a joke.

She turned to her left, blinking at the darkness. She started a prayer when her body bounced, shifting her slightly, piercing the blackness with a thread of light.

Karen blinked.

With some effort she repositioned herself to the left, drawing her face closer to the light. It was a seam no wider than the edge of a credit card, allowing her a narrow glimpse of the outside. Concentrating and pressing against it to widen it, she was able to see carpet.

She held her breath.

She was in an RV. Directly across from her was the veneer finish of the storage compartment that supported a twin bed. So she was *under* the twin bed at floor level. Under the storage area of one of the RV's beds at the rear. Maybe she could break out?

She forced her body against the wall to her right and pushed hard against the wall with the crack. Nothing. Like trying to push against stone.

Karen collected herself, drew her face back to the crack, pressing against it, widening it a little, to see what else she could see. Her eyes traveled from the rear, over the files, papers, maps toward the front. It looked as if there'd been a terrible struggle.

She saw the driver's head. His neck. Karen tried to swallow.

The reverend.

Cutlery, or what she thought was cutlery, rattled as the RV rolled over a bump, jolting Karen.

She heard a thud above her, saw something strobe across her shaft of light. When she focused, her scalp tingled.

A woman's arm hung over the edge of the bed above her.

9

Shortly after dawn the next day, a police helicopter hovered over State Route 539, a few hundred feet above Karen Harding's Toyota.

The yellow ribbon of tape marking the huge rectangle around her car quivered in the prop wash, lifting the pages on Hank Stralla's clipboard. Sipping take-out coffee, the Sawridge County detective faced the clear morning light painting the spot where Karen Harding had vanished.

Too early to tell exactly what the hell happened here.

The chopper pivoted to make more passes south along the shoulder. It had gone about half a mile. The break in the thumping allowed him to think. Was this a young woman who had simply hitched a ride when her car broke down, or a crime? One thing was certain: the circumstances were suspicious.

He looked up at the Cessna borrowed from Washington State Patrol. It made another pass, photographing the area and scouring the terrain for any signs of a body. Then he heard a yip from Sheeba, the Belgian shepherd emerging from the forest, snout to the ground, leading Chris Farmer, one of the state's best K-9 officers.

"The heavy rain won't make it easy for her to pick up a scent," Farmer had told Stralla at the outset.

"I appreciate that. Just do what you can."

Stralla watched the crime scene investigators in their white moon suits working on the Toyota. They'd been at it since daybreak.

"At this point, there's no sign of violence," said Cal Rosen, the lead criminalist, as he chugged a Coke. "No indication of a struggle or blood. No casings. Nothing. We got some partial latents, but the car's pretty clean. Strange she would leave the keys."

"Strange. What about mechanically?"

"We've got to get the car on a flatbed and over to the garage to process it further, give it a good going-over, and examine everything. At this point, it looks like she ran out of gas and got picked up, or walked away."

Stralla agreed, it was the most likely scenario. His attention went to her driver's license picture on his clipboard. She ran out of gas. She walked off, or someone stopped. Then what?

He scratched his chin.

They had zero so far, nothing to point them in any direction. Time was always a factor. Soon he'd start a shoulder-to-shoulder grid. And he would call in divers to check the Nooksack River.

He looked under Karen Harding's license and the

folded copy of the *Seattle Mirror*. That kid, Jason
Wade, had done all right on the story. Down the road,
a satellite news truck from Bellingham was lumbering
to the scene. More press were arriving.

Stralla sighed. During his time on the job he'd seen
it all.

Scams. Cons. Insurance frauds. People who
couldn't make car payments. Pissed-off spouses, adults
who had the right to lawfully vanish. Let people think
they disappeared into Canada, if they chose.

He was haunted by the case of a troubled housewife
who'd vanished a few years ago under similar circumstances. He had leaned so hard on a paroled convict he
believed had killed her that it nearly drove the man to
suicide. Then the housewife surfaced in Toronto.
Turned out she'd staged her disappearance to cover
for an affair. The case shook Stralla to his core. Angry
at himself, he vowed never to repeat his mistakes. Until
they had something concrete, Karen Harding was a
person missing under suspicious circumstances.

A large group of people had gathered at the perimeter. Karen Harding's college friends, including some
teachers. They'd volunteered to help search the scene.
The newspeople were interviewing them, taking pictures. He went back to his clipboard and reviewed his reports.

He wanted to talk to Luke Terrell, Karen's boy-
friend, and Marlene Clark, her sister. Luke had told
Tolba that Karen was on her way to visit her sister in
Vancouver, B.C., but her sister said it was news to her.

Something didn't sit right on that point.

Stralla needed to know more about Karen's state of mind when she left. Was she emotionally or physically impaired? Taking medication? Cal was right. It was strange that she'd left her keys in the car.

Chilling.

But Stralla kept that to himself, hoping for a mundane explanation as he scanned the rolling dark forests and the Cascade Mountains. Too much of this vast beautiful region was stained with blood. The Green River Killer, the Spokane Serial Killer, and the grisly cases up in British Columbia all jutted from its history like headstones.

Monsters loved to hunt here.

10

Jason's bedroom glowed with light dimmed through the tilted slats of the venetian blinds. He was trying to figure out what had awakened him when his phone rang again and he grabbed it.

"Hey, it's Astrid Grant. Oops, I woke you, didn't I?"

Jason ran a hand through his hair, guessing she was calling on a cell phone from a car. "What is it?"

"Good story today," she said. "Have you got anything more on it?"

"Why?"

"I'm on my way to the scene where they found her car and I don't know how to do these police stories. Can you help me out, Jason, please?"

And help myself out of a job. Right.

Among the interns, Astrid Grant was the best feature writer. She'd already landed several big stories in the paper. All of them came together with the help of another reporter. Astrid was a user and Jason was not going to be used.

"Sorry, I put everything I had into my little hit."

It was true.

"Well, whatever," she said. "This whole Harding thing seems odd to me. No sign of a murder. It's a story of an abandoned car. For all we know, she climbed into the cab of some trucker stud for a ride to Las Vegas."

Wade rolled his eyes. "That's right, Astrid."

In the shower, Jason grappled with the feeling he was being pushed off his story. He couldn't let that happen. After dressing, he seized two bananas and two apples for breakfast in his Falcon on his way to the *Mirror* and was near the door when his apartment phone rang.

"Did I catch you at a bad time?"

The clang of steel and the hydraulic whoosh of forklift trucks came across the line with his father's voice. Jason could almost smell the hops.

"I was on my way to the *Mirror*."

"I just wanted to say good job on the story. I must've bought twenty copies. I've been bragging to all the guys on the dock."

"Thanks."

"Listen, Son, I know you're busy but it's been a while since you dropped by the house. How are you fixed for this weekend? I can get us some steaks, we can watch the game. Shoot the breeze."

"I don't know, Dad. I might have to stay on this story."

"Pretty serious business. I understand."

"Dad, I promise. I'll get over to South Park when I can."

"All right, Jay."

* * *

On his way to the paper, Jason wondered what his father had on his mind. Whatever it was he wanted to say, he should just say it. As far as Jason was concerned, all of the bad stuff was far behind them.

Well, nearly all of it.

Stepping from the elevator into the *Mirror* newsroom, he searched for the assignment editor. Unable to spot him, he went to Phil Tucker, one of the *Mirror*'s Pulitzer winners. Tucker peered over his glasses from behind his monitor.

"Young Jason, the night stalker."

"Morning, Phil."

"What're you doing here? I thought you guys melted in daylight."

"Came in to work on the Harding story. Do you know who's on it?"

"Astrid Grant went up to Sawridge with a shooter. I think Nestor's got other bodies on it."

Tucker indicated the man approaching them. Jason turned to Ron Nestor, the metro editor, who supervised the thirty reporters in his section. Before becoming an editor, Nestor was a marine sergeant, who then became a reporter covering the military for the *Mirror*. He was six feet two inches tall. He had a brush cut, kept his collar unbuttoned, his tie loosened, and his sleeves rolled up. He was accustomed to having his orders followed.

"Good story. You can go home now."

"I've come in to work on it."

"You're on nights, I need you fresh for your shift tonight."

"I can handle it."

Nestor's eyebrows rose slightly as he assessed Jason, then he jotted an address on his pad, snapped off the sheet, and passed it to him.

"Your fellow intern, Ben Randolf, is at this place. Go help him work the neighborhood."

Jason stared at the address. "It's Karen Harding's apartment building."

"That's right. In Capitol Hill."

"What do you want from there?"

"Everything we don't already know. Otherwise known as news."

The street in front of Karen Harding's building was lined with police and press vehicles. On the sidewalk, a clutch of TV crews and radio and print reporters were talking to the uniformed Seattle officers while inside, plainclothes detectives were searching her apartment. Jason caught glimpses of their white-gloved hands and grim faces through the crack in the curtains as he joined the group.

Ben Randolf's smile evaporated when he greeted him.

"What're you doing here?"

"Nestor sent me to help you out."

Randolf led him out of earshot.

"I don't need your help. I've got this covered."

"So what're her neighbors saying?"

"Not much. Look, we're getting a police statement soon. I'm good here. Shouldn't you be sleeping or something?"

"I'm fine."

Jason took stock of the bystanders watching from across the street, then looked farther uphill. Half a block away, almost out of sight, in a patch of park under a tree, he saw two young women watching the scene. It appeared one was crying while the other rubbed her shoulder. Randolf hadn't noticed them; he was focused on the cops.

"You're right," Jason said. "No need for both of us to stand here. Besides, my bed is calling me."

"Good," Randolf said absently.

Jason took the long way around the block so none of his competitors would see where he was headed. As he neared the women, the one doing the consoling eyed him coolly.

"We have no comment."

The other woman's gaze was fixed on Karen Harding's building. A copy of the *Mirror* was folded next to her. She had blond hair and dabbed a tissue to her eyes.

"I noticed you sitting here watching and thought you might be Karen Harding's friends."

"Well, we still have no comment," the first one said.

"Sure." He reached into his pocket. "If you do, here's my card."

The blond-haired girl read it, then looked up at him.

"You wrote the story?"

"Yes."

"Do you know any more?"

"Only what the detective in Sawridge County told me."

"Stralla?"

"Yes."

"I just talked to him on the phone today," the blonde said, making Jason's pulse skip. "I reached him after I read your story."

"Trudy, don't say anything," the dark-haired woman warned.

"If you want to tell me stuff, off the record," Jason said, "I can keep your name out of the paper. And I'd be willing to trade information."

The women looked at each other, reading each other's expressions. Trudy looked at Jason's name in the paper, and on his card.

"All right."

"First. I have to know you are who you say you are." Jason produced his press ID, then asked to see their identification.

"I'm Trudy Moore," she said, showing him her school card. "I live directly under Karen's apartment."

"Have you spoken to any other reporters, Trudy?"

She shook her head and then Jason asked her to tell him what she knew.

"I saw her leave her place the night of the storm. She looked upset, like she was in a hurry."

"Did you talk to her?"

"No, she rushed by me. Then the next morning I

heard footsteps in her apartment. Someone was up there and it sounded like they were looking for something."

"Any idea who?"

"No, I never saw. It's so creepy." She cupped her hands to her face. "What've you heard? Do they know what's happened to her?"

"From what I understand, Karen was going to see her sister in Vancouver and had car trouble. They've got a massive search going on right now around where they found her car. But so far, there's no indication of any violence."

A few moments passed in silence and then Jason got ready to leave by getting all of Trudy Moore's contact information.

"You can use my name in your story. I trust you. I'm staying at my mother's house until I feel safe again, if I ever will."

"I'll be working the late shift tonight, so please call me if you hear anything."

Later that night, after filing what he had on the Harding story, Jason went to the night photo editor, who showed him the *Mirror*'s pictures of her car from the site. An array came up on the editor's large color monitor and he clicked through them. They were dramatic. Shots of Stralla talking to reporters, the helicopter, the white-suited crime scene people scrutinizing her Toyota. Volunteers helping search the scene.

Vic Beale called him over. "Wade, we've thrown

everyone's work into one big take. Astrid's copy from the scene is pretty thin. Seems like nobody's saying much. You're getting top byline because your stuff about footsteps in Harding's apartment is strong."

"Where's it going?"

"Page one."

Good, he thought, going to the window at the far side of the newsroom to look at the lights twinkling across Elliott Bay and puzzle over Karen Harding's disappearance. Keys left in the ignition. Belongings left in the backseat. No sign of a struggle. Footsteps in her apartment.

It was bizarre.

His phone began ringing and he strode to his desk. "Jason Wade, *Seattle Mirror.*"

"It's Trudy Moore, I talked to you earlier today."

"Hi, Trudy."

"Maybe you know this, but there's a new rumor flying around that someone at the college might have something to do with what happened to Karen."

"Like who?"

"I don't know. I'll ask around."

After the call, Wade thought for a moment before going to the photo desk. He shuffled through the prints of images taken at the search scene, coming to shots of Karen's school friends and teachers. A few dozen men and women near Jason's age, combing the area side by side with a handful of teachers and what looked like local volunteers. Jason moved on, concentrating on the cutlines, which identified most of the people in the pictures. He found what he was looking for, circled a face, then drew a line to the name.

Luke Terrell. Karen Harding's boyfriend.

This guy had to know something.

11

Jason was up early the next morning to roll the dice on a long shot.

He considered it as he guided his Falcon southbound on I-5. Odds were slim he'd break news. He had nothing to lose if he struck out, nobody had gotten this story yet. Besides, this was his own time.

He was listening to Hendrix, tracks from *War Heroes*, when he came to the edge of the campus. After double-checking his map, he wheeled into the Motherlode Village Court Apartments where Luke Terrell lived.

It was called Loader Village: a maze of motel-type units, one of several complexes built to handle the rising student population and aging buildings near Seattle's colleges and universities.

Terrell's address was Block D, number 231. Jason took the exterior stairs. The air hinted at sweet marijuana. As he approached Terrell's unit, music blared from across the earthen common area. Painful at this hour. Towers of pizza boxes and pyramids of beer cans flanked every door. He knocked on 231, got no response, and knocked again, louder.

"Who is it?" a male voice called from the other side.

"Jason Wade, I'm here to see Luke."

Muffled movement, then two clicks at the door. A guy about Wade's size but a few inches taller, wearing frameless glasses, a blue tie-dye T-shirt, and faded jeans opened it and studied him.

"Are you Luke Terrell?"

A nod.

"Jason Wade. I'm a reporter with the *Seattle Mirror*. May I talk to you for a few minutes?"

Luke's eyes were red-rimmed and bloodshot. His hair was disheveled, he was unshaven. Looked like he hadn't slept for two days. He stared at Jason. "Did they find something up in Sawridge?"

"No, I'm sorry, but can we talk?"

"I don't want to give any interviews. I was up there helping on the search, I'm beat."

"A few minutes is all I'll need to let you know what I've heard."

Luke weighed the offer, took a breath, exhaled.

"All right, a few minutes."

It was a studio apartment. A futon with messed sheets was in one corner. Shelving constructed of pine planks and cinder blocks, supporting a TV and sound system, stood against one wall. It faced a torn sofa and two unmatched chairs. A large desk with two laptops and a big freestanding hard-drive system occupied one end. The walls were covered with posters for classic horror movies.

"Nice poster collection."

"It's a hobby."

They sat in the chairs. Seattle papers, including the *Mirror*, were on the sofa. Karen's face stared from various angles.

"How are you holding up, Luke?"

He shrugged. "Anything new?"

"Maybe something." Jason pulled out his notebook. Luke's eyes locked on to it. "I'd like to take notes. I just need to be accurate for the story."

After a few moments passed, Luke nodded.

"What do you think happened to Karen?"

"I don't know. I don't want to think about it. I want her to come home."

"All police have said is that she was on her way to see her sister in Vancouver, yet she didn't call ahead. It seems odd that she'd set off like that without telling anyone."

"I don't know why she did it."

"You have no idea?"

Luke shook his head.

"I see." Jason checked his notes. "Trudy Moore, who lives below Karen, said she'd heard strange noises. Someone was walking in Karen's apartment the very next morning."

"I saw that today in your paper. The story sounded like some mystery man was rifling through her place. That was me in her apartment."

"Excuse me?"

"That was me in her apartment that morning. I went there looking for her when I couldn't reach her on the phone."

"But how did—"

"I have a key to Karen's place. She has a key to mine."

"I see."

"Police know I was there. I answered Karen's phone that morning when a deputy called saying he'd found her car near Laurel but no trace of Karen. I told the deputy that, given the car's location, Karen had likely been on her way to see her sister, Marlene Clark, in Vancouver. The deputy told me to call her sister in Vancouver and check. That's how it got started."

"Have the police given you any theories?"

"No. I've told them all I know, but they're not telling me anything."

"What about the possibility that someone from the college may've had something to do with it?"

"Like who?"

"Like anybody."

"I don't know anything about that."

"Why do you think Karen left Seattle without alerting anyone?"

Luke glanced at the movie posters as if for the answer, then looked back at Jason and swallowed. "I wish I knew. I don't understand it."

Jason let Luke's answer hang in the air long enough to signal that he doubted him.

"When was the last time you talked to her?"

"The night she left, just before her car was found. I work part-time tending bar at the Well and called her on my break to talk."

"How was she? Was she sad? Happy? Angry about something?"

"All right. I'd say she was fine."

"Really? A neighbor who saw her leaving said Karen looked upset."

"She was fine when we talked."

"What'd you talk about?"

"We just talked a bit about her upcoming trip to Africa."

"She's going to Africa?"

"For a year."

"First time I heard that. Tell me about Karen and how you met. I could profile her. Maybe someone will read a detail that might help."

Luke took a moment to consider the request. Jason thought it a little strange that he seemed reluctant. In his shoes anyone else would be calling a press conference every ten minutes asking for people to help find his girlfriend. Maybe he was exhausted with anguish and not thinking clearly.

"I'm sure the more people know of Karen," Jason said, "the more they'd be inclined to come forward with information, or help locate her."

Luke agreed.

"We met a few years back at a campus rally for Third World relief. She's studying African history. I'm taking software design. I told her I was concerned about globalization, poverty. I want to create advanced programs to bring remote regions of the poorest countries online."

"What'd she think?"

"She was cool with that. Her parents are missionaries in Central America. She said her mother's time in the peace corps had inspired her to devote a year in Ethiopia as an aid worker. One of Karen's professors in religious studies told her about an African fellowship. I told her to do it."

"You hit it off."

"We're unofficially engaged. After graduation I'm going to work here to establish things while Karen does her year in Africa. When she returns, we'll get married. She wants a small ceremony by the Pacific."

"When was she supposed to leave?"

"In a few months."

"The last time you talked to Karen on the phone, did you disagree on anything that would upset her?"

Terrell shook his head.

"What went through your mind when you picked up the phone in her apartment that morning and the deputy said they'd found her car on the side of the road not far from the border?"

"I thought it wasn't true."

"So she wasn't upset after you talked. You didn't argue?"

"No."

Jason was uneasy with Luke's account. It contradicted Trudy Moore's account. Was he lying? Jason had to confirm it with the investigators.

"So what do you think happened to her?"

"I think she was on her way to see her sister when

her car broke down and someone came along offering to help her." Luke paused. "She's a beautiful trusting person who doesn't preach, doesn't judge anyone, sees only the good in people."

Then Luke stared at Jason with a question.

"You tell me, how could she just vanish?"

He didn't have a quick answer, although he was familiar with the torment of losing someone. Sitting there in Luke's apartment surrounded by walls plastered with poster art from old horror movies, Jason was transfixed. Karen's picture in the newspaper bled into the unsettling images. Women's faces frozen in wide-eyed terror as they tried to escape deranged men, demons, or malevolent forces on the brink of destroying them.

12

Karen Harding was sinking in a bottomless, black chasm.

The darkness was overwhelming, tossing her between sleep and waking terror. Her mind swirled with wild uncontrollable emotions. She'd lost all sense of time, all sense of direction and perception. Why was this happening? It took prayer and every fiber of her being to stop her descent into the abyss.

Slowly, with deep breaths, her thoughts became lucid.

Turning to the crack of light, her thread of hope, Karen put her mind to work as she lay in the back of the RV listening to the engine's hum and the tires against the pavement.

This was what she knew. She was alive. She was not dreaming. She had been abducted by the reverend. And unless she fought back, this cell under the twin bed would become her coffin.

The steady drone told her they were moving.

On some road somewhere.

Her pulse raced, struggling to keep a heartbeat

ahead of fear, the way she'd seen the baby rabbit in a documentary fleeing for its life from a large wolf. Eyes wide, darting left, darting right, stumbling as the wolf pawed its legs, screaming as the hunter's fangs tore at its fur, staining it with blood, until the rabbit disappeared into dense bramble.

And lived.

Karen would fight back.

Her will to survive would be her ally. Still, she was calmed only slightly by her determination. She could not stop trembling. Could not slow the adrenaline coursing through her.

The hot breath of fear was gaining on her.

She swallowed hard and searched for strength. Searched for it in the memories of her mother and father. Marlene. Luke. She searched for it in the smallest victories.

Like the gag in her mouth.

By chewing and stretching the dampened cloth, she had worked it to the point where it had slackened enough for her to close her mouth. The relief for her aching jaw was immeasurable. She could breathe, swallow. *Call for help*. But if need be, she could open her mouth and let the gag slip back into place and bite down on it so it appeared secure.

The binding around her wrists was more difficult.

She used every conscious moment to work on it. At times she worked on it automatically, stretching with every degree of strength she could summon. She would beat this rope. By clenching her stomach muscles, and

Rick Mofina

those in her arms, she was loosening the rope. Almost imperceptibly. But she could feel it. It was going to take time, but eventually she might, just might, be able to slip her hands free.

She prayed.

Prayed that someone would come for her. But how would they know where she was? She was kidnapped but had no idea by whom. A stranger? She had no idea where she was. What time it was. What day it was. She was thirsty. Hungry. The wolf was gaining on her. Tears stung her eyes and she sank deeper into the darkness. As if she were buried alive.

Karen caught her breath.

The mattress above her had creaked.

The woman above her.

She remembered seeing her arm. There was a person above her. Karen heard a muffled groan. Was the woman a prisoner like her? But the wrist hadn't been bound.

Maybe she was another wolf.

Karen swallowed. Blinking as she thought. And thought. She could call out to her. No. Not now. Not while the RV was moving. The reverend could hear. And there might be others in the back of the RV.

Karen strained to listen.

She forced herself to the crack of light. Pushed hard against it, harder than she'd ever pushed before, so she could see as much as possible. She used her peripheral vision, exerting it until her eyes hurt. She scanned the rear, then the rest of the RV, all the way to the driver's seat where the reverend was behind the wheel. As best she could tell, no one else was in the vehicle but the three of them.

And it was night.

At that moment they slowed down. Karen was jostled as the RV slowed, then turned. Onto another road. A soft quiet road. Almost like sand, or soft earth. The motion rocked Karen side to side. They were definitely off road. A backcountry road? Driving slowly, they climbed, dipped, and turned. Going forever, it seemed. Karen's heart thumped against her ribs.

Where's he taking us?

The woman above her moaned.

Brakes creaked. The RV stopped. The engine was turned off and ticked down in the quiet. Karen heard crickets chirping. Heard the reverend get up from behind the wheel and walk toward them, his footfalls growing louder. She felt weight shifting as the mattress above her squeaked, then he walked off. The vehicle tilted as he opened the door and stepped from it.

Striving to listen, Karen was convinced he had walked away on the soft earth. Convinced she was alone with the woman above her. This was her chance. She swallowed and cleared her throat.

"Hello." It was her loudest whisper.

Silence was the response.

"Hello. I'm down here under you. In the storage space."

A woman's muffled groan.

Karen blinked and listened for any sounds of some-one approaching before trying again.

"My name's Karen. Can you hear me? Are you all right?"

There was movement on the mattress but no re-sponse.

"We have to get away from him. We have to help each other."

The whole frame and mattress began to vibrate above Karen. Then came a loud thud on the floor next to her. Karen gasped and thrust her face to the crack of light.

Something had fallen onto the floor.

Her heart stopped.

She was staring into the horrified round eyes of a young woman who appeared to be her age. Silver duct tape sealed the woman's mouth.

Oh God.

Karen heard the sounds of someone rushing to the RV. Heard the door being yanked open, felt the dip of someone stepping inside, stomping to the bedroom, halting at the sight of the woman splayed on the floor.

Karen's body tensed at the sudden loud clank of metal as something was dropped to the floor beside her. She strained against the crack to see a shovel and a saw.

13

Sawridge County Detective Hank Stralla had a kind, intelligent face, Marlene Clark thought, sitting across from his desk in his Bellingham office.

He set a ceramic mug bearing the county's logo in front of her. His wooden chair creaked as he sat down and sipped from his own cup.

The corkboard to his left was feathered with county memos, a calendar marking duty and court dates. In one corner she noticed a snapshot of him in a ball cap with a beaming boy who had his eyes. The boy looked to be about seven. They were holding up a fish. On the wall above Stralla there was a clock. Marlene could hear it ticking.

"How's the motel?" he asked.

"Good." Marlene had arrived the day before, insisting that her husband, Bill, stay with the children in Vancouver. She had to come alone.

Because if she came alone, it would be all right. It wouldn't be serious. Police may have found her sister's car, but it would turn out to be a mistake, a Karen thing, she had lied to herself as she drove, her knuckles whitening on the wheel. *God, let this be just a little Karen thing, please!*

Marlene had driven directly to the site on 539 and stayed at the scene. She'd watched the search late into the night, then gone to the motel where she found a Bible on the nightstand and read from it until dawn.

Day two, and here she was sitting in Stralla's office. He opened a manila folder identified with neat block letters in felt-tip pen: KAREN KATHERINE HARDING.

"Anything else come to mind today, Marlene?"

A trace of cologne floated toward her after he opened the folder, clicked his ballpoint pen, and dated a clean note sheet.

"I think I told you everything yesterday."

He held her in his gaze for a moment. Marlene's voice was steady. She had been an experienced trauma nurse before becoming an OR nurse. Stralla had been a cop for too damned long. In their professions, they had seen more human devastation than people could imagine, a fact that gave rise to an unspoken mutual respect.

"Have your parents been notified?"

"Yes. They're working with an aid group, delivering medicine in a mountain region of Guatemala. We've sent word through the embassy."

Stralla nodded.

"You told me Karen has visited you before without calling first."

"A few times, yes."

"So this isn't entirely out of character?"

Marlene thought for a moment. Stralla made a mental note of her hesitation. "No."

"What's your read on Luke Terrell?"

"Bright. Karen loves him. Why? What about Luke?"

"He told us he called her during a break at his job, they talked for a while, and everything was fine."

"That's what he told me, too."

"But shortly after that call, she leaves Seattle heading north. She left without her cell phone in a storm. It tells me she was distracted by something. And the next morning Luke is in her apartment. What do you make of that?"

"I know Luke and Karen had exchanged apartment keys. Luke told me he'd gone to her place to talk to her and was there when a deputy called looking for Karen. You think he's hiding something?"

"Maybe." Stralla shrugged. "I'm just trying to get a full picture of Karen's state of mind and the circumstances leading up to this." He stared at the little circles he was making in his notes. "We just need to be certain everyone's telling us all they know about Karen's case." He looked at Marlene. "Describe for me again how Karen was the last time you talked to her."

"Happy, looking forward to Africa."

"She mention any problems with debts, school, drugs, Luke? Any little thing or person that troubled her enough that she would've mentioned it?"

Marlene shook her head, then stopped.

"She'd mentioned one man, actually she thought it was funny, but he liked to touch women a lot."

"Touch women?"

"She said he just put his hand on their shoulders sometimes when he talked. Demonstrative. She thought it was forward, not rude. All women know men like that."

"She ever say his name, or where she knew this guy?"

"Honestly, I don't know. It was a little thing she'd mentioned about three months ago over the phone. I don't know but it's possible she'd met him through the college or one of her church charity groups. You think someone followed her?"

"We can't rule out anything."

Stralla collected his notes. Because Marlene had filed the official missing person's report and was Karen's closest relative, she'd signed off on Stralla to check her sister's bank and credit card activity. Nothing so far. Stralla closed the file folder. Time to return to the 539 site.

"Is my sister dead?"

Stralla hadn't expected the question.

"Because"—Marlene's voice was ragged—"you and I know how most of these cases end, so you tell me right now if you think my sister's dead. You tell me."

Stralla recalled images of corpses, autopsies, and funerals and knew the odds were against them here.

"We don't know if Karen's dead. No evidence has surfaced telling us she'd been hurt. Right now, all we know is that she's missing under unusual circumstances. Until we have answers, all we have are more questions."

Marlene searched Stralla's face for deception until she was satisfied there was none.

14

The Big Timber Truck Stop outside Bellingham was one of the largest in the Pacific Northwest.

It was a twenty-four-hour operation offering fueling, a restaurant, a store, laundry and shower facilities, a chapel, motel rooms, and customs preclearance. The perimeter was dotted with ten-foot chain-saw wood sculptures of bears, moose, wolves, and eagles, produced by Odell White, the former logger who had opened Big Timber twenty-odd years ago.

Detective Stralla rolled by dozens of idling rigs and stopped near the restaurant beside a Sawridge County Sheriff's four-by-four. It was Raife Ansboro's, a detective in the division who was helping him on the Harding case.

Ansboro had called Stralla just about an hour ago. He was a calm, monotone-voiced man who lived alone in a cabin. Nothing much excited him. But today Stralla detected a degree of optimism.

"Got something at Big Timber, Hank. Better get over here."

Stralla entered the lobby, went down the hall to

where Odell was telling Ansboro, "I got Percy working on it," then to Stralla he said, "You two go use my office. Everybody's here now, I'll go round em up."

Odell's office was cluttered with a battered file cabinet, a desk stained by forgotten cigarettes that had burned to the butt, and two swivel chairs upholstered with what looked like animal fur. There was also a small table with invoices, order forms, and catalogues specializing in truck supplies.

Ansboro held up a sealed plastic bag containing two credit card slips.

"She was here."

Stralla's eyes narrowed to Karen Harding's signature on both slips. In clear, neat, and almost cheerful script. One was for gas. A second for the restaurant. The information on the slips faded, but Stralla saw the date and time. Although he already knew, he opened his slim binder to his case log. The time was consistent with the phone-in report by a trucker who said he'd seen Harding standing next to her Toyota on 539.

The receipt's code indicated who had served her.

"Odell's got everyone coming in who worked that night."

"This is good, Raife." Stralla looked around the office. "Odell's got security cameras all over the place, doesn't he?"

"That's the good news. But Percy thinks they crapped out in the storm."

Stralla cursed to himself.

"He's in the back working on them."

One knock sounded on the door before Odell cracked it.

"All here."

Stralla and Ansboro followed Odell down the hall beyond the hum and soapy smell of the laundry rooms where truckers were folding shirts and jeans, to a small room where four people sat in metal chairs around a Ping-Pong table. The group of staff who had been on shift when Harding was at the restaurant. Two women, a man in his twenties, and a man in his sixties, who looked pissed off. They were studying the sketch of the restaurant floor plan Ansboro had made. Fingers tapping booths as they determined who sat where and who ate what.

"I told them what this is about," Odell said.

Stralla asked the staff to tell him all they could remember about Karen Harding and the others in the restaurant.

"She was here." Betty Dane tapped her nail on a booth by the window. "I brought her a chicken sandwich and side salad. That poor little girl."

"Describe her demeanor."

"Like she had plenty on her mind. I think she was writing a letter."

"She talk to you or anybody?"

Betty's hoop earrings chimed as she shook her head.

"And the other people?"

"You had truckers, here, here, here, and here." Lorna, the older waitress, tapped the tables on the drawing. "Here you had a man by himself, older, quiet, reading a book."

"Right," Betty agreed. "Looked like a minister. And next to him there was a retired couple. I think they're locals."

"Jimmy and Connie. Got a place in the country two exits south. Next to them was a woman and her daughter, who was maybe twelve or thirteen. Except for Jimmy and Connie, I think the others were travelers," Lorna said.

"And the truckers?"

"Most of them are regulars," Betty said and Lorna nodded. "We're on their route."

Stralla nodded to the young man who had filled Harding's gas tank.

"I can't remember much. We had rigs backed up in the other bays. It was busy because of the storm. And we had the power surge."

The cook had his large tattooed arms folded across his chest. He raised his craggy face and squinted at Stralla.

"You think somebody from here might've followed her?"

"Anything's possible." Stralla's eyes lingered on the tattoos. Maybe someone had tampered with her car.

"Well, let me tell you," the cook said. "You're searching for a needle in a haystack. We get a lot of people passing through here."

"Don't I know it? Thanks for helping us out. Please, everyone, call us if you remember anything, any little thing."

After the staff members left, Stralla asked Odell if

he'd volunteer all credit card receipts for the time surrounding Harding's disappearance.

"Sure."

Percy York caught up to Odell and the two detectives in the hall. The responsibility for maintaining Big Timber's security cameras fell to Percy, a part-time mechanic and self-taught computer geek.

"Anything?" Ansboro said.

"Come and see."

Stralla's cell phone rang.

"Stralla."

"Hi, Jason Wade from the *Mirror*. Do you have a second?"

"A second."

"I'm on my way to see you, as soon as possible."

"Why? We've got nothing new for the press."

"I want to confirm something Karen's boyfriend told me."

"Concerning?"

"His last conversation with her before she disappeared."

Stralla considered his watch and Wade's request. "Tell me now."

"I'd like to do this face-to-face. I'm on the road now."

"Suit yourself. Call me when you get to town."

Wade had captured Stralla's interest, he thought, slipping his phone into his pocket. The kid was a digger.

Big Timber's security system was shoehorned in a dark room near the arcade. Percy went to a table with several consoles, video recorders, and four small TV monitors. "The heads were dirty and we had a surge from the storm. I don't think it reset properly." A shape in a snowstorm began swimming on one of the monitors. Looked like a woman walking in the lot.

"I think that's her."

"Hang on." Stralla left, then returned with Betty and Lorna. "Run it again. Now tell me, is that her?"

Betty nodded.

"Yes, that's her."

The picture quality was terrible. A grainy figure moved between trucks, got into a car, and drove out of the frame. It could've been a Toyota.

"Take it back," Stralla said.

After taking several moments to line up the tape, Percy tried several times in vain to find a clean stream of footage.

"But you've got stuff from other cameras, other angles throughout the lot and the building, right?" Stralla asked.

"Yes, from a number of cameras. What I just showed you is the best."

Stralla turned to Odell. "You going to volunteer your tapes so I can take them to somebody who might clean them up?"

"Sure, Hank."

Odell and Percy gathered the tapes into a brown take-out bag for Stralla, who then walked to the lot with Ansboro.

"We could have something here," Ansboro said before starting his engine.

"We could." Stralla watched him drive off, turning at the lot exit marked by a ten-foot grizzly, poised to do battle. Then the detective studied the credit card receipts, thinking that the last thing Karen Harding might've written in her life was her name.

15

High winds from the Strait of Georgia tumbled inland over the stretch of State Route 539 where Karen Harding's Toyota had broken down.

Investigators were finishing the scene work, loading her car onto a flatbed before a line of news types and onlookers. Jason Wade walked to the far edge of the yellow tape, quietly took a State Patrol trooper aside, and asked for Detective Stralla. The trooper made a radio check, then nodded to a Sawridge four-by-four among the police vehicles. As Jason approached it, calculating the time he had to get back to Seattle for his shift, the driver's-side window lowered.

"I'm Jason Wade, from the *Mirror*."

Stralla remained in his truck, shook Jason's hand, observed his stubble and earring. Still, he warmed to the young reporter, maybe for his pursuit of the story, maybe for that '69 Falcon.

Jason recognized the woman who was sitting next to Stralla from news pictures. "You're Karen's sister?"

"Yes," Marlene Clark said before Stralla cut in.

"You said you needed to talk about Luke Terrell."

"You want to do this here?"

"Here's good."

"Okay." Jason flipped through his notes. "I've got a few questions, to confirm some things for a story. Luke told me he'd called Karen from his bartending job the night she left Seattle. Is that right?"

"That's right, he was working that night."

"He said that in their conversation everything was fine. Is that true? Is that what he told you?"

Stralla and Marlene exchanged glances.

"What people tell us at first is not always clear," Stralla said.

"So Luke gave you one story, and gave me another."

"He could be inconsistent on his conversation with Karen."

"So everything was not fine between Luke and Karen in the time before she left," Jason said. "I mean, he was in her apartment the next morning, looking through it aggressively, according to the noises her neighbor heard."

"What're you trying to say?" Stralla checked the time.

"I think they had a monumental argument, that he's not telling the whole story here, that maybe he lied to me."

Stralla was impressed with Jason. He was smart. "Could be Luke got mixed up a bit there. We're working on a time line," he said.

"Well, if that's the case, do you consider Luke a suspect?"

Marlene turned away and looked at the slopes.

"Hold on," Stralla said as his phone began ringing and he shifted to get it. "It's too soon to be pointing any fingers. We're still sorting through things." He took his call. "Stralla," he said, then ended it with a terse "we're on our way" and turned the ignition. "Jason, we've got to go."

Frustrated, Jason pleaded for a few more minutes. As the motor idled, Marlene answered a few quick questions about Karen, then removed two nice photos from her wallet for Jason to use in the paper.

When he returned to his car, he called the *Mirror*, leaving a message on Ron Nestor's voice mail telling him about the story. As he drove, he went over it in his head. Nothing made sense. Miles later, he was closer to Seattle but nowhere near the truth behind Karen Harding's disappearance.

In the newsroom, Jason looked at the pictures of Karen Harding.

There was one of her on the beach. In another, she was baking at a charity for an African cultural fair. In another, she was radiant beside Luke, arms around his neck, snowcapped Mount Baker behind them. A young woman who wanted to devote herself to helping the children of the world's poorest nations.

Vanished.

There's the lead, Jason thought, beginning his story when Astrid Grant tapped his shoulder.

"I get a shared byline on that story."

"Excuse me?"

"This morning Ron Nestor assigned me to find Harding's sister and boyfriend for a feature."

"Yeah, and you couldn't find them. You never left the newsroom."

"You're hogging this story, Jason. No one knew you were out there doing the same thing on your time. God, don't you ever sleep!"

"I broke this story and I'm going to stay on it."

"I could've been working on my lottery winners feature. I wasted my morning because you never called it in."

"I did. I called in once I had the interviews nailed."

"I made a lot of calls. I want credit for my time. I deserve a double."

"You *deserve* credit, even when you fail? Is that how it works for you?"

After glancing around to ensure that no one could hear, Astrid dropped her voice. "Listen to me. I'm going to get the job, understand? I intend to get away from L.A. and work here as a staff reporter for the *Seattle Mirror*."

"Good luck with that."

"You're the one who needs luck. From what I see, you're the local poster hire for the program. I mean, did you *read* everyone else's bio?" Astrid paused when a couple of senior reporters walked by, then resumed. "You'd be wise to stay out of my way."

Jason's jaw muscles tensed as he stared at his monitor. Without speaking he pushed himself from his keyboard and stood to face Astrid Grant, whose family lived in a Beverly Hills home valued at $3.3 million.

Maybe her upbringing conferred her with a sense of entitlement. Whatever it was, Jason had swallowed enough.

"Jason Wade!" Ron Nestor summoned him from his glass-walled office. Astrid rolled her eyes as Jason walked to Nestor, who was holding the door open.

"Have a seat."

One wall of Nestor's office was covered with plaques, framed photos of him with the president, the governor, and a couple of Mariners players. Also up there were two commemorative front pages and a collection of press tags. Nestor set down a mug of his final shot of coffee for the day, then joined Jason at the small table.

"I'm glad you got us the scoop on Harding's boyfriend and sister. Good legwork."

"Thanks."

"The next time you're inspired to enterprise, even on your own time, you give the desk a heads-up."

"I called you when I nailed the interviews."

"Yes, but I need to know what you're up to beforehand. It's my business to know. That's carved in stone."

Nestor studied Jason for a few seconds.

"Look, I understand six of you are competing for one job. I understand our intern program is insanely stressful. It's like this every year. Some people crack. It's the program's only way to determine if people are cut out to be *Seattle Mirror* reporters."

That night, after Jason filed his story he drove through the city trying not to think of Karen Harding. But she surfaced with the glow of each passing streetlight as he guided his Falcon over the bridge to Fremont. He kept thinking about her until he entered his apartment and heard his father's voice. The sole message on his machine.

"Hi, Jay. Sorry I missed you. I keep reading your work. Looks good. Drop by the house sometime?"

Sadness and shame rolled over him. Could've been because of Astrid, or his old man, reminding him of where he came from, or his need to prove himself at the *Mirror*.

Could've been everything.

He shoved it all aside, took a sheaf of stories and news photo prints from his bag, and headed for bed. He glanced at Valerie's bracelet on his bedpost, missing her again, before his mind returned to the story.

He stripped to his T-shirt and briefs and plopped on his bed.

He shuffled through photographs of Karen and Luke, then looked closely at the news shots of the groups of her friends who'd volunteered to search. Luke was there, alongside several good-looking women. Were they the reason Luke was holding back on him? Then there were the local people and, according to the cutlines, some of Karen Harding's college instructors and church group.

Jason came back to shots that included the man who had the black shirt and collar of a reverend. Odd. In each frame he seemed to be turning his head, as if shunning the camera. He was never clearly photographed and not identified in the information.

Who was he?

Jason shrugged, studying all of the pictures again before switching off his light. As he lay in the dark, sleep fogged his sense of reason as it began whispering that the truth might be closer than he thought.

16

Hanna Larssen, a seventy-three-year-old descendant of Norwegian pioneers, peeked through her lace curtain but saw no trace of her best friend. Where could that rascal be?

At daybreak, Cody, her shepherd, was usually yawning from his mat by the kitchen door, or he might've ambled outside to the front porch.

The timer chimed. Hanna turned to the stove, slid a hissing pot of boiling water from the burner. She spooned out her four-minute brown-shelled egg, sat alone at her table, and began her breakfast, a titch annoyed with Cody.

She didn't want to go looking for him. Last time this happened the silly thing had chased a squirrel for a quarter mile before he got himself snared in a thornbush. He cried like a baby. And his squirming didn't make it much easier for her to disentangle him from the prickly branches.

Such a male. Running off and getting into trouble, waiting for a woman to come to his rescue. Hanna finished eating, looked around for him, hopeful he would appear. No luck.

Her needlepoint for the museum would have to wait. After washing up, she stepped onto her veranda, slid her worn wide-brimmed hat on her white hair, shielded her eyes from the light, and surveyed her three hundred acres in the lower Yakima Valley. To the south were the Horse Heaven Hills, while on the north, where she lived, were the Rattlesnake Hills, with the Yakima River cutting through the valley, running east to west.

The sun was spilling over the treeless southern slopes where wild horses once galloped across the grassy hills. Hanna squinted, drinking in the panoramic view of the valley. Her keys jingled against her jeans as she climbed into her old Dodge truck. Might as well try the western slope first. Cody liked to wander out that way.

The access road to the remote corners of Hanna's property was not really a road. It was more of a path. Two dirt ruts divided by a rise of grass. It paralleled the local highway for nearly a quarter mile before looping north, climbing a rise, then disappearing over one of the gentle rolling hills.

Hanna was inseparable from her land. She was from a line of Norwegians who arrived to farm in the late 1800s. Her great-grandmother was born here in the family's first house, a homestead shack. Hanna was born here and like her dear late husband, whose people were from Yakima, she would die here.

But that was a long way off. She was healthy, sturdy, her teeth were good, and she had a lot of living to do. She had friends in Whitstran, Prosser, and she was a member of the Benton City Bridge Club. She had no intention of ever selling out and going into a home in Grandview. She guarded her independence. She was happy here with Cody. He was good company.

Except this morning.

The truck's brakes creaked as Hanna halted at the western slope with its wonderful view. She shut off the motor, called. Then listened.

Nothing.

All right, she'd head for the eastern coulee, that was the other favorite runaway spot for him. Recalling how she once spotted a big female cougar there, she telegraphed a protective thought for her dog. She also remembered the time a couple of carloads of teens came out from Toppenish and had a party along the creek at the isolated coulee.

Toddling along the path she scanned the rolling grassy hill for Cody. She continued on for another fifteen minutes, cresting a hilltop, the truck rattling and clanking, seeing nothing as she began to descend into the valley toward the creek. Here the road twisted around buttes and small rises that popped up, blocking the long view to the water.

Hanna heard a yelp. Or was it a cry?

Concentrating, she heard nothing and kept going. She rounded another small butte when a loud woof at her ear made her jump.

"My heavens!"

Cody leaped into the road, landing on all fours.

Hanna braked, opened her door, and after catching her breath shouted at him. "Get in here. Come on."

Cody stared at her, then made a noise she'd never heard before, a sort of whoop-wail-cry. Unease shivered through Hanna and she pictured her husband's Winchester rifle locked in the cabinet in her living room, wishing she'd brought it.

"Let's go."

The dog was spooked and wanted Hanna to confront whatever was over the butte and down by the creek. Hanna looked around and considered it, thinking this was silly. In all her days living her life on her property, Hanna had feared nothing. She turned off the truck. The day was so peaceful.

"All right, I'll look, then I'm picking you up."

The cab squeaked as she stepped from it. A pair of larks flitted by as Hanna ascended the small rise, followed by Cody. As she climbed the hilltop, she noted the wildflowers, the candleweed, Gray ball sage, Jim Hill mustard, and rip-gut. She could hear the water rushing below, saw the sun shimmering off the waves, drawing her to the object by the grassy bank some forty yards away

What a mess.

That was her first thought.

Garbage spread all over, some even piled in a heap, as if in defiance of respect for a person's private property. Heading to the site, Hanna decided that she would go to the sheriff and give him an earful about how these young hoods were out of control. As Hanna got nearer, her pulse quickened and her anger evaporated.

What is that?

For a few seconds she was confused, blinking to adjust her understanding, then her jaw fell open.

Oh, sweet son of Mary, this can't be!

17

An hour out of Seattle, Jason Wade watched the trees blurring by his window as news photographer Nathan Hodge pushed his Cherokee well over the limit east on I-90.

Destination: somewhere in the Rattlesnake Hills.

A radio station in Richland, on its noon broadcast, was first to report the discovery of a woman's body in a remote coulee near Whitstram. The Associated Press moved the story on the wire and soon every news organization in the Pacific Northwest had it and was speculating on whether it was Karen Harding.

When it reached the *Mirror*, Ron Nestor called Jason's cell phone.

"Where are you?"

"Supermarket."

"A woman's body's been found in Benton County. Get in here, hook up with Nate Hodge, and get your asses out there."

"Is it Karen Harding?"

"That's what you have to find out. Get as much as you can. File ASAP."

This was Jason's shot. A major breaking story.

* * *

His stomach lifted when Hodge braked hard coming up too fast on a slow-moving van as they entered the Snoqualmie Pass. In winter this was avalanche country. The Wenatchee Mountains rose in the east. Southwest, the highway threaded along the Snoqualmie National Forest with its alpine slopes and peaks shrouded by glaciers.

Hodge was hard to read. Bald under his Seahawks cap, the brim down low over his dark aviator glasses, he had been shooting news for some twenty years. When Jason climbed into the Cherokee, Hodge made it clear that he had no time to babysit interns. He also made it clear that Jason must never track mud into his Jeep.

As they drove, Jason fired up his laptop and scrolled to the contact list he'd dumped into it. He called Benton County for an update.

"You want Lieutenant Buchanan, but he's at the scene." The secretary recited his cell phone number. It rang through to Buchanan's voice mail. Jason left a message, then searched the landscape, wondering if Karen Harding had been murdered out here.

Around Ellensburg, they got on I-82.

"We're going to hit a fast food place in Yakima," Hodge said. "Use the washroom. It's going to be a long, long day."

After a pit stop at a Burger King, they got back on the road and were coming up on Outlook when Jason's phone rang.

"Lieutenant Buchanan, Benton County Detective Division."

He scrambled for his pen and notebook, opening it to a clean page.

"Thanks for getting back to me. Lieutenant—"

Hodge interrupted Jason to ensure that he got directions to the scene. Jason noted it before continuing. "Lieutenant, we're coming in from Seattle. Can you direct us to the scene?"

Hodge did, sounding as if he'd been giving the same directions all day. The way to the farm was uncomplicated. Wade asked his next question.

"Have you been able to identify the victim?"

"Way too soon for that. Nothing's been moved. We're securing the scene and forensic people will go over it."

"Any indication as to the cause and manner and time of death?"

"Nothing I can tell you right now. We're early on this."

"Well, can you rule out a link to Harding, the missing Seattle woman?"

"Can't rule on anything. You'll have to excuse me, I've got other calls."

"One last question, Lieutenant. The wire story says the body was found on private property. Can you tell me a little more? Who made the discovery? How did they make it? And do you have any suspects?"

"That's more than one question, son. Our people will bring you up to speed when you get here."

To get to the farm they exited 82 at North Prosser, taking the country road that parallels the canal to Whitstram. The property was a few miles east. There was no mistaking the remote house. Some two dozen police and press vehicles, from Seattle, Yakima, Richland, and Spokane, were there.

Jason noted the name, Hanna Larssen, on the mailbox.

Reporters and news crews were standing in small groups with sheriff's deputies. One of them handed Jason and Hodge a sheet—a summary of what had happened, lacking anything new. A map pinpointed the scene. Hodge cursed.

"Must be half a mile over the hills. There's no picture from here."

"Welcome, Nate. Misery loves company." A photographer from the *Seattle Post-Intelligencer* joined Hodge.

Jason left them for a deputy encircled by a group of reporters, assuring them the lead detective would hold an on-site press briefing in two hours. Jason decided to try to talk to Larssen, the property owner. But when he approached the porch, a deputy there raised his hand.

"I'd like to speak to Hanna Larssen," Jason said.

The deputy shook his head. "Sorry. Nobody's home at this time."

Jason didn't know what to try next. He joined the vigil with the press pack, making small talk. No one seemed to know much. If they did, they weren't sharing. Deciding to use the time to write up some bare-bones stuff and color about the location, Jason went off alone by an empty patrol car. Its radio was busy with chatter.

"Ryan, seventy-nine, wants you to pick up the additional statement, over."

"What statement? Over."

The dispatcher heaved an audible but friendly sigh.

"The property owner who made the find this morning."

"Hanna Larssen?"

Jason's head snapped up, cocked to listen.

"Ten-four."

"Okay, but what's her twenty?"

"Stand by."

Jason held his breath as the dispatcher returned.

"She's in Richland, at 344 Evergreen, with friends."

"Richland, well, that's where I am."

"That's why I called you."

"I'll take care of it, ten-four."

Jason jotted the address, then consulted his map for Richland. It was east and not far. He could get there and back easily in under two hours. He glanced around to see if any of the others had overhead the police dispatch. It didn't look like it. He closed his laptop to approach Hodge, but Hodge got to him first.

"Jason. I can't get a picture here. I have to take an aerial shot, so I'm going to Richland right now. I'm sharing a small Cessna charter plane with KING-TV and the *P-I.* I should be back in time for the news conference."

"Good." Jason kept his voice low. "I need to get dropped off in Richland."

"Why?"

When they were alone in the Cherokee, Jason told Hodge, who agreed to drop him off, then pick him up on the way back. He told Jason to be sure to find out if Larssen would agree to have her picture taken along with the story.

The address was for a seniors' home, a low-ceilinged one-story building with a community hall attached. It was well kept with a neatly trimmed hedge and beautiful shrubs and flowers. Some flowers had nameplates rising from them. Someone had put in a lot of work on the landscaping, Jason thought as he went to the front desk and asked for Hanna Larssen.

"Sorry, she's not a resident." Seeing the disappointment in his face, the receptionist added, "But she might be in the living center around the back with the card club."

Jason followed the sidewalk to the rear of the building and entered. A piano was being played for about twenty white- and silver-haired people, mostly women, who sat in the large room. Some rocked in chairs and chatted, others were playing cards, or working on needlepoint. Jason bent down to a woman with thinning hair.

"Excuse me, can you point me to Hanna Larssen?"

"Who?"

"Hanna Larssen?"

"What?"

"Hanna Larssen?"

"She's right there, with the checkered shirt." A man with a pencil moustache pointed to a woman with a very grave expression talking quietly with another woman. "Hanna's not a resident. She just visits. Are you a friend?"

"I'm here to speak to Hanna Larssen on business."

Jason glanced at his watch, mindful of the press conference and his deadline to get a story filed to the paper.

The man touched each side of his moustache. His eyes twinkled at the notion that Hanna would have business with someone so young.

"I'll tell her you're here. Your name?"

"Jason Wade."

The man bent slightly as he talked to Hanna, causing her to look at Jason. Her face was serious as she nodded. Then the man waved Jason to join them at the small table. Jason remembered Phil Tucker telling him how seniors, coherent ones, made the best interviews because they feared no one. They'd lived through wars, deaths, every hardship imaginable. Jason hoped that was the case as he told Hanna he was a reporter with the *Seattle Mirror*.

Strong, intelligent soft blue eyes assessed him.

"Ma'am, is that your property out by Whitstram where the police are investigating?"

She nodded.

"And are you the one who found the body this morning?"

"Yes."

"Can you tell me how you came to find it?"

"Lieutenant Buchanan told me not to speak to the press."

"I understand. But there's about forty reporters in front of your place and in a short time the investigators are going to hold a press conference. I'm just here to make sure I get the facts right."

"Who told you where to find me? Was it the deputy who just left with my report?"

"I protect my sources, but you can say I heard it through police circles."

She nodded as Jason opened his notebook and tapped it with his pen.

"Can you walk me through what happened and what you saw, please?"

The color drained from her face and she looked out the window.

"Cody ran off. I got in my truck and went to the coulee to find him."

"Cody?"

"My shepherd."

"I see. And was it Cody who found the woman?"

"Yes, she was in the coulee, by the creek." Hanna covered her mouth with her hand.

"Was the body in a shallow grave, on the ground, or in a plastic bag?"

"That would have been better, maybe."

"I'm sorry, I don't understand."

"Buchanan told me not to tell anyone the details because he needs them for his investigation."

Jason said nothing. He thought for a moment, then had an idea.

"Did you see the woman's face?"

She nodded.

Jason reached into his pocket and pulled out the snapshots of Karen Harding he had.

"I'm going to show you pictures of a woman and you tell me if the woman in the coulee is the woman in these pictures."

One by one Jason set down pictures, Karen on the beach, Karen in the kitchen, Karen with Luke. All the while he was studying Hanna Larssen for her reaction. Tears welled in her eyes.

"I can't."

"Is the woman in the coulee the woman in these pictures?"

She kept shaking her head.

"I can't. I just can't say."

"Ma'am, please, can you describe how she was situated?"

"It was horrible. The most utterly horrible thing you could ever see."

18

The Sawridge County Sheriff's Office was in a six-story brick and glass office complex, which also housed the county courthouse and short-term jail. It occupied a block of downtown Bellingham, mixing a Victorian and neoclassical theme. But its pleasant design and bubbling lobby fountain offered little comfort to Marlene Clark when she entered.

Escorted by a uniformed female deputy, Marlene and the officer did not speak as their elevator ascended. As the bell tolled for each floor, Marlene's heart screamed.

A woman's body has been found.

That's what Stralla had told her on the phone when he sent for her. Marlene trembled until the elevator stopped and its doors opened on the floor of the detective division.

"This way."

The deputy guided Marlene down the hallway, its walls adorned with maps, posters for crime prevention, and pictures of smiling children receiving awards from the sheriff. They came to an empty lounge room. It had a sofa and several cushioned chairs, a veneer-covered table with four hardback chairs, and a fridge. At the far end there was a television and VCR.

"Please have a seat. Hank will be right with you."

Marlene didn't feel like sitting. She turned slowly from the deputy and stared blankly at a watercolor of a Pacific landscape.

"Is there anything you would like?"

I would like my sister to be alive.

"Coffee, soda, water?"

"Nothing, thank you."

Stralla entered, his hand clamped around several videocassette tapes scaled in a plastic bag, a file folder tucked under his arm.

"Thanks, Lee."

The deputy closed the door and left. Marlene turned to Stralla.

"I'm sorry. There's still no word from Benton County," he said. "It's going to take time." His eyes were strong, clear, as he waited to make sure she was with him before he continued. "I know this is the hardest thing to go through, but I'm going to need your help."

Marlene caught her breath and nodded.

Stralla set the tapes and the file folder on the table. He began checking and signing the evidence sheet, then removed the first tape and switched on the video player. The tapes were from the Big Timber Truck Stop security system and had been cleaned up. He needed Marlene to confirm that Karen was on the tape and that it wasn't someone who might've stolen her credit card. He was also hoping the footage would show if Karen had encountered anyone there that night.

Anyone Marlene might recognize.

As for whether it was Karen Harding's body in the Rattlesnake Hills, well, without confirmation anything was possible. Buchanan at Benton County would call. And Raife Ansboro was there to observe for Sawridge. Stralla inserted the first tape, dimmed the lights, and turned to Marlene.

"Ready?"

She folded her arms, hanging on to herself, then nodded.

A color image of the Big Timber Truck Stop parking lot emerged with the time and date blinking at the bottom of the screen. Stralla accelerated it, making people move at high speed in and out of the entrance. Coming to the time Karen had arrived, he slowed the tape.

Karen.

There she was gripping the collar of her jacket in the rain, walking, almost trotting to the entrance. Marlene knew that navy jacket. She was with her when she had bought it at a boutique in downtown Vancouver last spring. They had shopped and had lunch together. Marlene recognized her sister's body shape, her walk, the profile of her face.

Stralla turned to her and she nodded.

"That's her. That's Karen."

"Any doubt?"

Marlene covered her mouth with her hand. Tears filled her eyes.

"None."

Stralla inserted lobby and restaurant tapes, showing Karen eating alone. No encounters. Then he inserted another tape where Karen exited, hurrying off alone into the night until she vanished from view.

Marlene gasped.

Her instinct was to reach into the screen and pull Karen back. Pull her tight to her. Was this the last image, the last memory she would have of her little sister? *No. Please.* Marlene's heart raced, her mind took her back through her life to when she and Karen were children.

Halloween night.

Marlene was a princess. Karen was a tiny fairy. Holding hands, walking through the dark among the ghosts and monsters. Karen was young. Her first time out like that with her big sister. Karen was a bit uneasy, clinging to Marlene at every door. Marlene was annoyed because she wanted to be with her friends, not saddled with taking care of her baby sister.

Then at one house three large groups converged. It was loud, chaotic with laughter, shouting and screaming, howling. Marlene and Karen were jostled and Karen's tiny hand slipped from hers. Marlene searched among the witches and demons.

Karen.

She lost her in the darkness.

Karen.

Marlene stared at the tape of the truck stop.

Stared at Karen walking into the night.

Marlene buried her face in her hands, turning away from the TV. She had found Karen that Halloween night. But would she find her now?

Oh, Karen.

A woman's body has been found.

Images from Benton County assailed Marlene. Corpses in the country. Her sister lost among the monsters. When Stralla had first told her about the body, Marlene's response was to rush to the scene. See for herself.

She needed to know.

Stralla had stopped her. It wouldn't be best right now. Nothing'd been confirmed. No one knew for sure who the victim was. Fear seized Marlene. She wouldn't go. Couldn't go. Because if she didn't go, if she didn't see with her own eyes, then it wasn't true.

Her sister hadn't been murdered.

Hope was the fine thread holding Marlene together. Sitting in the darkened room with Detective Stralla, she had no idea how much time had passed as he played and replayed the tapes, making notes. She was adrift until the door opened and she saw her husband.

"Oh, Bill."

Marlene sobbed when he put his strong arms around her. Only then could she fall apart. He held her tight for several minutes until she regained some control.

"How did you know I needed you? I never called."

"Detective Stralla called me."

At that moment Stralla's cell phone rang. He left the room to take it but returned in less than a moment.

"Please sit down," he told Marlene and her husband. "Nothing has been confirmed, you must bear that in mind. Benton County has asked for Karen's dental records."

19

By 5:45 a.m., Jason Wade had showered, dressed, and left his room for the lobby of the Saddleback Motel. The smell of fresh coffee and toast and the clink of cutlery drifted from the smattering of tables in the dining area. A few early risers were working on their free continental breakfast.

Some glanced at CNN flickering from the big-screen TV. Some read newspapers, consulted maps, or talked on cell phones. Those near the window looked into the gloomy mist rising from the morning rain on the Columbia River as it flowed through Richland.

Jason stepped outside to the row of news boxes and bought a copy of the *Seattle Times*, the *Post-Intelligencer*, the *Mirror*, and a Tri-City paper. The story was on the front page of each edition. Jason grabbed a large coffee, a bagel, a banana, a cherry Danish, and bottled apple juice, putting them on a tray before heading back to his room.

His story was the line, running six columns under the *Mirror*'s flag: POLICE PROBE WOMAN'S "RITUALISTIC" KILLING IN RATTLESNAKE HILLS.

That was the word Hanna Larssen had used. The article ran over Nathan Hodge's large color aerial photo, looking down on the white canopy covering the scene. White-gloved forensic investigators could be seen working on the desolate site, a remote island of activity amid a vast, grassy ocean.

Jason bit into his Danish as he devoured his story, recalling Hanna Larssen's account of what began as a search for Cody, her shepherd.

Although shaken by making a grisly find on her property, Hanna Larssen was a smart woman, unafraid to talk to Jason but not foolish enough to reveal details that might hurt Lieutenant Buchanan's case. She swore she was unable to identify the victim as Karen Harding. The remains weren't in good condition, she said, refusing to give Jason more details other than to say the scene was horrible and looked "ritualistic."

No other newspaper had the ritualistic angle.

It was critical, Jason thought. For if the woman was displayed in a ritualistic manner, then her murder went beyond a crime of passion, or, he cringed at the thought, a run-of-the-mill murder. It was the hallmark of a predator. A serial killer.

And Jason knew the subject.

He'd studied serial murder in his spare time for years, having read just about everything he could find on it. He fired up his laptop and went online to various law enforcement studies on crime scenes, profiles, and behavior of organized killers: those who were likely to employ a ritualistic display of their victims. Such killers would possess an ever-changing personality. They would blend in with society. They would take their time selecting victims. Be cunning, methodological, research killing and dump sites.

Jason bit into his bagel, chewed on his thoughts, then read the other newspapers heaped on his bed. All of them had pretty much reported straight-up versions of police investigating the discovery of a woman's body. All had speculated on whether the corpse belonged to the missing college student from Seattle. No one had the answer. That would come after an autopsy confirmed identification and cause of death.

If this was Karen Harding, did the killer select her from the highway to be killed in a ritualistic way? Did he preselect the Rattlesnake Hills as the place to leave her corpse? The Pacific Northwest had plenty of precedent for this sort of thing. Sure, but hold on. Jason was getting ahead of things. There was too much he didn't know. So much he wanted to know. He looked out his window at the dark overcast sky, the rain, and the river.

His room phone startled him.

"It's me." Hodge was awake. "Meet me downstairs for breakfast."

Hodge said little over his frosted flakes. He crunched while appraising the news pictures of the scene taken by his competition. Satisfied that no one had beaten him on anything, he began reading the story.

"What do you think?" Jason asked.

Hodge said nothing for a long moment. He began peeling an orange.

"I don't know about this ritualistic thing, but one thing's for sure. You have to be in the air over the site before it hits you."

"Before what hits you?"

"How far out it is. Isolated from everything. He could do anything he wanted to her out there because nobody would hear the screams."

Jason's cell phone rang.

"It's Buchanan, returning your call."

"Thanks, Lieutenant." Jason dropped his voice and pulled out his pad and pen. "Any word on identifying the body?"

"You tell me. You seem to have the jump on everyone."

"Excuse me?"

"Browbeating an old woman just so you can sensationalize a story."

"I'm afraid you're mistaken."

"You didn't go hunting Hanna Larssen down?"

"I looked for her and she agreed to an interview. I was doing my job."

"What's your question, Wade?"

"Are you talking to Sawridge County on the Karen Harding case?"

"It's routine to check cases against those in other jurisdictions."

"Any word on identifying the body?"

"No. We're going to be done at the site in a few

hours, then the coroner's going to remove the remains. Then we'll set out on confirming identification."

Jason told Hodge.

"I'll need that picture," the photographer said. "Even in this crappy light."

They packed up, checked out, and within twenty minutes were on the road in Hodge's Cherokee heading back to the Larssen farm.

Despite the early hour and the steady gray drizzle, Jason counted as many cars at the farm as there had been the day before. While most were familiar press vehicles, several had no news logos painted on them. Looked to him like members of the public had come to rubberneck. A group of people in colorful rain clothes were huddled near a deputy's car with a halo of TV lights over them.

Hodge rummaged through his camera bag, changing lenses. Pulling on a rain poncho and covering his camera with plastic, he cursed the weather and the havoc the moisture played with his digital. Jason didn't understand why Hodge was rushing until he saw the shapes in the distance.

Hodge got out and climbed to the roof of his Jeep.

Cresting a far hill was a Benton County Sheriff's four-by-four, followed by the coroner's van. Their red lights flashing, signaling a sense of violation. A sense of gravity. Against the backdrop of the sweeping hills, they moved slowly, almost solemnly along the earth in the surreal mist, like a funeral procession emerging from another world.

Jason made his way to join the huddled group of people who were not reporters. All appeared to be in their early twenties. It dawned on him when he glimpsed the college and university parking stickers on some of the cars that these were Karen Harding's friends.

A couple of the young women had single white roses in their hands.

"Can you tell me why you came?" Jason indicated the roses. "Nothing's been confirmed."

"We wanted to be here just in case this turns out to be Karen." The woman turned away, her expression grim.

A second woman consoled her, then, turned to Jason.

"Is it Karen? Do you know? The deputy won't tell us. We got up so early and drove all the way here to find out."

"No, I don't think they're going to know for a while."

Other students had quietly joined Jason's group and he found himself encircled by heartsick faces. He interviewed them. Hodge was taking pictures of a woman placing flowers on the roadside in the rain. When Jason finished he passed out his card, saying, "If anyone learns anything, give me a call. I'll pass on what I know to you."

"You should talk to Luke Terrell. He's over there." The man indicated the lone figure a few yards away, staring at the coroner's van inching toward the highway. He was wearing jeans, a navy windbreaker, and a ball cap pulled down nearly covering his eyes. Wade noticed they were red-rimmed when he came up next to him.

"How are you holding up, Luke?"

Turning and recognizing Jason, he shrugged, looking into the distance as if haunted.

"For what it's worth," Jason said, "it could be anyone out there, you know. I mean we're two hundred miles from Seattle, two hundred miles from Portland. Spokane and Boise aren't that far."

"Why did you have to write that the death was ritualistic?"

Jason was taken aback.

"That's what Hanna Larssen told me."

"I think that it's disgusting that you would write that."

"I understand. But I'm just reporting it."

Terrell looked to the horizon as a breeze nudged a curtain of fine rain toward them. Jason noticed a small group of teachers from the Sawridge search in the distance, and a clergyman. Who was he? He wanted to talk to him after he'd finished with Terrell.

"Has Stralla told you much new?" Jason asked.

Terrell shook his head. "He wants to talk to me some more, that's it. You?"

"He doesn't tell me much," Jason said. "Luke, I have to ask you, about that night, the night Karen left Seattle."

"What about it?"

"What really happened?"

"What're you talking about?"

"Are you sure something wasn't on her mind that night? Something that forced her to drive off without telling anyone? Maybe she argued with a friend or something?"

"And what difference would it make now?"

"I'm just asking. Maybe it would shed some light on what happened. Did you two argue?"

Terrell's shoulders sagged slightly as if he were bearing a terrible weight. Then he walked away from Wade without speaking another word.

Activity wound down at Hanna Larssen's farm with a press conference from Lieutenant Buchanan. Nothing new was expected until full autopsy results were known, which could take a couple of days.

Karen Harding's college teachers, including the reverend, had left before Jason could talk to them. He wrote in the Jeep as Hodge drove them back to Seattle. It was still raining by the time they'd reached the metro area. It was very late when Jason finally finished at the *Mirror*, got into his Falcon, drove to Fremont, and returned to his apartment.

Exhausted, he trudged to his bedroom, where he glanced at Valerie's bracelet, then snapshots of Karen Harding before falling into bed. He studied his stories and notes. It was after 2:00 a.m. when he closed his eyes. It felt like he'd slept no more than ten minutes when his phone rang.

Man, his body ached. Heavy as if he were underwater. Must be the poststress of a road-trip assignment. Wow, it was daylight and his phone was still ringing. The clock showed 11:23 a.m.

He rubbed his eyes and reached for the receiver.

"Yeah, what is it?"

"This Jason Wade, the reporter with the *Seattle Mirror*?"

"Yeah, who's calling please?"

"I know who was involved in Karen Harding's disappearance."

20

To Benton County, the victim was file number
05-6784-54.

To Brad Kintry, the lead detective, she was more
than a number. More than a Jane Doe, unidentified
white female victim of a homicide. She was someone's daughter. Someone violated.

She was his case.

Now he watched over her as Morris Pitman, Benton
County's coroner, and Pitman's assistant Cheryl
Nyack, were preparing to autopsy her remains in the
Benton County Justice Center, in Kennewick. No matter how he tried, Kintry never got used to the room's
chill and its ever-present smells of ammonia and for-
maldehyde.

Pitman tied off his apron and then he and Nyack
began the procedure, washing, weighing, measuring,
then taking X-rays of the victim before moving the gur-
ney to the stainless steel tray of the autopsy room.

Kintry's stomach clenched when they began trans-
ferring her to the table. He tried to control it. Like
Pitman and Nyack, he was paid to examine the

county's human carnage. All three were professionals who had witnessed the results of every tragedy on victims of all ages. Human beings reduced to charred, cooked flesh from fires and electrocutions, to pulpy, meaty masses from car wrecks, multicolored organs spilling from stomach cavities in stabbings, or gunshots, bloated and putrid from drownings, or suicides. In his early years on patrol, Kintry went home with nightmares. Over time his emotional armor hardened.

Today, as Pitman and Nyack carefully set the body on the table, Kintry's armor fractured.

The victim was in six pieces.

First, the complete right leg, severed at the hip, then the left leg, severed in exactly the same location. Together they set her torso down, leaving a wide space between the legs for examination. Next came the right arm, severed at the shoulder. Then the left, severed at the shoulder. Again they left distance between the limbs and torso for study.

Then came the head, severed at the neck.

Eyes open wide.

Frozen.

As if still registering the horror.

Her face was a sinewy mask. Much of the skin below the eyes was shredded, as if ripped from the skull in fury, exposing teeth. Her hair was pulled from the scalp in spots, shorn in others. Visual identification was impossible.

Kintry blinked at the outrage.

This was not like any other death. There was a cosmic breakdown between heaven and humanity on the table. As if some malevolent force had clawed from a dark world into this one. The killer had cut her to pieces. Destroyed all that was human limb by limb. The sheer magnitude of the act commanded awe, nearly eclipsing Kintry's anger. He steeled himself by taking notes, remembering Lieutenant Buchanan's order to pass every detail to Ansboro from Sawridge County for the guys working on the missing Seattle college student.

Maybe this was her right here.

Karen Harding

It was going to take time before they knew with certainty.

"Most of her fingerprints have been mutilated. He knew what he was doing," Pitman said. "We might have a shot with the right pinky."

He and Nyack spoke in soft clinical tones as they worked, dictating into the overhead microphone. Kintry caught snippets of terms like clavical, femur, trachea, femoral, and subclavian. He watched Pitman from time to time, consulting the state's form, protected in plastic, for unidentified remains, headed *Body Condition and Status of Parts*.

Pitman was thorough with the external examination before they began the internal examination. He and Nyack betrayed no emotion. They maintained a steady professional calm.

Then something changed.

Pitman's brow tightened with concentration as he

scrutinized a new aspect of the remains. A number of small distinguishing marks trailed along the upper shoulder and leg. Given the web of abrasions that covered the victim's flesh, they were easy to miss. Upon closer study, he determined they were the letter X, burned into the skin. In all he counted eleven stylized Xs. In the upper left quadrant, over the heart, he found, stylized in the same script, the letters VOV. Just one instance. A word, name, or abbreviation of some sort.

Pitman exchanged glances with Nyack and Kintry and continued. Perspiration moistened his brow as he reexamined the points of separation, drawing his face closer. Pitman's hand trembled and at that stage Nyack began blinking faster as if something terrible, something previously unencountered, had revealed itself to them.

Kintry searched their eyes for an answer.

None was offered.

They continued working. Only this time in silence.

After finishing, Pitman disappeared to the washroom for a time before meeting in his office with Kintry to discuss his preliminary observations. He worked at his computer with a neutral expression. Kintry had already gotten a Coke from the vending machine, grateful for the hint of orange blossom from the aromatic machine Pitman's secretary had insisted on.

The phone in Pitman's office rang. His chair squeaked when he took the call.

"Coroner," he said, then, "Yes, who's calling please?" Pitman looked at Kintry as he listened for several moments before saying, "No, I'm afraid I can't confirm anything like that at this point. You might want to try the Sheriff's Office in the morning."

"Who was that?" Kintry asked after Pitman hung up.

"Jason Wade from the Seattle Mirror. Looking for an ID."

"He's the joker who ticked off Buchanan."

"He's tenacious. I'll give him that. All right," Pitman turned to his report.

"We have a female. White. Approximately five feet four inches or five feet three inches. Twenty-one to twenty-five years of age. One hundred ten to one hundred twenty pounds. Brown hair, blue eyes. No confirmed identity."

"Who's going to do that?" Kintry was taking notes.

"We'll get you the fingerprint to bounce through AFIS and I've got Seth Lyman, our forensic odontologist, coming in. Should be an hour. He'll look at the X-rays and Karen Harding's dental chart for a comparison. If Seth says it's Harding, then you can bank on it. If not, well, it's not."

"Cause?"

"Loss of blood from the trauma."

"Approximate time."

"A couple of days."

"So it would fit with the Harding case."

Pitman nodded.

"All right, Morris. Give me the rest of it."

Pitman removed his glasses. He was in his sixties

and had worked with the U.S. forces in Vietnam and Iraq. Retirement was close. Today, he wished it were closer. He ran a hand across his face.

"I saw something I've never seen before." He looked to the ceiling. Then at his clipboard. "It's *how* he did it that's shaken me."

He touched his notes lightly with his fingers.

"From the condition, from what I could see, he started with the right leg. I suspected he used a hack-saw. Not a surgical bone saw, because the cut would have been finer. Nevertheless, it was a clean amputation. Quite good. But he did it while she was alive, then attempted to cauterize it while he moved to the left leg. He repeated it with the arms. Cutting, then cauterizing."

"Why?"

"He wanted to reduce blood loss so that she'd be alive and conscious of what he was doing. He had removed her limbs and wanted her to witness and experience the fact he was reducing her to a mere torso."

"So she would've been conscious through all of this trauma?"

"Yes."

"Jesus Christ."

"She would've passed out, or gone in and out of consciousness from shock, but I believe she would've been aware."

Kintry looked off.

"I think he removed her head as slowly as possible, so she again would be aware."

Kintry closed his eyes.

"He tortured her first. I found a series of the letter X seared into her skin here and here." Kintry touched his pen to a generic body sketch among his notes.

"Seared? Like branded?"

"Yes, and there was something else that was chilling. Here, over her heart, were the letters VOV."

"VOV? What does that mean?"

"I'm just speculating, but it could be someone's initials, a message, or a signature."

"A signature?"

"At the outset, it appears the style of the script is late sixteenth to mid-seventeenth century. Xs were sometimes symbols of the church at war, an all-out defense of God."

"You've lost me."

"What you have here is evocative of torture techniques used by executioners during the Inquisition, against heretics, sorcerers, enemies of the faith. It looks like he used a pear, a Spanish or Venetian pear."

"What's that?"

"It's a metal device that emerged in the 1500s. It's thrust into an orifice like the mouth, rectum or vagina, then enlarged with a screw mechanism. It rips away all tissue."

Kintry tried to comprehend what he was facing.

"I've got to do research on his techniques and signature, which might yield a lead for you," Pitman said. "It's obvious the killer here wants his victim to suffer as much pain and torment as possible. And by the way he displayed her, he wants people to be aware of his work. He's a proud artist."

Kintry nodded.

"Brad, I don't think this is the first time he's done this and I don't think it will be the last."

"Why?"

"The cutting technique."

"What about it?"

"He's practiced."

21

The caller's name was Erika.

She'd refused to give Jason any more details over the phone, except a time and place to meet.

He debated on whether he should do this. If Erika had credible information, why didn't she call the police? Maybe she was involved. Or had a criminal record. Or was a whack job. But his rookie instincts urged him to follow this through. He had nothing to lose.

He had ninety minutes to decide.

After showering, Jason sat at his kitchen table peeling an orange while reading the *Mirror*'s front page.

His story was there. Along with one by Astrid Grant on a little boy who'd survived a ten-story fall by landing on a mattress in a Dumpster. Ben Randolph had an investigative take on some city tax rip-off, and Gretchen Saunders, who'd written for the *Washington Post*, had a feature on Seattle-Tacoma International Airport. Plenty was happening beyond Karen Harding's story, and the other interns were scoring major play. Jason needed to keep breaking news.

Some ninety minutes later, he was sitting on a park bench holding a copy of the *Mirror*, as Erika had instructed. Like something out of a B-movie. He decided to give it twenty minutes.

"Jason?" a woman said from behind him.

She had short, spiky brown hair and looked about the same age as Karen Harding. Fair face, good figure. Her left eyebrow was pierced with a ring. She wore faded jeans, sneakers, a long-sleeved black cotton shirt under a pink T-shirt with a small hummingbird embroidered on it.

"Erika?"

"Yes."

She sat beside him, clasped her hands together, and held them between her knees. "First," she asked, "is that body in the hills Karen?"

"The police don't know yet."

She closed her eyes for a moment, then looked toward the skyline.

"Here are my rules. You didn't get any of this from me and you can't use it. I'm just telling you where to look."

"All right, but we'll negotiate everything when we're done."

"Agreed." Erika took a deep breath. "I'm a student at Karen's college. A few weeks before they found her car, she told me one of our instructors was creeping her out."

"Who?"

"Gideon Cull."

"Spell it?"

Erika unfolded pages torn from the *Mirror* and circled grainy news pictures of Cull with search groups at the scene. *The mystery man.*

"He's a part-time instructor," Erika said, "an ordained reverend who's involved with the ecumenical group and charities. He's also a toucher."

"A toucher?"

"He stands close to you when he talks. At first it all seems innocent, like he's an affectionate, warm conversationalist. But when he talks to you he'll touch your shoulder, your arm, your hand, whatever. He touches."

"Has he been reported?"

"No, because it's so subtle. Some of the women ignore him, but he makes others uncomfortable."

"And Cull was giving Karen the creeps?"

"She confided to me that he seemed to be touching her more and more and inviting her to his office for counseling, insisting she come. I think she went to see him to talk about her plans to do aid work in Africa after graduation."

"Did she ever tell anyone else about this guy?"

"I don't know."

"So what happened?"

"Well, a few of the women got talking about Cull one night and it came out how he had a nickname, Creepy Cull, because of his creepy past."

"Creepy how?"

"We think there was an incident at some other

school and he'd been charged, maybe went to prison. Or, it was a complaint that he'd sexually harassed a student. And how he had strange books on satanic worship, murder, criminal psychology. He also had some scary friends who visited his campus office because he worked on helping ex-cons and did some spiritual work in prisons and in soup kitchens. He traveled a lot."

"I can see how all of that might make you a little uneasy."

"And there was his tattoo, on one arm, something like a Reaper's scythe over the words *The Next Life*. The story was that he got that in prison."

"Sounds like quite a legend around this guy. Any of it confirmed?"

"Not much, but we think most of it is true."

"Thinking it and knowing it are two different things, Erika. It's all quite a leap to connect him to Karen."

"There's more. Karen told me that one night she had this feeling she was being followed by a stranger. I don't think she did anything about it. She said it was just a feeling."

"Has anyone told the police any of this stuff?"

"No. We don't think they'll believe us, because we're relying more on instinct than what you'd consider facts. We think they'd hush up things."

Ah, there it was. The conspiracy rumor panic that swirls after a major tragedy hits a community. He'd read a *New York Times* piece on it.

"Why would they hush things up?"

"There's a story that he's connected to the governor

because he'd helped the governor's daughter through his Samaritan work or something."

Jason was skeptical but said nothing.

"We read your stories and thought you could do some investigation on Gideon Cull's background, see what you could find out."

He thought it over.

"Give me some time, I'll see what I can do."

22

Gideon Cull's office was hidden in a far-flung campus annex to the social sciences department. Jason Wade approached it, unsure he was doing the right thing.

He was out on a limb here, investigating Cull simply because Erika had leveled wild accusations against him. Two other students Jason had reached by phone backed up Erika's claims, but it was Erika who'd provided their numbers.

This was a risk.

He hadn't told Ron Nestor about his tip and he had no experience with this sort of thing. For all he knew, Erika was using him in a student vendetta against a teacher. Still, his gut was telling him to chase this down. If he was dead on the money, it'd be a helluva story. If he was dead wrong, it'd be a helluva lawsuit.

Here we go.

The nameplate on the wall read: GIDEON CULL. INSTRUCTOR, ANCIENT RELIGIOUS STUDIES. *Be cool. Feel the guy out. Relax.* Odds were, this would amount to nothing. He rapped on the door frame.

"Come," a voice said.

Cull's office was cluttered. Floor-to-ceiling shelves overflowed with books and papers next to a pair of avocado four-drawer file cabinets. Framed certificates, diplomas, photographs, and mementos were everywhere. In one corner, hanging from a hook, he saw what appeared to be a costume. A robe and what looked like a wig.

"You must be Jason, the reporter who called?"

"Yes, from the *Mirror*."

"You got here fast, have a seat." Cull set down his copy of a book by Camus. A page was folded to a chapter on the guillotine.

He looked to be in his early fifties and was a couple of inches taller than Jason. Maybe six two, with a solid, athletic build, large hands. He was clean shaven. An imposing figure. He coughed.

"Can't seem to shake this cold. I got caught in that storm the other night." He coughed again. "My apologies for not responding to your call earlier. I was helping in the search for Karen. Then I was out of town. I'm a part-time instructor and my volunteer work keeps me on the road."

"Not a problem."

"I'm afraid I can only give you twenty minutes before I have to go."

"That should be enough time." Jason opened his notebook.

"I've been following your reporting." Cull cleared his throat. "What's happened is horrible. I've tried to help with the search and prayers. Have police in Benton County made an identification?"

"Not yet."

Cull nodded, blinking thoughtfully. "I pray for Karen. Only a few days ago, she sat in the chair you're sitting in, anxious about her one-year mission to Ethiopia. I helped arrange it through our worldwide faith agency. She was nervous about the impact it would have on her life."

"She came to you for counseling?"

"Unofficially."

"What do you mean?"

"I'm not a counselor, but students talk to me about problems. Course load, careers, relationships. In addition to the people I help off campus, I've come to be something of a confessor to young people here."

"I see."

Jason's focus shifted to the robe, drawing Cull's attention there too.

"Oh, that?" Cull asked. "A little inside joke with our drama teacher. I play Moses in a church pageant. That's my garment and my beard. He likes me to remain close to my character." He smiled.

Jason nodded, making a note as he formed a question arising from Erika's accusations. "So students come to you with their personal troubles. I understand you're known to them as someone who is"—*Careful. Be very careful*—"as someone who cares a great deal about their welfare."

Cull's smile weakened slightly.

"I admit, I show an interest when they come to talk to me. College can be stressful, as you know." Cull glanced at his watch.

"Did Karen mention any problems you think might be related to her disappearance? You know, anything troubling her?"

"Not really, other than what I've already told you."

"Tell me about her, the kind of person she is."

"She's an outstanding student. Conscientious, altruistic, selfless. I was ordained as a pastor years ago. I belong to an ecumenical group on campus. Karen's part of the group and she volunteered for every one of our fund-raising events. A totally giving person. I can't understand how this could happen to her."

"You're obviously concerned about her."

"As I said, I like to watch over my flock, if you will." The phone rang.

"Excuse me, I'll have to take this."

"I can step outside."

"Stay. I won't be long."

Jason used the interruption to look at the shelves and titles of some of Cull's books: *Guided by the Light, Life after Life, Psychology of Faith, Reflections on the Ritual, Morality of the Confined Soul, America's Theological Quest.*

Heavy stuff, he thought, making notes, then noticing the collection of papers and letters on Cull's credenza. Next to folded copies of Seattle newspapers, he saw student papers on seventeenth-century persecution of believers in obscure religions.

Fanned across the desk were letters, envelopes of all sizes addressed to Cull. Jason's eyebrows edged upward at the return addresses. Prisons and parole offices in Washington, Montana, Idaho, Oregon, British Columbia, and Alberta.

He saw a couple of framed photographs of Cull smiling with a large group of people before three RVs of different sizes, each painted with inspirational messages. There were pictures of Cull and volunteers at fund-raisers. Luke Terrell was among them in one. In another, Cull had his hands on a woman's shoulder. *Karen Harding*. Hanging from the peg was a minister's white collar.

"Sorry," Cull said after hanging up. "We've got a couple of minutes and then I've got to get going, got a long drive ahead of me."

"I appreciate the time you've made for me."

"Hope it helps."

"Just quickly, can you give me a bit more background on yourself?"

Cull sighed. "All right, before I came here, I used to minister at a small church," he said, collecting papers. "I taught courses at a local college and I would minister in prisons. I counseled troubled souls in shelters, missions, the street, highways, wherever they were."

Jason nodded to the letters.

"Yes, I still help inmates and guys on parole. I still minister in prisons to people who've had hard lives, who've committed atrocious sins. We've all sinned, Jason, wouldn't you agree?"

"I guess."

"No doubt you've discovered that I'm far from perfect, that I've learned from the mistakes of my past." Cull snapped his briefcase shut. "I do my best to help people benefit from my errors, to see that things are not always as bad as they seem, that there's something perfect waiting for you."

"Where?"

"In the next life."

Cull smiled, then reached for his white collar.

23

At his office in Bellingham, Detective Stralla answered his phone.

"Hank, this is Buchanan. The ID should be on your fax now."

Stralla snatched the pages, reading quickly. Lines formed at the corners of his eyes, his jaw tightened as he digested the result. His first thought went to Marlene Clark, and then he glanced at the time.

"No one knows the official results," Buchanan said. "We'll sit on it so we can make notifications. Say, four hours, then we'll release it."

"Are you going to hold a press conference?"

"No, we'll just put out a statement. How's that sound?"

"Good. I've got to tell the family in person." Stralla was checking his cell phone, reaching for his jacket. "The sister went down to wait in Seattle at the apartment. On my way. I'll call you once I'm done."

Stralla collected the coroner's faxed pages, then his file on the Harding case. He slid them into his valise, alerted the division secretary to his plans, then headed to the elevator. He strode from the building to his four-by-four, knowing they had a monster on their hands.

The white-haired woman who owned the Seattle building where Karen Harding lived had given Marlene and her husband, Bill, a key.

"I'm praying for Karen," she said before leaving and closing the door behind her.

Standing in the middle of the deathly silent apartment, Marlene was overcome. Bill held her. They looked out the large bay windows at the city's skyline, the Space Needle, and the mountains until Marlene collected herself.

Then Luke Terrell called. He'd heard from Benton County that an update was coming and wanted to join Marlene at the apartment. Although she was growing frustrated with Luke because she believed he was hiding something, she agreed to meet him.

To be honest, she was glad they'd come here. Detective Stralla had warned her to prepare for the worst. That they could have an answer today. She couldn't bear another minute in her dreary Bellingham motel. Grateful she had Bill by her side, she decided Karen's place was where she needed to await the news.

Marlene had always loved the apartment and the way Karen had decorated it. The living room had a handcrafted Egyptian area rug over the hardwood floor. Above her studio sofa, she had framed prints by Picasso and Rembrant.

Bill went to the window, Marlene went to Karen's bedroom.

She looked through the four-drawer dresser, then the closet jammed with clothes, shoes, books, boxes of cards, letters, and treasured items from their childhood. The bed was made. Nothing seemed to be amiss. Karen was very neat. Very organized. Always had been.

Marlene traced her fingers along the pattern of the quilted down duvet on the bed. Then she picked up the large pillow, hugged it tenderly, breathing in Karen's fragrance.

In the bathroom, towels were clean and hung neatly from the rack next to the tub and shower. Marlene inspected the medicine cabinet. Her sister's toothbrush, toothpaste, and other toiletries were gone, indicating she'd definitely packed for at least an overnight stay.

Why didn't you call me and tell me what was on your mind?

In the kitchen, Bill sat at the table going through all of the Seattle newspaper stories about Karen that Marlene had collected. Since he'd arrived, he'd studied each one several times as if the answer to the mystery of her disappearance was buried in newsprint.

Marlene stood over him, staring at a recent *Seattle Mirror* story, the one showing the aerial photograph of the tarp in the middle of Hanna Larssen's windswept property in the Rattlesnake Hills.

No one had disclosed any details about Benton County's case to her. She knew what the public knew and little else. "Ritualistic" was the word Hanna

Larssen had used to describe the horror that had befallen the woman whose body she found on her property.

Ritualistic.

Her little sister.

Bill steadied her and helped her to the sofa, her fear and grief palpable as they looked out helplessly at Seattle.

As he drove along I-5, Stralla's mind was drawn to the details he'd read in the coroner's report. The savagery of the crime, the markings. Nothing had prepared him for this.

He thought of Marlene, what she'd been through. What she might yet go through. His heart went out to her, but his thoughts returned to the case, reexamining every aspect he knew, questions rushing by like the broken line on the highway. Was she lured away by a stranger she trusted? Did she walk away and accept a ride? What compelled her to hurry from Seattle? Did Luke Terrell tell them everything? Stralla gnawed over the case until he pulled up to Karen Harding's building in Capitol Hill. He buzzed her unit.

Bill let him in.

Sober-faced, Stralla shook his hand. He was surprised to see Luke Terrell sitting in the living room with Marlene.

"He called me," she said, coming to her feet.

"I needed to be here," Terrell said.

Stralla nodded. "Please, everyone sit down."

Bill sat next to Marlene. She clasped her hands in

his, blinked, and steeled herself. Stralla sat near them, holding his valise with the case file and coroner's report inside.

"It's not Karen."

Marlene sighed, tears flowed, and Bill pulled her tight.

"Thank you," Terrell whispered, loud enough to be heard, before he stood and paced to the window.

"Comparison of dental records," Stralla said, his eyes following Terrell, "rules out the possibility that the victim found in Benton County could be Karen Harding."

Somewhere, another family was going to be devastated, Marlene thought.

"Do you know who it is?"

"Possibly a woman missing from Spokane."

"Is there anything connecting Karen's case to this one?" Bill asked.

"Nothing immediate. There's a lot more work to do."

"This means Karen could still be alive," Marlene said.

"Yes, until we find evidence that proves otherwise."

Marlene slid her arms around herself and began rocking slowly. Lack of sleep, overwhelmed by worry, she felt numb. "This puts us back to where we started, right?"

"Essentially, yes."

Marlene turned to Terrell. "What happened that night?"

"What do you mean?"

"Why did she run off like that? What happened between you and my sister, Luke?"

"We talked on the phone." He shrugged. "Everything was fine."

"Everything was not fine! Something upset her. What did you say to her that night?"

"Nothing."

"I can't stand this," Marlene said. "I can't stand this not knowing. Luke, why did she leave Seattle to see me?"

"I don't know, Marlene. I swear I don't know."

Stralla watched Terrell's reaction, his breathing, his body language.

This guy knew more.

A lot more.

24

After leaving Cull's office Jason drove straight to the Mirror.

He needed to catch up on a few things. And start digging into Cull's background, he thought, stepping into the newsroom.

He stopped at the bulletin board to consider a front-page tear sheet with Astrid Grant's child survivor feature, displayed next to Ben Randolph's investigation on city hall. One of his own stories from Hanna Larssen's farm in the Rattlesnake Hills was up there too.

Astrid's piece was circled with bold, red marker. Next to it, a large handwritten note said *Terrific, moving read! Superb writing, Astrid!* A thick red arrow pointed to Ben Randolph's article and an accompanying note. *Solid, first-rate, hard-hitting investigative work, Ben!* The notes were signed by Neena Swain, the *Mirror*'s assistant managing editor. *Our interns raise the bar!* Swain had added.

It was known to the staff that Swain thought little of crime reporting. Understandably, Jason's story had not warranted a word of praise. It was just there.

Jason shook it off.

The newsroom was humming. It was crunch time for the day side. Reporters and editors were typing at their keyboards, talking in small groups, or on the phone. Faces tense with concentration as they tried to wrap up the stories that would fill the pages of tomorrow's paper.

The police radio chatter increased as Jason arrived at the cop desk. Leo Johnson, a stone-faced staffer, was typing at the desk adjoining his.

"You in early to take over?"

"Might as well." Jason adjusted the scanners. "Anything shaking?"

"A house fire. Nobody home. And some rush-hour fender benders."

Jason settled in, then scanned the wires for anything new on the Harding case. He scrolled through all of the stories that had moved over the last four hours. A press conference, a statement, anything. Nothing new came up. All right, time to move along to Gideon Cull.

Jason wanted to start digging into Cull's background and relationship with Karen Harding. He'd give Erika credit for one thing, Cull was a bit creepy.

"Jason Wade." Ron Nestor had a sheet of paper in his hand. "You're early. Got anything on your plate right now? Anything I should know about?"

Jason wasn't ready to tell him about Cull.

"No, I'm just poking around on the Harding story."

"Just got this fax from Benton County. The body's not Harding's."

Jason read over the fax. "This is it?" he said.

"That's it. Now, I've got you down to do this tonight. Get reaction from everyone. What does it mean for the Harding case? Relief for her family, et cetera. This might take the Harding story down a notch because it seems unrelated."

"I'll try to reach everybody."

"Don't sweat that too much." Nestor loosened his tie. "It's a Spokane case, a little outside our area of interest. We lost the Seattle peg because it's not Harding."

"But a person's been murdered."

"I know. Do what you can. Space is tight."

The press statement was short.

The Benton County Coroner's Office has identified the remains found on private property off County Road 225, near Whitstran, as those of Roxanne Louise Palmer, aged 24, of Spokane, Washington. Positive identification was confirmed using dental records and fingerprints.

The manner of death has been classified as homicide. Cause of death is not being released at this time.

Friends indicated Palmer had not been seen for approximately three to four days before her remains were discovered by a property owner searching for her lost dog.

Jason called Lieutenant Buchanan in Benton County. "We can't add much more at this time. We're working with Spokane police in an attempt to trace her last movements."

"Can you say if this is linked to Karen Harding's disappearance?"

"Check with Stralla in Bellingham on that."

"Is there anything you can say about the ritualistic nature of her death?"

"Ritualistic is your word, Mr. Wade."

"Actually, sir, it's Hanna Larssen's word. The woman who found her."

"We're not releasing any details about her death. What you have is what you have."

"Can you tell me about Roxanne Palmer, a little biographical stuff?"

"Try Spokane for that."

It took Jason several calls before he reached the Spokane detective assigned to assist Benton County on the Palmer file.

"She worked as a prostitute. We understand she was addicted to cocaine and heroin and had run up a sizeable drug debt before she was last seen on the street."

"Do you think the debt is a factor in her homicide?"

"Everything's a factor at this point. She could have gone off on a bad date. Her murder could be related to her drug problem. We don't know."

"Any link to Karen Harding?"

"On the face of it, no."

Jason asked if Roxanne Palmer had any family or friends who might offer some kind words about her.

"Doubt it," the Spokane detective said. "From what

we know, her mother's in prison. Girls on the street here are a bit edgy to talk to anyone right now, as I'm sure you can appreciate."

Jason tried Stralla up at Sawridge County. He got his voice mail. Then he tried Marlene Clark and Luke Terrell. No luck. He flipped through his notes, began writing up the county fax and what the Spokane detective had given him. It was going to be a thin story. He was cobbling it together with some sourced stuff and background from other stories, when his phone rang.

"Hank Stralla."

"Hey, thanks for getting back to me. I'm working on the release of ID from Benton. Have you ruled out any link to Karen Harding?"

"Until we determine what happened to her, we can't rule anything out."

"Well, have you got anything suggesting a link?"

"Nothing we're prepared to release."

"So you've got something then?"

"I didn't say that, Jason. We're going to work with all the agencies in the Benton case to ensure that nothing is overlooked."

"Any suspects?"

"Let's say we're following all leads."

Sounded like a big fat zip.

Jason call-forwarded his desk phone to his cell phone, then hurried downstairs to the *Mirror*'s cafeteria before it closed. His cell phone rang just as he returned to his desk with a cheeseburger, fries, and soda.

"This is Marlene Clark."

"Hi. Thank you for calling back. I wanted to get your reaction to the identification of the case out of Benton County. Do you feel a sense of relief that it's not Karen?"

A long uneasy silence passed.

"It's hard to describe. Yes, there's a sense of relief, but our hearts go out to Roxanne Palmer's family." Marlene cut herself off as she struggled to control her emotions. "We're still praying Karen will be found safely."

"Have police told you any details of the Benton case? Or suggested if there's a link to Karen's case?"

More silence. "No, we're not privy to any details."

"What do you think happened?"

"We don't know."

"Is there anything you'd add on your sister's case?"

Marlene thought about it, then said, "If anyone knows something, anything, about my sister's case, or the case of Roxanne Palmer, please, I'm begging you, call the police, because…"

Jason waited for Marlene to finish her sentence, but after seconds passed he prompted her.

"I'm sorry. Because…?"

"Because in my heart I feel my sister is alive."

25

In Eugene, Oregon, in the upper-floor communal bath-room of the New Halo Women's Mission, Julie Kern was drying herself off with a towel, grateful to have bathed in private.

It was the first time in weeks she didn't have to shower with strangers. The water was hot here, the pressure strong. Halo was a good place.

No sleeping mats on the floor. No fears about some-one swearing at you, punching, robbing, or raping you. No reek of body odor or urine. It was a safe place to work on her plan, she thought, walking to her private room.

It was small and barren, except for a cot. Halo's policy and mission statement were posted above it. Among the rules, "guests" were to immediately report all communicable diseases; they faced instant eviction for possession or use of contraband, such as alcohol or illegal drugs. Halo also offered a range of services including help to those seeking it for times of "suffering, loneliness, sorrow, turmoil, danger, and fear."

Same old, same old.

Abide by our rules, we offer a helping hand with a touch of the Good Book. The shelters Julie had known were all the same that way. Their conditions were another story. Some were so bad, Julie preferred the street, or sleeping under a stairwell, or in a bus station toilet stall, which was where Eugene police found her before they brought her here.

Julie dug deep in her backpack for fresh underwear, jeans that were fairly fresh, and a top that was pretty clean. She'd use the laundry room tonight. At the mirror she combed her hair and struggled to ignore the ravages of acne on her blotched skin and the scar that shot like a lightning bolt from her temple along her hairline, fading toward her right ear.

The mark of her fate.

Her mother and father had died in a train wreck that had left her in a coma for seven months. At age fourteen, Julie emerged orphaned and brain-damaged. She had no family to take care of her. The little insurance her parents had went to Julie's medical bills and she lived with a succession of distant in-laws. In her last home, her aunt's boyfriend abused her.

Julie was sixteen when she fled.

She didn't know what she was running to, only that she had to escape. Eventually she descended to the street, becoming addicted to alcohol and crack. She turned to prostitution and small crimes to survive as she drifted aimlessly across the country. At times Julie felt she was a ghost.

Her sliver of hope was her plan.

An older cousin, the only good person she knew, lived somewhere in California. He had a successful car wash business and Julie wanted to work for him. Get off the street. Get her life together. Trouble was, she couldn't locate him. Each time she got close, seizures from her injury and her addictions would take control and confuse her. Julie would often awake in a park, a shelter, a hospital, or a jail.

That was the extent of her life since the night her parents died.

Julie was now twenty-six. Still clinging to her plan, the only thing she owned in this world. Here she was in Eugene, Oregon, trying to get to California. This time she believed she could make it.

Halo would let her reside rent-free for sixty days. Counselors would help her find a job, one where she could save enough to get to San Diego.

Julie was certain her cousin lived there.

After brushing her hair, Julie was feeling optimistic and decided she would treat herself to a cup of tea. It wasn't too late in the evening when she went downstairs to the basement and the large dining hall. Nearly empty except for a few women, hunched over a card game.

The walls featured colorful paintings done by children. Pictures of sunshine, rainbows, and happy-faced stick people. Above them, enlarged postings of rules and Scripture. At the far end of the hall there was a table with a coffee and tea service. Reaching for the teapot, she tilted it over a cup to pour. It was empty with nothing else in sight. She was too late for tea.

"Shit."

"Can I help you?"

Julie turned, startled by the man who'd come up behind her.

"Oh, Father." Julie guessed that's what he was by his white collar. "I'm sorry. I didn't see you."

He was holding an old leather-bound Bible in his hand.

"Just doing some reading." He indicated the table in a corner near the piano. "You looked a bit lost."

"I'm new here. First time."

"Can I help you?"

He had a warm smile under his beard. A soft whispering voice that went with his kind eyes. Suddenly Julie was self-conscious, feeling her face blush, aware how it exacerbated her skin condition.

"No, I—thank you, Father." She carefully set the empty teapot down.

"Anything on your mind, dear? Anything you'd like to talk about?"

Julie didn't know what to say.

"You wanted some tea?"

Julie nodded. He glanced about the room. The women at the far end hadn't noticed them.

"I'll get you some. Come with me."

He turned. Instead of walking to the kitchen door, he led Julie from the dining hall, making her a bit curious before she reasoned that maybe he was taking her to his office or a counseling room.

None of the cardplayers saw them.

As they climbed the stairs to the main floor he asked over his shoulder, "What kind of tea do you like, dear?"

"I'm not fussy."

"Well, I have quite a selection."

He went to the main entrance, stopped, and opened it to the street. The creaking door yawned to the night.

Julie stopped in her tracks.

"It's in my wagon." He smiled. "I have some donations there. I thought perhaps you would help me move a few small boxes into the Mission."

She considered his request. It was common for shelters to ask the people they helped to help them with light chores. He gestured with his Bible hand and smiled.

"I'm just parked down and across the block."

Julie smiled and stepped outside. Fog had rolled up from the Willamette River, clouding her vision as she walked with him. A shiver rippled through her mind. Funny, he would park such a distance and out of sight from the shelter, especially when he had boxes to carry.

"Not much further."

They crossed the street to an alley as Julie recognized the outline of an RV. Keys jangled, he inserted one, then opened the door for her to step inside. It was dark. She took a few steps from the cabin area. The door thudded closed behind them and lights came on.

Looking toward the rear, Julie took stock of the RV, its lamps, its veneer paneling. What she saw next raised the tiny hairs on the back of her neck as the reverend raised his arm high, growling as he smashed his fist against Julie Kern's head, sending her into a world of darkness.

26

Jason Wade led his story with Marlene Clark's belief her sister was not dead.

It was human nature to hope. An act of faith, until proof to the contrary stared back at you from a crime scene, a morgue, or a coffin.

Forty-five minutes later Jason filed to Vic Beale on the night desk. Then he polished off the cold remainder of his burger and fries, ruminating on Marlene Clark's resolve, floating back to his timeworn hopes of seeing Valerie again, or learning the truth about why his mother had walked out on him and his old man.

Jason shook it off as he crumpled his burger wrapping.

He had work to do. He pulled out his notes of his interview with Gideon Cull, then ran Cull's name through the Internet. He got about thirty hits. Most were from the last five years, for conferences, lectures. A couple of color profiles in community weekly papers on his ecumenical and charity work. A few years back, he was with a group that traveled the Pacific Northwest in RVs helping homeless people and motorists stranded on the Interstate.

Helping stranded motorists. Like Karen Harding?

Man, he was getting a bad feeling about this guy. There had to be something more to Cull.

Astrid Grant and Ben Randolph stopped at his desk.

"Jason, you're back from your trip to the hills," Astrid said.

"Here I am."

"I liked your stuff," Ben Randolph said. "How was it out there?"

"A beautiful but lonely place to die."

"How can you stand writing that murder stuff? I can't even read it," Astrid said. "It makes my skin crawl." She pointed at the emergency scanners. "And how can you write with this incessant noise going on? This is inhumane. God, it would drive me absolutely insane."

"It's my job," Jason said. "You two are working late."

"I'm wrapping up an exclusive," she said. "Animal surgeons at the zoo are going to perform an organ transplant between two lions."

"Cool."

"We have great pictures. Neena loves it. It's going on page one tomorrow," she said. "Oh, Ben's got a big one coming."

"Yeah, what's that?" Jason asked.

"Finalizing permission to ride along in a 747 to Tokyo and back," Benjamin said. "Security's been tough, but a source of mine from the FAA is making calls. I'm going to do a feature on a day in the life of a charter pilot. If clearance comes, I'll leave in a few days."

"Wow."

"Just read your latest on the Benton County body," Ben said. "Looks like a drug-addict hooker from Spokane had a bad date."

Astrid suppressed a giggle.

"She was someone's daughter, you know," Jason said.

"That sounded cold, I know, but judging by your piece there's no link to Seattle at all. And unless something breaks, it looks like the missing college student story could sputter."

"I wouldn't be so quick to dismiss it."

"We're going to the cafeteria," Astrid said. "Can we get you anything?"

"I'm good, thanks."

It was clear to Jason they didn't consider him or his work competition, he thought, watching them walk away. To hell with them.

All seemed quiet, so he resumed pursuing Cull, informing the night desk he was going to the newsroom library, tucked in the far corner of the floor. Nancy Poden, the sole librarian on night duty, raised her head from her monitor when he leaned on the counter.

"Oh, a customer." Nancy was thirty-one, had a pleasant, well-scrubbed face, brown hair with a jawline page cut. "You're one of the interns. Jason?"

"Yes, hi. I was wondering if you could help me with a search. But keep it confidential."

She poised a sharp pencil over a small pad. "What're you looking for?"

Jason glanced around to be sure they were alone.

"The man's name is Gideon Cull." He spelled it. "He's in his fifties, a minister or chaplain. Also a college teacher of religion. Here's a page from the school's Web site. He might be affiliated with prisons, street ministries, stuff like that."

"What do you need?"

"I need to know as much about him as possible, going back as far as you can go. He lives here now but could be from anywhere."

"You want a shotgun search then?"

"Exactly, any criminal convictions on the database. And check old wire stories, profiles. Anything and everything, no matter how obscure."

"I'll get started right away."

"Thanks. Please keep this just between us."

It would be good to get something concrete on Cull. Something he could check out, he thought. As he walked back to the newsroom he thought he heard someone call his name.

Someone familiar.

He dismissed it until he was actually in the newsroom and heard a commotion.

"Jason!"

He froze.

Heads turned to a man trudging through the newsroom. He was in his fifties, wearing an open plaid work shirt over a T-shirt, worn jeans, work boots, and a ball cap.

"Jason Wade! Somebody please tell me where he is!"

It was his old man.

Jason hurried over to him, keeping his voice low.

"Dad, keep it down. What is it?"

His father's bloodshot eyes widened in stunned recognition. He swayed, then his expression contorted as he focused on Jason, raising his arm to point a finger. "How come you don't call me back? Huh? Whatzamatter, huh, Jay!"

"Please lower your voice, Dad."

"Answer me!" Spittle shot from his mouth.

"I'm sorry." Jason looked around the newsroom. Concerned night staffers had stood, bracing to come closer. "Dad, let's go sit down over there." He nodded to a darkened, empty reception area.

"No!"

Two female copy editors peered from behind the half-opened door to the women's restroom.

"Dad, please."

"You listen to your old man!"

Jason took his father's shoulder, but he shrugged it off hard, nearly losing his balance. "Don't I matter to you anymore, Jay!"

"Dad."

Beale rushed up with more men who'd emerged into a circle around them. Jason's face burned. Astrid, Ben, and a few others were back from the cafeteria in time to witness the scene. Astrid was picking at a muffin. Ben was eating an apple. Keys jingled as a security officer trotted up.

"I'm sorry, folks. He just got by us." The officer extended one hand. The other went to his utility belt and pepper spray. "Sir, you'll have to come with me now."

Beale raised his hand.

"Hold up, Larry." Beale looked at Jason. "I think it would be a good idea for you to take your father home now."

Jason was paralyzed with humiliation.

"Jason," Beale repeated.

Jason approached his father, who surrendered in silence, satisfied he'd made his point. As he hurried to collect his things to go, Jason noticed Astrid smile in disbelief at Ben.

"Ben," Beale said. "Can you pull some overtime at the cop desk, listen to the scanners for a couple of hours?"

"Sure."

"I'm so sorry," Jason said to Beale and the others as he escorted his father from the newsroom, the security guard walking closely behind them. "I'm really sorry."

Jason managed to load his old man into the backseat of his Falcon.

Driving through the city, he felt everything slipping from him. Felt all he had worked for had died right there in the newsroom. His skin prickled at the faces of the night staff who'd witnessed the spectacle.

"Jay," his father mumbled from the back. "I just wanted to tell you how proud I am of you, son."

Jason stared out at Seattle's skyline. Then out at the

bay as he rolled south on 99, south beyond the airport until the brewery loomed, with its somber cluster of brick buildings, their stacks rising into the night, capped with the blinking red strobe lights. Then came the stench of hops. It invaded the car, coiled around him, slithered inside him, angering him, for he now realized it was something he could never, ever escape.

He wheeled through his old south neighborhood, familiar with every turn, every bump, every pothole, every timeworn, weather-beaten tree, fence, and landmark that had been there since he was a kid.

He parked his Falcon in the driveway, found his key to the house, and got his old man into bed. After working off his father's boots, Wade covered him with a blanket.

On the floor, a few ancient snapshots faced upward.

Wade's father smiling in uniform. Before Wade was born, his old man had been a Seattle cop. He had to quit the force after two years. Wade never knew why. It was something he never, *ever* spoke of. His father then failed to make a go of it as a private investigator before he ended up working in the brewery.

There was another photo of his parents beaming, his mother's arms around Wade, who was glowing. He was seven with his new red bike. Their faces, all of them, radiant on a day when his world was perfect.

Wade wouldn't leave tonight, in case his father needed him. But he refused to sleep in his old room. He had left this house. He had a place of his own. Still wound up, he found an old Bogart movie, watched it with the lights off, trying not to think about anything. When it ended, he pulled out a blanket and pillow and stretched out on the couch, his skin still tingling over what had happened.

He could hear his father snoring.

Here they were, two men who had pushed away the women in their lives, alone in darkness. And it was going to get darker. He sure as hell expected to be fired from the *Mirror*. Suddenly he was gripped by the image of the brewery. If he didn't rise above his circumstances he would be drowned by them. He stared into the night, thinking of Karen Harding and Roxanne Palmer.

27

That night, hundreds of miles away at an isolated exit off I-5 that led to a mist-shrouded mountain range, Gideon Cull sat in a lonely roadside diner studying a newspaper, thinking of his Samaritan work and his sins.

No matter how many people he'd helped make their peace with God—and there were many—his work was forever enlaced with his transgressions.

It was his cross to bear.

But now, as he'd feared since Karen Harding's disappearance, a liability had surfaced, threatening to destroy all that he'd accomplished.

Cull stroked his white collar and weighed his problems. He'd underlined parts in one of Jason Wade's articles in the *Mirror*, then said a silent prayer for Karen, as the light suddenly dimmed over his table.

"We meet again, old friend."

Cull looked up from his newspaper, saw a white collar, and met familiar eyes.

"Ezra."

"It's been a long time."

"A long time. You've been busy ministering?"

"Very busy." Ezra sighed as he sat. "You receiving my letters concerning His message? I've been sending them every two weeks, but your response has been, shall we say, erratic?"

"I read them but I too have been consumed by work," Cull said.

"I understand, my brother, but what we're both facing is a matter of urgency. Let's come to the point of this meeting. *I know what you did, Gideon. And you know what I did.*"

Cull shut his eyes.

It was true.

"Our secrets are the chains that bind us," Ezra said. "We did what we did and we do what we do, *for Him.* We're two halves of the same man, God's hammer—"

"—and God's shield." Cull finished the sentence. "Yes, Ezra, we are His instruments, but I'm troubled by the ramifications, the risk of detection. It leads me to think that perhaps we should leave things as they are."

"No, that is an attempt by the enemy to bewitch you. Shun the darkness, Gideon. Look to the light. Our cause is just. Isn't that what you've said?"

"Are you not as conflicted as I?"

"We are following His message. We have a sacred duty. We have no time to lose." Ezra tapped the news story. "Look, you've recognized that forces are aligning against us. Do something."

Cull had noted several points lower in Wade's article: that detectives wanted to talk to Karen's teachers;

that police wanted to clarify inconsistencies given to them by Luke Terrell, her boyfriend, who lived in a campus community known for illicit drug use and Internet fraud schemes.

"We're at war and we're running out of time," Ezra said. "Sooner or later it could all fall to ruin."

The air tightened as if a weapon had been drawn.

"Just as before, this is a test of our faith. A test neither one of us can fail." Ezra stared hard at Cull. "I have to go, old friend."

Cull sat alone in the empty diner.

Ezra returned to the night.

They were indeed two halves of the same man shackled by the sins of their past. Everything each man had worked so hard to achieve was now hanging by a thread because one of them failed to grasp the enormity of the glory.

Because one of them was insane.

Action had to be taken.

Too much was at stake.

28

Marysville was an hour's drive north of Seattle, near the Snohomish River Delta, the Cascade Mountains, and the Puget Sound. A pretty community known as the Strawberry City.

For the Washington State Patrol, Marysville had another meaning. One of its crime labs was located there.

In the garage, Van Cronin, a criminalist with some fifteen years' experience and a passion for T.S. Eliot, had been tasked to analyze Karen's Toyota. He discovered that three fuses had loosened and likely led to the car performing erratically, producing false readings on the instrument panel, or shutting down on her.

Theoretically, it was quite possible that the car simply had a mechanical failure. However, it was also conceivable someone could have tampered with her electrical system to cause a breakdown, Cronin noted.

Ned Vecseno, a fingerprint specialist, processed the car's interior, trunk and exterior, recovering as many usable latents as possible. Meanwhile, investigators, aided by Seattle police, developed for Vecseno a set of elimination prints. They included Karen's and those friends who would likely have been in the car at one time or another. Vecseno compared them with a few unidentifiable partial prints he recovered.

He then submitted the unidentified latents to a couple of databases holding millions of known prints: AFIS, Automated Fingerprint Identification System; and WIN, the Western Identification Network. No hits emerged.

Blame it on the rain.

It was raining when the car stalled and the hood was touched, and it continued raining for hours afterward. The rain would have first formed an obstruction between the car's surface and the skin, severely reducing chances of sufficient residue to be left and detected. If anything was deposited, the rain would have diluted it, or washed it away.

The lab still hadn't processed everything from the scene. Casts, debris, etc. There was a lot yet to do on tire impressions. A lot of the material was in poor shape, but there might be enough to compare with that found at the Roxanne Palmer scene in Benton County.

Throughout the Marysville lab's investigation, Vecseno moved between the car and his workstation where he sat next to Blair Brady, an expert on physical, chemical, and biological trace evidence.

She had collected and inventoried every item found in Karen's car—sunglasses, CDs, tissue, maps, fast-food coupons, lip balm, lotion, and a receipt for a parking ticket. All of her belongings, every item in the trunk, her spare tire, the tools, gas can, and an old rag.

Then she vacuumed and scoured the interior, probing the seats, the ceiling, side panels, and carpets for microscopic traces of anything that might shed light on what had transpired. Brady found traces of ketchup, spilled coffee. A handbook of inspirational teachings, a pocket guide to Africa. Things she probably glanced at in traffic. As a picture of Karen Harding's lifestyle began to come into focus, Brady looked for inconsistencies, aberrations, something that didn't belong.

But nothing seemed out of place.

Brady went through Karen's bag. A few pairs of underwear, fresh socks, dress slacks, two pressed tops, a vest, two T-shirts, a pair of sweatpants, toiletries. Some makeup. Not too much. Brady examined them all several times over. She passed items to Vecseno to check for suspect latents.

Then Karen Harding's umbrella caught her eye. Sealed in a clear plastic evidence bag, it was mangled. The theory was it was twisted in the storm. Brady picked it up and studied it. What if she'd used it to strike someone? To defend herself. After tugging on surgical gloves, she removed the umbrella to have a closer look. The webbing was twisted, consistent with a strong wind, but the main post was straight. It would have shown signs of stress.

Thinking, Brady tapped the plastic handle in the palm of her hand. It felt strange. The weight seemed off just a titch. A hard plastic handle. Brady gave it a little turn. She blinked. It shifted. Tensing, she turned it again, only harder. She heard a crack. The handle was threaded to the receptacle at the post. She'd loosened it. She kept turning until she'd managed to work it off completely.

The handle was hard plastic but hollow. A clear plastic bag of white powder, about the capacity of a bath-size soap bar, had been shoved inside. *One guess what this is,* Brady thought, making notes in her file. *One guess what we have here from little Miss Save the World.* She cleared her workstation and reached for her kit.

The analysis came through, putting it at some 14 to 15 percent purity.

Cocaine.

Brady shook her head. Then reached for her phone to call Detective Hank Stralla.

29

Thunder drummed in Karen Harding's ears, growing louder until she realized it was not a storm.

It was her heart.

Pounding with fear, images twisting and curling through her waking mind.

Remembering the face of the woman who had fallen on the RV floor next to her, the panic in her eyes before the reverend took her outside. He hadn't taken her far. Karen flinched as the woman's screams began piercing the night. Bloodcurdling shrieking, pleading for mercy. Karen couldn't bear it. *Make it stop, please make it stop!*

Karen had seen nothing. But had heard everything. Whatever he had inflicted upon her was beyond comprehension. The torment went on forever before blessed silence.

Dead silence.

Then the reverend returned to the RV.

Alone.

Walking slowly, as if exhausted, to the back. The floor thudded as he dropped an object, metal and heavy, on the floor. Karen pressed her face to the crack, seeing his hacksaw. Her scalp tingled. The blade was bloodied, flecked with tiny bits of bone, hair, and visceral matter.

Oh no. No. No. No.

Frozen with fear, she closed her eyes tight. She didn't move. She didn't even know the woman's name, but her terrified face was seared into her memory.

Why was this happening?

The reverend got behind the wheel and they drove and drove, for hours, maybe days, the woman's cries echoing in Karen's ears. Karen prayed for her. Then she shut down. Went numb. The trauma of what had transpired pressed down on her.

Surely the same fate awaited her.

But was it possible that her death was near? As time and miles rolled by, she felt death coil around her, waited for it to begin constricting and crushing her. Then she heard the RV door open.

Her senses snapped alert.

People were entering.

A grunt, a sigh, a brief commotion as if someone had fallen.

Heavy steps neared her. The mattress above her squeaked again.

Oh no. Karen swallowed.

This wasn't happening.

Her breathing quickened. Her pulse picked up. She forced her mind to grapple with a barrage of emotions, battling herself to find her resolve. *Don't give up. Think.*

Do something. There was moaning, the mattress creaked.

He has another woman.

Karen hammered the fact into her brain. They had to escape. Like the rabbit fleeing the wolf, Karen had to find the bramble. Had to summon her strength, her will to survive. No matter the cost. Her body trembled with adrenaline.

Think, she told herself, as she heard the RV ignition start the engine.

You have to plan, scrutinize everything you know, it's your only hope. All right. They were driving again. Karen knew the motions, the sounds, fragments of the reverend's routine.

The woman above continued moaning as Karen concentrated.

By the movement, the speed, the sounds of traffic, the hum of the RV's wheels, the rumble of its motor, Karen could tell when they were driving in a town or city, or when they were on the highway or a twisting back road.

Now, it was stop and go. They had to be in a city.

He was listening to the radio. Judging by the distant sound of KK, or KL, something, which had "the latest in Eugene's news, weather, and sports," she guessed it was Eugene, Oregon.

She couldn't hear any details.

They were making their way outside the city. Speeding up. It felt like they were on the Interstate.

Since her abduction, she had drifted in and out of

sleep so much, she had no concept of time. Or where they had traveled. She suspected he had been drugging her food.

He fed her irregularly. As if she were something less than human.

She remembered the first time, keys had jingled and a small door about the size of a hardcover book opened near her head. Light flooded in, forcing her to squint. His large powerful hands unfastened her gag. He thrust something inside at her face, letting her smell it. Cooked hamburger, pickle, onion, mustard, a bun. His hand shoved it into her mouth. Karen chewed fast, almost choking from hunger. Then a soda. Sucking on the straw, spilling it. He replaced her gag, then locked her back up in the darkness.

He unlocked another small door by her legs, slid in a bedpan and tissue. In her confined space, with her hands and legs bound, it was difficult to use. He rarely came to empty it. Leaving her to endure her own waste. In the beginning she wept at the degradation. She felt soiled, filthy, unclean, until eventually she no longer noticed.

He slept in the front of the RV where he had converted a bench seat to a bed. He read, studied documents, maps, newspapers, and he drove.

They drove endlessly.

At times the RV would stop and remain absolutely still for what seemed like hours. The air grew cool and she sensed he had driven into an enclosed garage or a storage space to park overnight.

Hiding.

At other times when they were mobile, she would struggle to guess if they were at a gas station, highway rest stop, or campground. Praying that maybe someone was near, a police officer, a tourist, a trucker, a savior, she ached to push away her loosened gag and scream for help.

But she was afraid. Afraid that her cries might alert him and remove all hope of her ever escaping. He would discover her loosened bindings, take steps to secure them, or punish her.

Or kill her.

She couldn't see beyond her corner of hell. She had to wait until she was confident he was far from her, confident she could kick herself free and run. Like the rabbit.

She would only have one chance.

The ropes around her wrists were snug, but she had managed to loosen them more over time. He never checked them. He never spoke to her. Once, when he'd opened the food door, she tried talking to him, pleading when he removed her gag.

"Please, sir. Please let me go. I won't tell anyone anything. Please."

He shoved a snack food cake into her mouth, waiting until she finished it, then replaced her gag and slammed the small door and locked it.

Now he had another woman.

The woman above Karen shifted on the mattress.

Karen pressed her face to the crack, but couldn't see

anything above. The hacksaw on the floor was gone. Had there even been one? Had there even been another woman? Maybe her mind was deceiving her?

God help me.

Her thoughts shifted.

The RV was slowing.

How long had they been driving since she'd heard the new woman? Karen didn't know. The mattress above her creaked.

The RV was almost crawling now. Cars, doors slamming. The smell of gas. The clank of fuel nozzles and gas pumps. The reverend stepped out to gas the RV. Karen heard muffled voices, heard the fuel hose nozzle being inserted into the tank, the hum of the pump, and the flow of gas. She pushed her gag from her mouth, swallowed, then whispered as loud as she could.

"Hello, on the bed. Can you hear me?"

The woman shifted her body and groaned.

"Don't be afraid," Karen said. "He's locked me down here under you. In the storage space."

Another shuffle and muffled groan.

"My name is Karen Harding. Listen to me. We have no time. Knock once gently for yes, twice for no. Can you hear me?"

A knock sounded and Karen's spirits soared.

"Are you hurt badly?"

Knock. Knock.

"Are you gagged and tied?"

Knock.

"Do you know him?"

Knock. Knock.

"Can you run if I can get us free?"

Knock.

"I think I can loosen my ropes and kick myself from this space. We'll wait for the right time. Keep calm, okay?"

Knock.

The RV shifted.

The reverend stepped back inside and they resumed traveling on the interstate. Again, time passed by unmeasured. Karen drifted in and out of sleep. While she was awake she felt and heard no movement from above as she continued working on straining her rope.

Soon she would be able to slide her hands free.

30

When he first woke, Jason Wade didn't know where he was or what had happened.

Part of him tried to block his memory the way a cop tries to block a relative from looking under the sheet.

Something in the air struck him. The smells of cologne and fried onions, the sounds of a creaking window frame and a neighbor's wind chime, the familiar pall of desperation and despair. Recent history came into focus and then he knew.

He was on his father's couch, in his father's home on the fringe of South Park, in the aftermath of last night's humiliation in the newsroom.

Don't think about it, he told himself, heading to the bathroom. *Flush the whole damned thing away. He would apologize.* Explain that his father was sick. He stripped off his clothes and took a shower, scrubbing until his skin was raw.

He hated being here. Hated being jerked back to this house of misery, he thought while taking stock of the kitchen. The same kettle, the same toaster, the dishcloth folded and hung the same way, after all these years.

Time stopped after she walked out.

Jason plugged in the kettle for coffee, then wandered through the small house, hearing his father snoring, then stirring. He went to his old bedroom.

The musty air took him back. Nothing had been touched. The same posters, his model planes, cars, and ships. His small desk where he did his homework. His window where he had sat for hours and hours searching the street, hoping she would come back.

The day before she left, she'd hugged him, her eyes flickering, as if she were seeing something far away. He thought of his old man's worn swivel rocker and his big hands, scarred from working at the brewery, how they covered his face on the long nights he sat in his chair after she left.

Jason wanted to know how his mother could walk out on her son and her husband. How could anyone do that? She had worked alongside his father in the brewery and one night at dinner, Jason noticed how her face had aged with sadness.

"You know," she said, "a person can see their whole life on the factory line. There are young people there, fresh from high school, then those a bit older. Then some like us." She nodded to his father, who chewed on his pork chop as he listened.

"Then you get those like Ida and Frank, a bit older. Kids grown. Then Rob and Aileen in labeling, and Edna and Butch almost going to retire. You see all generations, all the stages of life, right there on the line, with your life over at the end of it. Makes you realize that's all there is."

His father said nothing. Jason said nothing. Maybe because they didn't quite understand. Jason remembered the window frame creaking in the wind that stirred the neighbor's chimes.

A few months later, she was gone.

In the years after she left, Jason secretly searched for her. He'd go to the library, look for her name, and maiden name, in out-of-town phone books. He'd search obituaries and news stories about deaths. He'd keep records of those he checked, thinking the day would come when he would find her and she would tell him what went wrong and he would forgive her. Maybe that was how his journalistic dream truly started for him. Born out of his mother's desertion.

It was a different story for his old man.

After his shift, he would sit in his chair saying nothing, staring at nothing. Then Jason noticed that his father, who never drank, would be holding a beer as he sat there. Then he noticed how the number of empties increased. And one night his old man told him, "She'll be back. I can fix it, Jay. Just wait. She'll be back. You'll see."

And his father got up every day and went to the brewery. As if it were an act of faith, as if by keeping everything precisely as it was, as if by not upsetting the balance of their fractured lives, she would return.

The kettle's whistle pulled Jason from the past to the kitchen where he made coffee and toast, then went to the door for the paper. He saw Astrid Grant's feature on the animal surgery. Then he thought of Gideon Cull, wondering what he should do next on the Harding story. Maybe it wouldn't matter, he thought as he heard his father rising. He had been kidding himself to think that he could compete with the other interns for the one job at the paper.

Jason was ready. He seized the phone book and plopped it on the table, just as his father's bedroom door opened and he shuffled into the kitchen.

"Jay," he started, as he poured himself coffee. "I meant no harm, I—"

"Stop right there, Dad."

Jason opened the phone book to the listing for A.A., stabbed it with his finger, held the book to his father's face, and said, "Go."

"But, Son, I—"

"She's never coming back. *It's been years!* Get over it and get some help."

His father's face deflated and he drew his hand over it.

"I'll take you. I'll go with you for the first few sessions."

His old man turned and gazed out the kitchen window.

"It's just that after she left, you were all I had. And now, you're on your own and doing well. I've lost you, too."

"Stop it. I'm right here. You're going to get some help. All right?"

His old man said nothing. His head turned when a phone started ringing. Jason's cell phone.

"Jason, it's Ron Nestor at the paper."

"Listen, about what happened last night."

"I'd like you to come in as soon as you can. We need to talk."

Jason felt something cold shoot up his spine and he swallowed.

"On my way."

Nestor was sitting at a computer in the metro section, talking on the phone and making notes. Spotting Jason, he pointed his pen to his glass-walled office, hung up, then followed him there.

"Sit down, Jason." Nestor loosened his tie, then appraised him. "Look, I'll come to the point—"

"I'm sorry about last night. My father's sick. He's going to get help."

"Good. That's good. Now, I want to talk to you about your performance."

Jason's stomach quivered. *This is it. It's over.* But he felt a perverse relief that it wasn't about his father.

"It seems you've been doing a lot of work on your own time—and in some cases not informing your supervisors—*even after I advised you to do so.*" Nestor glanced at his notebook and interrupted himself. "Look, you did it again, Jason."

"What do you mean?"

"I just got a call from the college director of public affairs regarding Gideon Cull, an instructor you went to see on the Harding story."

"Yes."

"Apparently you were supposed to go through public affairs to arrange any interview of faculty. He claimed you ambushed him, started grilling him at a time he was anxious about his missing student."

"*What?* That's bull! Cull agreed when I called him. The guy shook my hand. He was totally cooperative."

"Did you tape it?"

It hit him hard—he simply had forgotten to tape it. How could he have been so stupid? "No, I didn't."

"A big mistake. Now it's his word against yours. Furthermore, you didn't tell me what you were up to. I had to get an earful from the college."

"This is strange. It's all wrong."

"Look at me. You disobeyed my explicit instructions to keep me informed. You can't go around enterprising and representing the *Seattle Mirror* on your own time, without me knowing what you're doing."

Something's not right. Why would Cull complain?

"Are you listening? Given the college thing, and your father—"

"My father's sick and getting help. That should be my business."

Nestor leaned close to Jason.

"When he comes into the newsroom smashed and is a potential threat to our staff, it's our business. Understand?"

Jason understood.

"Jason, I know it sounds like we're being hard on you. Beale and I are in your corner. You have talent. Take a few days off and try not to read anything more into this. I know it's hard but don't read this the wrong way."

"I'm being fired."

"No. To be frank, Neena Swain wanted you gone. Vic and I got in the way. Are you taking in what I'm telling you?"

"What about the Harding story, the Benton County connection? I was checking some leads…"

"We'll take care of it."

Nestor's attention was drawn to some people at his door. Ben Randolph and Astrid Grant. Jason took it as his exit cue.

Before he left the newsroom, he turned and glanced over his shoulder. Nestor gave him a wave. Jason felt everything was coming apart. Lost in his trouble, he nearly bumped into Nancy Poden, the librarian.

"Goodness, Jason."

"Sorry."

"Did you get the material I got for you on Gideon Cull?"

"No, I didn't."

"It's in your slot up front. Have a look. He didn't have any criminal convictions."

"No criminal history?"

"Nothing came up on the Washington Access to Criminal History database, but there's a complaint out of Spokane."

"I'll look at it later. Thanks, Nancy."

He went to the washroom, splashed water on his face, and stared at his reflection. What was he going to do? How could he get himself out of this mess? He stopped by the newsroom mailboxes for the documents Poden had left. Without looking at them, he rolled them into a tube, got into his Falcon, and drove home.

Dinner that night was cold baked beans eaten straight from the can, while watching his tropical fish gliding in the tank.

No one else for company.

He thought of Valerie, but not for long. It hurt too much. He went to his fridge and stared at his lone beer, contemplating it before grabbing a soda. He had to see himself through this. There were more important things, like Karen Harding and Roxanne Palmer.

He began flipping through Nancy Poden's research.

Most of the items were of no consequence—conferences, lectures, academic papers, nothing that he was really interested in. Not even a conviction. So much for confirming anything about Creepy Cull. Professor Touchy. And why had he griped after the interview? What was up with that?

Jason was still puzzling over Cull when he came to a tiny citation that blurred by. Right, Nancy had mentioned an incident of some sort. It was several years old and came out of Spokane.

Cull had been under investigation following a complaint by one of his college students who alleged that he had sexually harassed her.

31

Karen Harding's face beamed from three different color snapshots, taken at three distinct places.

Indoors at a friend's house, on the water at the railing of a ferry, and one in front of the Space Needle. Her eyes brimmed with warmth and happiness from an ordinary sheet of legal-sized paper.

MISSING, in bold, black letters, crowned the pictures.

Below them was Karen's description, her date and place of birth. Her gender, her hair and eye color. Her height, weight, and race.

Then came the details.

Marlene Clark traced her fingers over her sister's face before nodding her approval of the poster. Her husband, Bill, put his arm around her as she looked through the restaurant window of their Bellingham motel at the college students from Seattle who'd gathered in the parking lot.

Karen's friends.

They had produced the flier and were circulating it along the route she would've taken to Marlene's home.

They wanted Marlene to know they were helping. She turned to Kim Metzer and Sophie Lacosta, two students sitting across from her, and cleared her throat.

"It's good. Please keep doing this. I wish I'd thought of it sooner."

"We're making more," Sophie said. "And we're setting up a Web site."

Kim reached for her phone. "Luke is with a group handing out the fliers at the Lynden and Sumas crossings," she said as she dialed. "Then they'll work their way back along Route 539, hit every gas station, store, and house they see."

Marlene took a deep breath as Sophie pulled out a folder.

"We've contacted student and church groups in Canada."

Marlene was touched by their determination. "Thank you," she said.

Departing hugs were exchanged with Kim and Sophie. Marlene watched the student caravan leave the parking lot, then struggled with her exhaustion as she gazed down at the posters the girls had left on the table.

"Let's go to the spot," Marlene said. "I want to go the same way she went again. Starting from the truck stop."

It wasn't long before they'd driven by the chain-saw sculptures of the Big Timber Truck Stop, then got on Route 539. Looking out at the same scenery her sister had passed only days earlier, Marlene thought of how devastated her parents were going to be. She was almost grateful that they were incommunicado in such a remote mountain area.

The embassy had said it would take a few days to actually get word to them. Then a few days for them to trek safely out, maybe longer, depending on the region's severe weather. Torrential rains were expected. And by the time they got to a city, then an airport, then on a flight to the U.S. with a connection to Seattle, it would be another few days.

Maybe by then they would have found her, Marlene hoped.

Hang on, Karen. Please hang on.

As the highway rolled under them, Marlene realized why she was convinced Karen was still alive. It was a stirring in her heart that arose after Detective Stralla had informed them that she was not the victim found in the hills.

It was the same stirring Marlene had felt the time Karen *did* die on her.

No one ever knew.

They were kids and they'd gone on a river camping trip with friends. Marlene was fourteen and responsible for looking after Karen. They'd gone swimming at a small reservoir that had a dam. Just the two of them. It was pretty the way the water curtained over the dam, whirlpooling below.

Karen had chased a butterfly that was skimming the surface, running and splashing in knee-deep water, unaware of the drop-off until it swallowed her. Horrified, Marlene rushed out, swimming underwater some ten feet to see her sister pinned against the dam by the whirlpool's undertow. Karen's mouth had opened and her eyes were glazed. She didn't respond to Marlene's effort to help her.

She was drowning.

Marlene surfaced for air, then returned, and using every ounce of strength, pulled Karen from the dam to the riverbank. *"Hang on, Karen! Hang on!"* Marlene screamed over the rush of the water.

Karen's eyes were closed, her lips were blue. Her chest was not rising. Marlene was hysterical. *"No. No. No. You're not dead! Hang on, Karen!"* She fumbled at it, but Marlene performed CPR on her little sister, refusing to quit, watching her chest rise and fall as she breathed air into Karen's lungs. Praying and sobbing for her to hang on. Marlene didn't know how much time had passed before Karen's eyes fluttered and she coughed, spat up water, and came to.

Marlene kept it secret for fear she'd get into trouble. She told Karen she had slipped under and had swallowed a bit too much water. Only Marlene would know it as the time she came within a breath of losing her sister. Yet deep in her heart, she had refused to give up on her. Deep in her heart Marlene believed that Karen had refused to let go.

Hang on.

Bill slowed down at the site along 539 where Karen was last seen. Students had marked it with bows of yellow ribbon tied to the trees.

"Looks like Luke's here." Bill indicated the vehicles

and a group of young people studying large maps on the hood of a pickup truck. Luke turned as Marlene and Bill approached.

"Hi." He nodded. "We're just finishing up on who's going where. I'll catch up with Pete at Sumas," he said, waving off his friends as they drove away.

The highway whined with passing rigs and cars, the breeze lifting the yellow ribbons. During lulls, the area was tranquil.

"So, how are you holding up?" Luke asked.

"Doing our best. And you?"

He looked at the forests, rubbing his chin with his fingers, saying nothing.

"We know, Luke. It's hard, very hard, on all of us." Marlene stood toe-to-toe and looked him in the eye.

"What happened that night?"

"What do you mean?"

"Why did Karen run off like that? What happened between you and my sister, Luke?"

"We talked on the phone," he said. "Everything was fine."

"Everything was not fine! Something upset her. What did you say to her that night?"

"Nothing."

"I can't stand this. Why did she leave Seattle to see me?"

He searched the hills for an answer as Marlene searched his face for the truth.

"I don't know, Marlene. I don't know."

Marlene closed her eyes.

"You're lying. You never told us everything about that night."

His face reddened, eyes stinging. He bit his lip, shaking his head, then glared at her.

"All right! I never told anyone everything that happened."

"Why not?"

"Because at this point, my sins don't matter."

"*What!* What did you say? Don't you walk away from me!"

He'd broken into a trot to his car, the engine turned, the tires screeched, echoing over the treetops, rolling up the foothills that overlooked the last place Karen was seen alive.

"Luke!"

Marlene stared in vain as his car vanished.

She heard the soft beeping of Bill's cell phone. He was calling Detective Stralla.

32

At the instant of his birth, his teenaged, drug-addicted mother tried to flush his tiny body down the toilet of an Amtrak terminal between Philadelphia and Washington, D.C.

Alarmed by the screams, a young Jesuit priest rushed into the washroom, to the blood-drenched stall, and saved his life.

His mother was taken to a psychiatric hospital where she later died.

An orphaned bastard, he was placed with social services.

Throughout his infancy and early years he rarely cried or spoke. Concerned by his silence, foster parents regarded him as "the eerie one." He was passed through a succession of families whose capacity for love diminished with each new address.

When he turned nine, two older foster sisters used the promise of seeing a bird's nest to lure him to the roof of their building. He searched amid the vents and fans in vain while they smoked and drank from a bottle wrapped in a paper bag.

Look at the idiot.

"You hardly ever make a sound, do you?" They stood over him, grinning before flicking their butts at him. "We know a way to make you scream."

They pushed him down, each girl grasped one of his small ankles, then they held him upside down over the roof's edge some thirty floors up.

"Scream, you little bastard!"

He remained silent.

He'd shut down, extended his arms outward and arched his head to the world below. At that moment, suspended between life and death, his fate had been revealed. It began to crystallize what his bright, young mind had long believed. That part of him had died at birth; and part of him had evolved into something greater than what he was.

He was fearless.

God was with him.

God had selected him to battle evil

In all of its forms.

Like the two witches above doing all they could to make him cry out for mercy. They let his hand-me-down shoes come off, then his socks, as inch by inch he slipped from their grip.

"Scream!"

Silence was his response.

"Scream!"

Grunting in frustration, they jerked his body but he never made a sound. Instead, he raised his head, looking up at them, his rage seething beyond measure.

Defeated, they dropped him on the rooftop.

"If you tell, we'll kill you."

He never told.

Not after the abuse at the hands of his female foster family members continued. Not after their beatings, not after their sexual assaults, or dunkings in the bathtub and their favorite, special brandings with the curling iron and the terrible places they would insert it.

With each new torture they inflicted, he drew strength, the way an archer draws his bow, slowly building power, calculating the perfect moment to release it.

Once, they told him the tuna in his sandwich was actually brain matter from a cat they'd killed to cast a spell that would turn him into a toad if he told anyone about the things they'd done to him.

He never told.

Judgment Day for the witches would come.

Vengeance would come.

As a young man, his rage lay dormant as he roamed the country, first working hard to live a normal, exemplary life, one that would hold immediate meaning. But along the way, he stumbled.

Because of a woman.

He refused to dwell on the circumstances. It made him angry. One fact was undeniable. A woman was the wellhead of every episode of suffering in his life.

It was what led him to prison.

It was what led to his enlightenment and the further revelation of his destiny; that he and another he'd encountered in prison, a man whose life had followed a similar course of events, had both been dispatched by heaven.

To unite in battle.

Together they would eradicate the world of malevolent forces.

And it was at this stage of his life, as he looked back upon all he'd endured, all he'd overcome, that he embraced the righteousness of the part he would play in history. God had rescued him from death in a rail terminal toilet and had sanctioned him to exact full retribution against His enemies, the heretics, sorcerers, blasphemers, proud demons, liars, whores, and witches who committed sacrilege.

It was predicted. It was predetermined.

All encoded in the ancient text he and his friend had discovered.

Reflections on the Ritual.

An ancient text derived from letters, trial transcripts, and the diaries of a sixteenth-century executioner.

The executioner's soul, as old as time, had been reborn in his body, so that his work could continue, so that the world would know God's Wrath.

33

Seattle Police headquarters sits downtown at Fifth and Cherry, the stone portion of a half-block, twelve-story complex it shares with the city's municipal courts building with its monolithic glass facade.

Inside at his desk, Seattle Narcotics Detective Willie Heintz stroked his Vandyke beard, concentrating as he continued clicking through file after file on his computer monitor for Sawridge County Detective Hank Stralla.

Stralla was on the other end of the line in Bellingham, frustrated by cross-jurisdictional hurdles he had to jump. Heintz stuck out his bottom lip and shook his head.

"Nothing in our records for Karen Katherine Harding."

After the lab had alerted Stralla to finding cocaine in Karen Harding's umbrella, he called Heintz for a favor.

"Nope. Nothing for us, Hank. Her name doesn't come up. No traffic, no parking tickets. No hits. A good girl. You thinking, maybe too good?"

"I don't know."

"Let me try something with her address. That's in the East Precinct."

Heintz's keyboard clicked as he entered Karen's address into a number of department data banks. The screen scrolled with results of his query on complaint, call, and offender history for Karen's apartment, her building, and the surrounding addresses.

"Nothing at all for her. It's all been checked, even her neighbors have been canvassed and run through."

"Willie, would you run her boyfriend, Luke Terrell?"

"Sure, but I've got you down for a big-ass favor."

Heintz's computer beeped with his query.

"Nothing on the name. He's clean with us. But his address could hit the cherries for you. Could fit with the coke in the umbrella."

"What do you mean?"

"Hold on." Heintz typed. "That's Loader Village. Active. Mostly kids who buy and some small-fry dealers." Heintz clicked into several other data banks, went quiet, then grunted. "Hold on, Hank."

Stralla heard Heintz call out to another detective, asking about the status of something at Loader Village. He couldn't hear the response.

"Keep this under your hat, but a DEA task force is working with us, King County, and East Precinct people. Loader Village comes into play. Seems some serious threats have been made about outstanding drug debts."

"Does Luke Terrell come up in any of this?"

"Not from what I can see. But he lives in Block D, and Block D's mentioned from time to time in one of the files."

"Really?"

"There are sixty units in Block D. Your coke could be related to him or any one of them. I'm just giving you the atmosphere."

Stralla thought for a moment.

"Listen," Heintz said. "I have to go. I've got some pals on the task force. Give me some time, I'll make some discreet checks for you. Maybe talk to some of our CIs."

"Thanks, Willie."

Stralla hung up, tossed his pen on his desk, and sighed. It was clear, long before Bill and Marlene's cell phone call this morning, that Terrell was lying. Trouble was, none of the detectives had anything strong they could use to challenge him with.

It might be time to go at him with what they had.

Stralla swiveled his chair and caught a glimpse of one of the big double-decker ferries departing the Bellingham terminal. Soon it would be threading its way through Rosario Strait to Friday Harbor or Victoria.

He went back to Luke Terrell's statement and his notes. There was something in here. Stralla was pissed off by the delay, but Karen's phone records had finally arrived.

Before Karen left, she was on the phone with Terrell,

who said they talked and everything was fine. Yet Karen took off. The next morning, Luke used his key to enter Karen's apartment. Right. Why was he looking for her?

Karen's phone records showed that the first call from Luke Terrell came early in the evening of the night she left. But, and here was the kicker, it was followed by, Stralla counted, nine calls, then another six in the morning. Fifteen after the first call.

All from Luke.

Fifteen damn calls.

Then he showed up in her empty apartment the next morning. Why? The neighbor below heard a lot of noise. What was Luke really doing in her apartment? If everything was fine, why was he so aggressive in trying to reach her? That reporter from the *Mirror*, Jason Wade, had it right. Was Terrell searching for Karen?

Or something else?

Stralla turned to the far wall and the large white marker board. It was busy with Karen's picture, a running time line punctuated with notes, maps, and highlights of key events, like her stop at Big Timber. It was neat, orderly, the foundation for building a court case.

Stralla got up, uncapped a green marker, and drew a thread through the entire case to represent the latest development.

Drugs.

Say they had a blowout that night—maybe something to do with drugs. Karen's upset. They argue. She flees. Maybe, on an earlier occasion, he's hid some of his coke in her umbrella and now he rushes to her apartment to find it. But the umbrella's gone. Maybe Luke was holding it for somebody? Or, owed a heavy hitter? Maybe he'd been threatened? Maybe Karen got caught up in it, or was taken because of a debt? Maybe she was being held? There was no ransom call. None that he knew of. What if she was a mule or dealer? She'd have cash. Maybe a lot of cash. It would explain how she could vanish and survive.

Stralla's jaw tightened. He wanted to talk to Luke Terrell again.

He stood up, studied the board, then looked out to the bay.

The ferry had shrunk in the distance, like Stralla's logic. He was so stymied by this case. Nothing made sense. He glanced at Raife Ansboro's empty desk. He was pounding the street questioning registered sex offenders on their whereabouts after one of the Big Timber waitresses looked at a photomontage and said one of them resembled a man who'd been in the restaurant the same night Karen was there.

There was still a strong chance Karen was stalked, abducted, or taken in a crime of opportunity. It could be linked to Roxanne Palmer, the drug-addicted hooker from Spokane, chopped up and displayed in the Rattlesnake Hills.

Damn it.

This thing refused to crack.

Stralla snatched his jacket and trod off to catch up with Ansboro.

34

A million worries gnawed at Jason while he showered.

Fragments of Karen Harding's and Roxanne Palmer's cases that didn't fit. Gideon Cull. Luke Terrell. And pieces of his life that were coming apart.

Little made sense to him.

After cold cereal for breakfast, he sorted through the documents Nancy Poden, the news librarian, had pulled for him on Cull.

Very obscure.

A news brief out of Spokane reported that Gideon Cull, a local chaplain and lecturer at Tumbler River College, was under investigation arising from allegations that he had sexually harassed a female student in Spokane.

It was undated but had to be around ten years old.

Jason read it again. It was serious stuff, and this piece fit so well it was scary. It could be the reason why Cull was edgy, then had complained about the interview. He had an old sex complaint against him from a female college student in Spokane, and now one of his students was missing.

And Roxanne Palmer was a street hooker from Spokane.

But why hadn't anyone picked up on any of this? Shouldn't he call Nestor? Right, so he could pass it to Astrid Grant or Ben Randolph? No, he'd follow it up himself.

Jason read it again. There it was, plain and simple. All those years ago, a female college student had said Gideon Cull, *known as Professor Touchy, or Creepy Cull to his Seattle college students*, Jason added, had harassed her. And now, one of his Seattle students was missing.

Jason searched through his notebook with Cull's interview.

"No doubt you've discovered that I'm far from perfect, that I've learned from the mistakes of my past. I do my best to help people benefit from my errors, to see that things are not always as bad as they seem, that there's something perfect waiting for you. In the next life."

This was a hell of a thing.

And what about Karen's boyfriend, Luke Terrell? What was he hiding?

Jason downed his coffee, picked up his phone, and called Nancy Poden at the newspaper. While it rang, he took stock of his situation. Nestor had warned him that he was suspended indefinitely, not terminated. That he could not represent himself as a *Mirror* reporter to the public without the *Mirror*'s permission.

Well, nothing prevented him from doing research, or working for himself as a freelancer.

"Library, Nancy Poden."

"Hi, it's Jason Wade. Thanks for the research material on that little secret file."

"No problem. Did it help?"

"Very much. I was wondering if you could follow up on one for me."

"Shoot."

"Can you search everything in Spokane related to the one on the harassment complaint, document thirty-eight?"

"Hold on, let me call it up." Poden was fast. "Oh yes, that one. I'll do what I can, I'll search the *Spokesman-Review*, the local community papers, some of the law data banks, alumni, stuff like that. Where can I reach you?"

"Here's my number and here's an e-mail address where you can send me anything you find."

Jason covered his face with his hands to think. Surely something would come up in the archives on this. A chaplain who also lectured at a local college was alleged to have harassed a student. That should've been covered. Surely, police would've been involved. Jason switched on his laptop and searched the site for the Spokane Police Department. Even if the case was a decade old, the collective memory of the detectives would have to recall it.

Jason found the site, then reached for his phone.

Before he punched the number he hesitated. Was he willing to risk everything by secretly pursuing the disappearance of Karen Harding while suspended? Somebody had to chase this thing. Had to try to connect the dots. Maybe there was a reason that he was the one who broke her story. He certainly had nothing more to lose.

Jason met Karen Harding's eyes pleading to him from a news clipping.

He pressed the numbers.

35

The pain shooting along the nerves and muscles of Karen Harding's wrists and arms now reached to her shoulders and neck.

With every ounce of strength she worked against her restraints. She couldn't stop.

Push. Push. Push. Come on. You can do this. You can beat this. Push. Push. Push.

Then it happened.

In stretching and straining the rope around her aching wrists, Karen had succeeded in working enough play to pull the base of one palm over the other. Her stomach fluttered. She was astounded.

Raw and sore, her hand slid free. The rope dangled around her wrist. Karen cupped her face. Tears came. And with them hope.

Thank you, God.

The RV slowed. Then swayed. They were turning. From a paved road to a gravel road. Stones popcorned against the undercarriage, and Karen felt the ping-pong of direct hits beneath her. The RV tottered as the road rolled with hills, dipped with sudden valleys, twists, and turns. Branches slapped and brushed against the body. They must've entered a forest. The motor growled and the RV's suspension sagged as they drove deeper into it. She sensed no other traffic. No civilization.

Only isolation.

Like the last time.

Her stomach muscles clenched and she began trembling, forcing herself not to remember the panicked face of the other woman.

Forcing herself to silence her screams.

Don't think of the saw.

Karen prayed. They kept moving as the time passed. She could only guess at how much. An hour. Ninety minutes. Two hours. They were still on a back road. Where on earth were they? She pressed her face against her viewing crack. Daylight dappled under a canopy of trees and she sensed it was late afternoon, maybe early evening. As the RV continued deeper into the woods, the mattress overhead creaked. The woman above her groaned.

She was awake.

Good, Karen thought, forcing herself to subdue her fear and work on her plan. She started by trying to bring the feeling back into her hands, drawing her fingers into fists, driving her nails into her palms, massaging her wrists, her arms. Slowly, she felt warmth and strength trickle back into them.

It was impossible to reach the bindings around her ankles. She began rubbing at the numbness in her hips, thighs, and upper legs when, without warning, the RV jolted and shuddered.

The motor stalled.

In the quiet, Karen now heard the rush of water. A river. Birds. She looked through the crack. Still daylight. The motor restarted and the RV proceeded slowly, inching along, as if in a treacherous area. They took dramatic turns as they continued on for what seemed like half an hour before the RV stopped and the engine shut off.

The rush of water was louder now. Birds chirped. The RV vibrated a little as the reverend stepped from the driver's seat, opened the door, and began working outside. She could hear and feel him adjusting the levelers. He was settling in.

Where were they?

The doors to the exterior storage bins opened and she heard him rummaging for tools, a lawn chair, and other items. Humming. She actually heard him humming. He must be confident that they were completely isolated. She strained to detect any sounds of other people.

Nothing.

A branch snapped and she heard his footfalls fading. Except for the water, all was quiet. As if the place were airless.

This was her chance.

Karen swallowed. Her pulse began to pick up as she whispered: "Hello, up there. Can you hear me?"

Knock.

"This is our chance. I've got my hands free. Can you see if he's gone far?"

The mattress squeaked. It sounded like she was stretching, pressing against the window next to the bed. A blind swayed. The mattress creaked.

"Is he gone far?"

Knock.

"Okay, listen for him."

Karen pressed her hands against the crack that paralleled the small door he used to give her food. It sprang a bit, leaking more light as she put more weight on it. She turned on her side to face it, bending her knees, wedging her legs and entire body against the back wall. Turning herself into a coiled spring, she leveraged all of her strength through her hands against the split. The wood gave way.

Crack!

She was startled by the noise.

"Is he still gone?"

A creak. The blind brushed. Knock.

On her first effort, Karen pushed the small wall by a few inches. She inhaled, summoned even more strength, and pushed even harder.

Crack-Crack!

Another few inches. Without pausing she harnessed a sudden searing anger and pushed for her life against this outrage. Pushing. Pushing. Gritting her teeth. Pushing. Almost crying out when the wall gave way and shot along the floor, presenting her with a jagged hole about the size of a phone book. She caught her breath and sent her arm through it. Reaching up for the bed above, Karen nearly sobbed at the warm touch of another human being as the woman clasped her bound hands around hers.

Karen cocked an ear for the reverend.

Nothing.

She resumed working on her door to freedom, using her shoulder and elbow to smash away bits of wood until it looked big enough to pass through. Her head went first, clearing the pointed, splintered sides. Her shirt got snagged as she worked her torso out, but she dismissed the pain, quickly dragging her bound legs from her foul coffin-prison.

Pulling herself to her knees, Karen stifled a scream.

The woman was about her age. She was clothed, gagged, and bound on the bed. She had been beaten badly. Her face was a grotesque mask of bloodied bruises. Cheeks and lips swollen. Her eyes swelled with fear.

"We're getting away," Karen whispered, gently brushing the woman's hair. "My name is Karen Harding and we're going to escape."

She pulled off the duct tape around the woman's mouth.

"Oh God," the woman whispered, then sobbed.

Karen worked on the silver duct tape wrapped around the woman's wrists. "Tell me your name."

"Julie. Julie Kern. He's crazy. He's dangerous."

"I know. He's killed a girl already."

Julie gulped air.

"No! My God! Oh Jesus!"

Thud!

Both of them froze. The sound was near. He had returned from gathering firewood. Karen quickly found the tail of the tape on Julie's wrists and began unwrapping it until Julie's hands were free.

Thud.

"Do your feet," Karen whispered, going to her own bound ankles.

Thud. He was out there chopping wood.

Freeing themselves fast, Karen and Julie crept toward the RV's door, holding hands and holding their breath. Their bodies were weak, shaking from shock. Karen glimpsed the reverend's back. He was alone, swinging an ax a few yards away.

She swallowed.

Near him she saw loops of chains and other tools.

He stopped swinging his ax and turned his head toward the RV as if listening. He approached, still gripping the long-handled ax. The women were paralyzed. Could they fight him? He was a big man. He stopped at the door. He didn't enter. He bent down and disappeared from view. They heard a commotion from a storage bin as he retrieved a plastic bucket and headed for the riverbank, down a terraced slope, some thirty yards away.

Karen watched the top of his head bob in and out of sight.

Finally it vanished as he crouched to scoop water with the bucket.

Gently, she turned the RV's door handle. The women stepped out in silence, closing the door soundlessly behind them. As the rush of the river water filled the air, they padded to the rear of the RV, then around it, out of sight, coming to the road.

They ran for their lives.

36

At his desk in the Benton County Sheriff's Office, Detective Brad Kintry absorbed every word of the Spokane Police Department's most up-to-date file on Roxanne Palmer.

It had been sent that morning by the Spokane detective handling Roxanne's case there. Kintry had been waiting for the report on Roxanne's life in Spokane, to enhance what they knew about her murder on Hanna Larssen's farm in the Rattlesnake Hills.

Kintry would spend the rest of his day, as Lieutenant Buchanan advised, submitting Roxanne's case to several critical databases designed to help track repeat violent offenders, including serial killers.

He went to his computer and called up the site for the Washington Attorney General's Homicide Investigation Tracking System, known as HITS, a statewide computerized database used to analyze violent crimes committed in the Pacific Northwest. It drew upon cases in Washington, Oregon, and parts of Idaho.

Using his law enforcement password, Kintry logged into the site and entered data on Benton County homicide file number 05-6784-54. He was a fan of HITS, one of the most respected crime-fighting systems in the world, because it worked.

It had emerged in the 1980s, in the wake of the hunt for people like Ted Bundy and the Green River Killer. The fact that serial killers were often mobile, crossing into different jurisdictions, drove home the need for investigators to quickly share key data that could link cases and result in an arrest.

HITS catalogued murders, rapes, and missing persons, holding data on thousands of cases. Information included crime scene evidence, characteristics about geographic location, weapons, vehicles, suspects, and the victim.

Kintry liked how the system made it easy for agencies to search and analyze information on their case, while comparing it with cases submitted by other agencies. If you got a hit, bingo, you were on the line to the investigator handling a case linked to yours, opening the door to more information and a chance at solving the thing.

Another advantage Kintry liked was how HITS acted like a case file checklist, ensuring that you covered the basics, such as the victim's known associates, which in Roxanne's case was being handled by Spokane. They'd already provided a list in their report. Mostly prostitutes, pimps, drug dealers, customers, and social workers. Kintry took great care to ensure that he entered their names with the proper spellings, and their aliases. Benton County could look for a link to those names here.

The system also called for checks on all known convicted killers and sex offenders. That would include those living in Roxanne's Spokane neighborhood and surrounding counties. And those residing in Benton County. Buchanan already had some of the other detectives in the division going hard on that, shaking down the sex offender registry, parolees, checking alibis, rumors, and any data from informants.

Kintry paused to consider Karen Harding's case in Sawridge County. Detective Hank Stralla had told him they were going to submit it to HITS. Kintry would check with Stralla soon, to again compare Roxanne's case against Karen's. They were looking for a thread, a link, anything, no matter how small, to determine if the two cases were connected.

Nothing had surfaced.

Nothing except that the women were similar victim types. The same body type, age, race, and last seen outside, in an environment that made them vulnerable to just about anyone who happened by, Kintry thought.

Finished entering his data, he queried the system.

No hits.

He got a fresh coffee and returned to begin submitting his case to the FBI's Violent Criminal Apprehension Program, known as ViCAP. Similar to HITS, the FBI's national computerized database also analyzed, collated, and searched for links in murders and violent crime cases submitted to it.

Kintry was fascinated by the history of the FBI's system. It was conceived by Los Angeles Police

Detective Pierce Brooks in the 1950s. He was investigating a killer who was luring his victims by placing ads in Los Angeles area newspapers seeking women to model. The killer would tie them up, photograph them, rape them, then hang them. Brooks suspected the killer was likely committing murders beyond his jurisdiction, so he went to the public library to look for similar murders in out-of-town newspapers. Sure enough, his theory paid off. He discovered other cases with enough links and evidence to track, identify, and arrest the killer.

Brooks conceived of a system where details in crimes of neighboring jurisdictions were stored in an easily accessible system. The FBI picked up on his idea and worked with him over the years to create a central computerized system for police to quickly share information on mobile suspects. The guy was a visionary, Kintry thought.

ViCAP asked investigators to answer close to one hundred questions detailing every known aspect of the victim, the suspect, the crime scene, including key fact evidence, known as holdback. Once a case was submitted, FBI analysts continually compared all submitted files with others from across the country, searching for matches, signatures, patterns.

When they got a hit, detectives were alerted.

The most unique aspect of Roxanne's homicide was its ritualistic nature, the series of Xs, burned into the skin and the letters VOV, over the heart. Kintry was a little nervous providing his holdback, but if it was key to solving the case, then he'd give it up. Besides, the FBI was constantly assuring investigators that their holdback was secure.

Dismemberment, full or partial, even mutilation, was not uncommon in stranger-on-stranger homicides. No, it was the markings the killer had left on her body, his signature, that flagged the case.

The mark of a monster.

Not far from Kintry's office, Benton County Coroner Morris Pitman removed his bifocals as he ruminated over the gruesome violation the killer had inflicted on Roxanne Palmer.

Massive tearing of vaginal and rectal tissue was consistent with the application of a sixteenth-century torture instrument known as a Venetian Pear. Then there were the amputations, the decapitation.

The strange markings were familiar to Pitman, but just how and why, he couldn't say. Increasingly, his secret frustration had been turning to anger at himself. He couldn't sleep, he'd lost his appetite.

He went back to his autopsy report and photographs, zeroing in on the manner in which the killer had branded her. There were eleven small distinguishing Xs, about a quarter to half inch in scale, which trailed along her upper shoulder and leg-hip areas.

There were the letters VOV, about an inch in scale, burned over her heart. What the letters signified was a mystery to Pitman.

He stared long and hard at the autopsy photos and

kept staring until a small light of hope glimmered in the corner of his mind. The wounds were consistent with ancient torture practices and variations during the sixteenth and seventeenth centuries. In some corners, the X signified the church at war during the Inquisition. An executioner would brand his name, or mark, into enemies of the faith as a warning to others, an effective, terrifying tactic.

But how did Pitman know this? How did he specifically know this?

He scanned his office for his textbooks. A memory was coming. He thought back to his conferences, classes, his own university days in Seattle at the University of Washington. He had first come across ancient torture during his student days. Now, was it a lecture? Or a textbook? He was going back some forty years. He remembered a reference to this very specific phenomena. Where? Where had he seen it?

Damn. This was futile. Pitman reached for his phone, pressing the number for his office assistant.

"Kathy, can you do me a favor?"

"Yes, Morris."

"Call the University of Washington's history department and get them to look up a course reading and textbook list from the mid 1960s on a course called the History of Torment and Torture."

"My word, they had such a course?"

"They did. And I need the complete lecture and reading list faxed to us right away."

"Okeydoke, boss."

A few hours later, Kathy stood in his doorway holding the faxed pages.

"Don't go away."

Pitman slid on his glasses, studied the list and the titles, maybe a dozen in all.

"This could be it." He half smiled, passing the list back to Kathy.

"Call the University library, the state library, and the Library of Congress if necessary and see if we can arrange an emergency loan on each book, and I mean each and every title on that list, and get them shipped to us ASAP."

37

"Luke Terrell. Luke Terrell." The motel clerk repeated his name as she shuffled nervously through her registration cards for Detectives Hank Stralla and Raife Ansboro.

Terrell had not returned to Seattle.

He was among the group of Karen Harding's friends who had stayed overnight to distribute more fliers this morning at stops along I-5 to Blaine. They had checked into the same Bellingham motel where Marlene and Bill Clark were staying; where Stralla and Ansboro were now waiting with poker faces until the woman at the front desk said: "He's in room twenty-three."

"Thank you," Stralla said.

The two big men filled the narrow hall as they headed to Terrell's room. Before this day ended, Stralla wanted answers from him. Arriving at room 23, they heard voices coming from the other side of the door. They listened for a moment. Ansboro rapped softly on the door.

After it cracked open, a woman said, "Yes?"

Stralla and Ansboro flashed their badges and identified themselves.

"We'd like a word with Luke Terrell," Stralla said.

The chain was unhooked and the door opened wider. The woman was in her twenties, jeans, T-shirt, blond, pretty. Judging by the color, length, and cut of her hair, Stralla pegged her as the woman in news pictures comforting Luke Terrell at the Benton County murder scene. Well, well, well. Stralla exchanged a quick silent glance with Ansboro.

"He's in the shower but he'll be done soon," she said.

"Can we come in and wait, please?"

She moved aside.

Terrell stepped from the bathroom, hair damp, unshaven, dressed in faded jeans and a flannel shirt. He stopped when he saw the two visitors, then nodded. "Do you have some news?"

"No. Actually, we need your help. We'd like you to come to our office. If that's all right with you."

"Your office?" Terrell's anxious eyes went to the woman.

"We need to clear up a few small matters."

"Why not just ask me here? We're heading out to put up more fliers."

"We'd prefer you come with us."

"Maybe you should go," the woman said. "It sounds important."

"All right."

"We'll take my car," Stralla said.

A fine rain was falling.

The wipers and talk about the Seahawks and Mariners

filled much of the silence during the drive downtown. The interview room had a chrome-legged table with a wood veneer top. Two hard-backed chairs on either side. On one wall there was a mirror, about four feet by four feet. The room was painted off-white. The fluorescent light in the tiled ceiling hummed.

"Have a seat." Stralla slapped his file on the table.

"Do you have any leads?"

"Nothing substantial."

Terrell pulled out a chair, put his arms on the table, clasped his hands. He pressed his thumbs together, moving them back and forth until he felt Ansboro's eyes on him.

"Nervous?" Ansboro asked.

"I haven't been sleeping much."

"That blonde's cute," Ansboro said.

"Carmen? She's a good friend."

"I betcha." Ansboro winked.

"What's this? What's going on here?" Terrell asked.

"Tell us what happened that night you spoke with Karen," Stralla said.

"I've told you everything. We talked and everything was fine."

Ansboro's hand slapped the table.

"Liar!"

Terrell stared at the detectives. Stralla held up a copy of Karen's phone records. "If everything was fine, why did you call her fifteen times after your first call?" he asked. "Nine that night and six the next morning?"

Terrell gauged the intensity in Ansboro's face and in

Stralla's questions, blinked several times, then swallowed.

"We argued, all right?"

"Speak up."

"We argued. First, about her charity work with her church group. It took so much of her time, we were never together."

"You wanted her to stop?"

"I was getting worried, she was spending more time in shelters, soup kitchens, street missions, she dealt with a lot of ex-criminals and creeps."

"Any one in particular give her trouble?"

"No. I don't know, then that argument led to another one about her plan to go to Africa."

"What about it?"

"I got thinking about how dangerous it was for aid workers, how the experience would change her and that she wouldn't want to marry me when she came home. I told her I didn't want her to go because it would be over for us if she went. I told her she had to make a choice. Africa or us."

"You pressured her to make a choice that night?"

Terrell nodded.

"She cried. She said I was wrong and begged me not to force her into this type of decision."

"Then what?"

"She left." Terrell closed his eyes. "Then I realized I was being stupid. That I was wrong. After I hung up, I called but she didn't answer. I tried her cell but it must've been off. I let things cool overnight. I called in the morning. I called a lot. Still no answer. So I went to her place to beg her forgiveness, but she was gone."

"Why didn't you tell us this at the outset?"

"I was ashamed."

"Ashamed?"

"Ashamed that possibly the last words—" His voice cracked. "That possibly the last words I spoke to Karen were spoken in anger. That I'm guilty of making her run off that night. I couldn't bear anyone knowing that I may have been responsible."

Stralla exchanged a look with Ansboro, and then they glared at Terrell for a long moment before Ansboro said, "Bull. Shit."

"Excuse me?"

Stralla pulled a page from his file.

"You live in Loader Village, right?" Stralla said. "We all know what goes on there, especially in Block D."

Ansboro stood and drew his face to Terrell's.

"We found the dope, Luke."

The flicker in Terrell's eyes, in the microsecond of hesitation, the near imperceptible muscle twitch along his jawline told them that he knew about the cocaine hidden in Karen Harding's umbrella.

Knew all about it.

"Was that Karen's dope? Is that what you want us to think?"

Terrell's eyes went around the small room, searching for something he could mentally grasp to steady himself with. Finding nothing, he said: "Am I under arrest?"

"No."

"Why," Stralla said, "did you wait until now to tell us your concerns about Karen's work with street people and criminal types?"

"Can I leave?"

"Yes, but we'd regard your departure as being uncooperative," Stralla said.

"As in, what're you hiding from us?" Ansboro said.

"Maybe I'd like to have a lawyer before I answer any more questions."

"You want a lawyer?" Stralla said.

"I think that maybe I do."

"Well, doggies." Ansboro leaned back, folding his arms across his chest. "The woman you want to marry vanishes after you argue with her, and when the police ask you for a little help, you ask for a lawyer."

"Hold off, Raife." Stralla opened the door for Terrell. "It's just his way of showing how much he cares and really wants to find Karen."

"I bet he's showing Carmen there how much he cares."

"I'm leaving."

Terrell got up from the table and headed down the hall. Stralla and Ansboro followed him. At the reception area, all three men stopped. Waiting with her husband was Karen's sister, Marlene. Upon seeing Terrell she stood, blocking his exit.

"I want you to tell me the truth about you and my sister, Luke. *The truth, do you hear me!*"

38

Karen and Julie ran.

They ran as twilight pulled darkness down over the forest and the cries of unseen creatures pierced the air.

They didn't dare stop.

Legs numb. Sides aching, lungs sore, throats dry and ragged from panicked breathing, they ran, trotted, and walked as fast at they could. Fear compelled them to keep moving. For he must surely be behind them.

Hunting.

The images of his ax, the chains, his blood-flecked hacksaw, and the echoes of the other woman's screams consumed Karen.

Once they had fled the reverend's campsite they followed the twisting gravel road, expecting to hear the growl of the RV behind them at any moment. They veered into the woods where they struggled through the thick growth as branches and needles tugged at their clothes and skin.

The terrain was wild with scrub, small rocky cliffs, and hills fractured with tiny cracks waiting to swallow a foot, wrench an ankle, or launch them into a dark ravine. They bought distance but paid dearly, stumbling, bruising legs, bloodying fingers. But they kept moving. At times they held hands, careful not to speak or cry out while they continually cast frightened glances behind them.

Was he behind that tree? Was he over the next rise?

Karen had no sense of what direction they were moving. No sense of where they were. As it grew darker, it became more dangerous to continue.

Karen began scouting for a safe spot to hide for the night, leading them down a slope and into a thick grove until they came to an overhang at a small rocky hillside. It had a soft, dry grassy floor, while above, a rock roof jutted out. Inside there was space enough for the two of them. Protected by the forest, it offered shelter, and safety should someone approach up the steep incline.

"We'll sleep here," Karen whispered.

In silence they quickly gathered leafy branches for a blanket. Baseball-sized rocks and a couple of sturdy, pointed sticks would do as makeshift weapons.

As they sat in the stillness, adrenaline flowing through them, feeling their hearts pumping, Karen reflected on mistakes she'd made. They should've memorized his license plate. Should've grabbed food and water. Or they should've tried to knock him out and drive away. Yes, but her first instinct, her basic human instinct, was to flee. Remain positive, she told herself. They were alive and they were free.

Karen and Julie were pressed against each other,

warming themselves with their body heat in the blinding blackness. They remained alone with their own thoughts until Julie asked, "How did he get you?"

Her question took Karen back to another time, another world.

"I was going to visit my sister in Vancouver when my car broke down in a storm near Bellingham. He stopped to offer help. He seemed like such a kind man. A reverend," she said bitterly.

"It was almost the same for me," Julie said. "I was staying at a shelter in Eugene. He was in the dining hall. I'm good at spotting creeps and freaks, but he was so friendly, a chaplain to me." Her voice held dismay, sounding small. "He offered me tea. Said it was in his RV. So, like a fool, a stupid fool, I went with him. Stupid. Stupid. Stupid."

Karen tried to console her.

"Listen, our family and friends will have police looking for us."

"No. I have no one. No one will miss me."

Karen put her arm around her as Julie told her about the death of her parents, a life of being shuffled between foster homes, the abuse, and her heartbreaking search for her cousin in California.

"You're not alone," she said. "You have me. I'm your friend, and my friends are your friends. You're not alone, you got that?"

Karen felt Julie's head nodding slowly. Felt her spirits warm a bit, until Julie pulled away and said to the darkness:

"You said he already killed a woman?"

"Yes."

"Do you know much about her?"

"No."

"What did he do to her?"

"We shouldn't talk about it."

"Karen, tell me. What happened to her?"

"I never saw." She cleared her throat. "I only heard. We shouldn't dwell on it. I mean, it's horrible, but we've got each other and we've got to get to a road, a house, someone, right?"

"Yes."

Karen suggested they take turns keeping vigil and opted to let Julie sleep first. In the chilling darkness, amid the animal noises drifting in the forest, the warmth of another human being was psychologically comforting for both women.

But alone in the night, Karen's thoughts floated to her mother and father in Central America. Her sister, Marlene, and her family. Her boyfriend, Luke, her friends. She sent them a prayer.

I love you. I feel you with me. I'm alive. I miss you with all my heart.

Even Luke?

Yes, even Luke. Even though he'd hurt her. Even though the last thing they did together was argue. His sudden change had broken her heart. Made her doubt their relationship. Deepened her suspicions that he had taken up with that crowd at the complex where he lived. Drugs were common there. So was sex. And there were a lot of pretty girls there constantly, making Karen fear that Luke might be tempted. Because sometimes when she was with him, he let her know how difficult it was for him to hold to their decision to wait until their wedding night. She wiped her tears. And here she was preparing to go away for a year.

Had she asked too much of him?

What was happening to her?

She stared into the abyss, her head dropping, her eyes closing until finally, sleep took her.

39

Jason Wade pressed his phone to his ear.

Waiting for his long-distance call to connect, he stood and went to his aquarium. Watching his fish helped him think. He had to do this. He had nothing to lose now. The line connected.

"Spokane Police Department."

"I'd like to speak to someone in Major Crimes."

"One moment, I'll connect you."

The line clicked to a Johnny Cash song, a ballad about regret.

"Major Crimes. How can I direct your call?" a woman said.

"I'm inquiring about an old case of sexual harassment. I'd like—"

"I'll put you through to the Sexual Crimes Unit. Hold please."

Johnny Cash came back but not for long.

"Sex Crimes. Lange."

"Detective Lange?"

"Sergeant."

"Sergeant, I'm calling from Seattle to inquire about an old sex crimes investigation."

"What about it?"

"I'd like to know the outcome, or status, anything like that."

"And you arc?"

"Jason Wade, a freelance reporter. I'm researching a possible story."

"You should go through our press office, Mr. Wade."

"I know, I just thought your people in the unit might recall this one."

"What can you tell me about it? Have you got a suspect's name?"

"Gideon Cull. It was maybe ten years ago. He was a chaplain and guest lecturer at Tumbler River College. A female student complained that he'd sexually harassed her. I needed to know if the police took her complaint, what happened, that sort of thing."

"Ten years ago. Spell his name."

Wade heard Lange typing on a keyboard.

"Got his date of birth?"

"No."

"I've got nothing showing. If there was a case, it could be archived in Records. Not all of our older cases have been transferred into our system. Look, we're swamped here. Give me your number, and maybe we'll get back to you. Or you can try Records."

Jason hung up, realizing that he was on his own now. And without any sources in Spokane, chasing Cull's past was going to be an uphill struggle. He needed help from someone connected in Spokane, someone he could trust. He contemplated his fish for a few minutes before a name surfaced.

Carl McCormick.

McCormick was a crime reporter for the *Spokesman-Review*. Last summer, Jason had done freelance legwork for him on the Seattle angle to a story on a Spokane armored car heist. He wrote up some color under a tight deadline about the lead suspect's family. Got a clipping, a check, and a promise from McCormick. "Jason, buddy, I won't forget this. I owe you big time. If ever you need help with anything, let me know."

McCormick was a big gun who'd won several awards for his coverage of some of the biggest stories in the region, many of them becoming national stories. The Spokane Serial Killer, the Unabomber, Ruby Ridge, White Supremacists.

Jason went to his desk, sifted through his top drawer until he found McCormick's card. Tapping it against his chin, he thought for a moment, then typed an e-mail to McCormick.

Hi there:

Hope you remember me. Last summer, I filed you material from Seattle on an armored heist. Since then I've been reporting for the Seattle Mirror. As you know, I've been writing on the case of Karen Harding, the missing college student, and Roxanne Palmer, the Spokane woman, whose body was found in Benton County.

This is confidential, but

Jason hesitated to make some calculations, regarding money, distance, and driving time, then continued.

I hope to be in Spokane soon to do more research on these cases. Was hoping you might have time to get together to point me in the right direction and possibly share information that might be mutually beneficial?
Regards,
Jason Wade

After sending his e-mail, Jason went to his kitchen and washed his dishes. He grabbed his canvas suitcase from the closet in his bedroom and tossed in enough clothes for a few days. As he packed, he thought of his father. He made a mental promise to take him to A.A. when he got back from Spokane. This trip and time away from the incident would help Jason cool off. He took care of his fish, then checked his e-mail.

McCormick had already answered.

Hi, Jason:
Of course I remember you. Yes, I've been reading your stuff. I'd love to get together to talk about Harding and Palmer. Below are my office, cell, and home numbers. Call me when you get in.
Cheers,
Carl

40

The twitter of birds woke Karen and Julie at first light.

They were stiff, sore, and cold as they pushed away their blanket of branches. They stood and moved their tired arms and legs to replace the morning chill with the warm flow of circulating blood. There was little they could do about the hunger that scraped at the walls of their empty stomachs. Or the disgusting feeling of being coated with grunge.

As quietly and carefully as possible, they resumed their blind attempt to trek from the deep woods and contact help. They didn't run, but moved at a good pace, having quickly become reacquainted with the terrain. Karen estimated it took them about two hours to find the edge of the gravel road. They remained concealed in the bush, careful to keep the road in sight.

By the time the sun was directly above them they had gone a great distance. Still, Karen was uneasy. Had they gone the right way? Her unease was underscored by the fact they had not come upon a single sign of people, or vehicles, or buildings. She could only pray they had chosen the right direction.

A branch cracked loudly, then another. Then Julie cried out as Karen turned and saw her fall and slide down a rugged hill for thirty yards in a noisy avalanche of rocks and undergrowth. Karen rushed to her side. Julie's pants were torn and her leg was cut.

"Anything broken or sprained?" Karen helped Julie to her feet.

"I don't think so. I think I'm just banged up but OK. Just give me a minute."

Julie rubbed her leg, glanced up, and froze.

"Look," she whispered.

It took Karen several seconds to follow her gaze and focus through the tunnel of trees and branches. But far off in the distance it was there.

A flash of color from an object.

Hikers? Hunters? Something solid. A vehicle maybe?

The women exchanged glances. Karen cast around. Then spotting a stone and earthen rise, made a decision.

"You rest here. I'll go up there and see if I can get a better look, see exactly what it is before we go over, OK?"

Julie nodded. Then, for the first time, she smiled.

Karen patted her shoulder, then slowly began to ascend the rise. It was difficult, but the view would be the payoff. She figured the rise should take her above the grove and give her a clear line of sight toward the flash of color.

Karen lost her footing a few times, sending a trickle of stones down the slope behind her. She stopped, waited, regained her footing, then continued. She had to do this a few times before she reached the top and disappointment.

At this angle, the foliage was dense, nearly obstructing the view. She took her time focusing her eyes, trying to discern what the patch of color belonged to. It appeared to be a vehicle. A camper tent trailer, or car, or truck. After considering it for a moment, Karen decided she and Julie should get closer to it to see what sort of people went with it.

Carefully, she turned and began to make her way down the incline. It was just as tricky going down as it was going up. It took longer than she'd expected. When Karen arrived at the bottom she was confused.

Julie was gone.

What the heck? Not a trace of her. Did she walk off? "Julie?"

It grew quiet. No birds in the area were chirping. Karen took tiny steps from the area, then she saw Julie and was relieved. There she was, on the soft grass in the shade of a tree, on her back. Resting.

"What we should do is—"

Karen halted as Julie groaned, her head lolled to her side, revealing that half of her temple was a bloodied pulp. Karen heard a branch snap, a swish of fabric, turned in time to see a large branch block out the sun as the reverend brought it down on her head.

41

"Did you hear me?" Marlene Clark said. "You're not walking away from me until you tell me the truth about you and Karen."

Detectives Stralla and Ansboro let the standoff play out. The wheels were turning now. They saw it in Terrell's worried face.

"Everything, Luke," Marlene said.

Resigned to defeat, he lowered his head slowly, then brought it up.

"OK."

"And them." She indicated the detectives. "Whatever you tell me, you tell them."

"All right."

"Let's go back in the room," Stralla said. "Luke, do you waive your right to a lawyer?"

Luke looked at Marlene.

"I do."

"Hold on." Stralla pulled a sheet from his file. "Before you say anything, sign this, confirming that you're waiving that right."

Terrell rubbed his lips with his fingers after he

signed it, then said: "First, the dope, the coke you found in her umbrella, is mine."

"Cocaine! Oh God, this is about drugs?" Marlene said. "You've got her involved in drugs?"

Stralla shot a look to Bill, who understood immediately.

"Marlene," Bill said.

Terrell buried his face in his hands.

"I love Karen. She makes you better than you are. She's got a moral backbone stronger than steel. She's an angel but—"

Stralla and Ansboro, arms folded across their chests, stared at him.

"Because of her beliefs, and they're mine too. Only her conviction is deeper. But we didn't do drugs and she didn't want to have sex—" He stopped, looked at Marlene. "She wanted to wait until after we were married. And she didn't want to move in together. I was good with all of that. But my course load was getting overwhelming. I saw less and less of her. My friends at Loader gave me some pills to help me pull off some marathon work sessions. I liked it.

"Then I tried cocaine. Karen noticed a change in me, started to question me, started to wonder if I'd be able to survive a year apart before we got married. We began to bicker. I started to confide in Carmen."

Ansboro snorted, *"Confide?"*

Terrell let a beat pass.

"I started using more dope, I started running up debts with a dealer. I got scared and I got some cash together to put on my debt. Then word whipped through the Village that there were going to be big busts. I panicked, so I hid my dope in Karen's umbrella without her knowing.

"After I did it, I got thinking how I was just wrecking my life. I thought of Karen going to Africa, I thought if I could get her to stay, get married and be with her, everything would get back on track. Then one night Carmen came over. We did some coke and things happened. We made love. Later, I felt horrible, felt guilty. Then I got angry and blamed Karen for frustrating things by having such high standards. I called her that night. We argued about Africa, and—"

Marlene cupped her hands to her face and wept.

"Did you tell her about Carmen?" Stralla asked.

"No, but she suspected it," he said. "That's the truth. It's why I never told you everything. I drove her away."

"Who else knew you hid dope with Karen?" Stralla asked.

"Not a soul."

"Not even Carmen?" Ansboro said.

"No one, I swear. I couldn't risk anyone knowing."

"And what were you looking for the morning you went to her apartment?"

"Her umbrella."

Marlene shook her head in disgust.

Ansboro slid a blank sheet to Terrell.

"Write down all the names and numbers of your dealer and dope connections."

"Are you going to charge me?"

"You're such a bastard," Marlene said.

"Just do it," Stralla said.

Ansboro studied the information.

"Did you ever clear your drug debt?"

"No."

"Do you think any of these people would harm Karen as leverage against you? Or go looking for your stash, do something as payback for your outstanding debt?"

The thought hit Terrell like a blow to his midsection. He blinked several times.

"No. I don't know."

"From what you're telling us now," Stralla said, "Karen was far more emotionally distraught that night than you led us to believe. She likely felt her whole world was coming apart, because of you."

It was true.

"Makes me wonder if you would've ever told us the truth, if we hadn't found your cocaine."

"I'm sorry," Terrell whispered. "It was my dope and my cash and my fault she ran."

"Cash?" Ansboro repeated. "You hid your cash with her?"

"Yes, three thousand to pay the debt. I thought you'd found it, too."

"Where did you hide it?" Stralla asked, already flipping pages in his file folder.

"In her car, under the hood, between the battery and the battery tray."

Stralla looked at him, then Ansboro, as he punched

a number into his cell phone. It was for the crime lab in Marysville.

"Hi, this is Stralla, can you get me Van Cronin, right away?" Stralla continued turning pages, even though he was certain of the answer. "Van, Hank in Bellingham, on the Harding Toyota. Did you find cash hidden under the hood under the battery? No? All right, hang on."

Stralla asked Terrell details about how he'd hidden the cash, relaying them to Cronin, who actually went and checked the car again.

"Thanks," Stralla said, hanging up. "No cash."

42

Karen's head was a mass of pain.

Her mind sparked like a live wire burning a hole through her skull. Agony for her to think. Her ears throbbed.

Everything was black.

Her jaws were locked open with the gag clamped between her teeth and tied excruciatingly tight around her head. The pressure made her dizzy. Cord bit into her wrists, her ankles. She didn't know where she was. What had happened. Tears stung her eyes. Her aching body, her filthy, famished, exhausted body, sagged in utter defeat as the realization slowly crushed her.

No.

Let this be a bad dream. This can't be. Don't let this be, she pleaded in vain as it all came back upon her, driving her deeper into the darkness.

She and Julie had escaped from the reverend. Had gotten free and had fled into the woods, running for their lives. For how long? She didn't know. A day? A night? She didn't know. They had seen no one. Heard no one. They'd run and run until Julie slipped noisily down a slope. That's when they saw the object. Through the trees. A colored object. Someone to help them? Karen had climbed a hill to see better, but when she came back down Julie was...

In that horrible nanosecond Karen had understood what had happened to them. They had traveled full circle, back to his RV. The reverend had come upon them. He had clubbed Julie with a tree branch. When Karen turned, he clubbed her.

Oh no. No. No. No.

The fear returned. Where was she now? What had he done with Julie?

Karen opened her eyes, blinking to adjust to her surroundings. It was dark. Some diffuse light had pierced the roof of her enclosure. Where was she? She was not moving. She was not in the RV.

A shrill twitter.

A bird.

Her nostrils filled with the smells of dirt and cedar. Hard earth beneath her. Beside her. Cool, damp earth, branches and boughs above her. She couldn't move.

She was encased.

In a shallow grave.

He'd put her in a grave! Left her in an isolated woods to die!

A tremor went through Karen as she fought to cry out. For her mother. Her father. Her sister. Luke. *Somebody! Please.* Marlene. Karen thought of Marlene.

She could hear Marlene's voice telling her to hang on. Like the time they were kids on that camping trip near the river and the reservoir. They'd gone swimming. She'd swallowed water, slipped under. She couldn't breathe, couldn't move. Then she saw an angel and dreamed she was being pulled from the water. It was Marlene.

"No. No. No. You're not dead! Hang on, Karen!"

Hang on, Karen told herself as she lay in her shallow grave, her heart thundering against her rib cage as something began wriggling over her stomach. Oh God. It was large. She felt it moving! Something slithered under her wrist, its scales scraping against her skin as it constricted and contracted.

A snake! A big one! Moving over her body!

Her stomach clenched. Gooseflesh rose on her skin as she tried to scream. As quickly as it began, it ended as the snake slid away. Her pulse continued galloping for several horrible moments. Then her face twitched. Tiny, tiny legs scurried across her cheek, down her jawline toward her ear.

A spider.

Tears rolled from her eyes.

She stopped breathing at the sound of rustling. A branch snapping. Someone was approaching. Someone big. Heavy. Human. Getting closer. Karen had nothing to lose. She made muffled cries. Squirmed. Writhed. Struggled to be heard. The footfalls made the ground near her vibrate.

The light above her darkened. All went silent.

Karen froze.

In her heart she prayed it was a savior.

In her head, she knew it was the reverend.

He'd buried her. The way a cougar will bury its kill and return later to feast. Karen understood. The reverend had come for her. Her terror gave way to anger, outrage, and fury. *How can you do this to people?* What had he done to Julie? Whatever he was planning to do with Karen, she would fight him. She would...

She held her breath.

The light grew intense as he removed the branches and boughs above her. His face was silhouetted against the sky as he gazed upon her for the longest time before he walked around her. Karen then felt his big hands under her arms, as he hoisted her to her feet. Grunting, he hefted her over his shoulder. She weighed nothing to him.

Her head swirled, dizzy from fear and hunger.

His upper body was solid, powerful. He moved at a fast, surefooted pace over the rugged terrain. Karen strained to see more, but her aching, weakened body, her position over his shoulders, gave her a blurry upside-down view of trees, earth, and small hills.

Soon she heard the river flowing, saw the RV, the campsite. He grunted, knelt, and stood Karen upright.

Less than ten feet away was Julie Kern.

Chained to a tree.

Mouth gagged.

Hands bound.

Eyes open wide in horror.

43

Morris Pitman hefted the box that had been delivered by special courier van from the University of Washington to the Benton County Coroner's Office.

Inside he found a dozen or so textbooks of all sizes. Most of them likely out of print, he thought, carefully placing them one by one on his desk. The look and smell of their covers, spines, and pages took him back forty years to his college days. The History of Torment and Torture was one of the stranger but more fascinating courses he'd taken.

Pitman got busy with his investigation, which arose from the disturbing evidence of the letters *VOV* seared into the flesh of Roxanne Palmer, above her heart.

The killer had left his mark in keeping with the ancient method of branding victims. Pitman needed to find the reference to the practice. Not branding in general, but branding whereby the torturer leaves his name, or mark, as a tactic of terrorizing other potential victims.

This was what Pitman suspected was at play in the Palmer homicide. If he could find the reference in an obscure book, it might provide a building block in the pursuit of her killer. This unique ritual, this specific methodology, was his signature. Of that, Pitman had no doubt. But if he could point to the exact source of this signature branding, the inspiration, it would shrink their potential suspect pool to someone who would have to be familiar with such a practice.

If Pitman's memory was correct, the reference to signature branding stemmed from the course he'd taken and was buried in one of these books, most of which had indexes that cited branding methods. The reference could also have been mentioned briefly in a nonrelated passage.

He sighed.

This was going to take time. He'd have to go through each textbook. Better get started. He began flipping through the first book, which braced him for a refresher on the darkest dimension of human behavior.

He scanned through the illustrations—pricking of accused witches with needles, water dunking, stretching limbs on the rack, ripping away fingernails, gouging out eyes, acid wash, crushing bones. It went on. Disembowelment, inserting white-hot rods into rectums, vaginas, ears, or mouths, the gallows, whips, hacking off of limbs, and branding.

Pitman searched through passages on branding in book after book. There were references to letters signifying the crime or offense of the victim being seared with red-hot irons into their flesh, usually on cheeks, heads, necks, or other areas. But he failed to find the reference of a signature of the executioner. As he continued looking, he considered the psychological characteristics of those who inflict acts of depraved cruelty on other human beings.

In many instances, they themselves have been tortured, or come to believe in the righteousness of the cause. But studies had indicated that whatever the motivation of tormentors, it becomes easier for them each time to commit such unspeakable acts. They develop a pathological hatred for the victim, someone to be regarded as subhuman.

But what was at work in the case of Roxanne Palmer? Pitman asked, turning to his computer, clicking through his report and the photographs of her remains. What savage urges were driving her killer? Judging from the near surgically precise skill at amputation he demonstrated, he was certainly practiced. Meaning, of course, he'd done this before, and most certainly would do it again. Judging from the way he displayed Roxanne, he wanted the world to know what he'd done. And judging from his signature, he wanted to communicate an identifier, wanted people, and perhaps other potential victims, to know it was him. He enjoyed his power. Pitman looked hard at the picture showing his signature branded into Roxanne's skin.

VOV.

What did that mean?

And where had he seen reference to this specific

practice? Pitman clamped his jaw shut and resumed searching through the course material. It was among these textbooks. It had to be. Or was his memory playing games with him?

Damn it. No.

He remembered reading an ancient work. Was it a novel, or was it a paper, put together by Jesuit scholars? As he recalled, it was drawn from trial transcripts, letters, and the secret diary of an executioner-torturer. A European who signed his work by searing his initials or mark into the flesh of his victims. He'd gained notoriety with a greater audience. Not unlike what was at play here.

"Now, why can't I find it?" Pitman said aloud in frustration.

"Morris?"

Lieutenant Buchanan and Detective Kintry were at his door.

"You all right?" Buchanan asked.

"Yes, just working on something challenging. How about you?"

Buchanan was holding a sheet of paper.

"Just got off the line with the FBI's ViCAP section chief. They have a match on Palmer. An unidentified unsolved of a white female in Oregon, near the California line. They want to set up a meeting ASAP. I'm going to talk to the investigators there. What do you make of that?"

Pitman removed his glasses.

"Could be another piece of the puzzle."

The fact of the matter was, he feared the prospect of a rising body count. He replaced his glasses and scrutinized his old textbooks. The answer had to be here.

44

Excerpt from *Reflections on the Ritual*

In the year of Our Lord, A.D. *1557*
Somewhere in Europe

At dawn, a hungry crow made several final strike bites to remove an eye from the corpse putrefying at the gallows outside the city gate.

Under cover of darkness the souvenir hunters had already picked over the remains of the heretic. They took teeth, locks of hair, fingers, and snippets of fabric, to be sold in the backward provinces as cures for everyday maladies, perhaps talismans for unrequited love.

Such was the status of last month's judgment.

For those who had missed out, this morning held greater promise. Anticipation was in the air, carried on the smoke from the bakers' ovens, the iron works, and the market fires that curled beyond the walls to the far reaches of the community, inviting all citizens to gather near the square.

For today, they would bear witness to a rare event.

The judgment and sentencing of two young sisters charged with having succumbed to devils. The practitioners of sorcery and witchcraft would be compelled to bow to the glory of God.

A local holiday had been declared.

Every stratum of the region partook. The poorest of country folk, servants, artisans, and rich merchants, rose early from their beds and dressed in their best clothes. They had set all the day's duties and business affairs aside to make their way to the city, through the market to the center. In every corner of the town, the streets swarmed with activity.

The smells of fresh bread, produce, and slaughtered poultry and swine mingled with those of goat heads boiling in blackened kettles and the stench of urine and excrement from the chickens, pigs, cattle, and horses, who also trod along the busy streets.

Minstrels performed, jesters joked and juggled, while hawkers claimed to offer genuine items belonging to the young witches. "This is her comb, I assure you, Madame." Crowds gossiped and speculated as their numbers swelled in the shadow of the church spire where necks craned to watch the local tradesmen make final preparations.

The clock tower chimed and the square fell silent.

Those knowledgeable in the proceedings of these matters quietly explained to their neighbors that the accused, being held in the jail, would at this very moment face a chance to renounce Satan, confess their crimes, name those who also sinned, and convert. If they confessed, it would be deemed false. If they refused to confess, it would be an admission of their heresy. Don't worry, their guilt is assured.

The penalty is a certainty.

A rumor rippled through the square. Only a rumor, mind you, because the statute guaranteed the anonymity of the executioner to thwart those dark forces that would attempt retaliation. As you know the rumor arose from the relative of a chambermaid at the inn, or was it the boy from the stables, or the old guard at the court? No matter, the story being that the presiding executioner was Xavier Veenza, the hermit monk from the distant mountains.

In all of Europe, few were as skilled at the ritual.

"If we have Veenza, then we are to behold something, to be sure, eh?" Winks and nods were followed with enthusiastic nudges.

The prosecution of the heretics began a fortnight ago when the girls were given the summons. They were roused from sleep and brought at night to the government building for questioning. They were urged to confess, to renounce the *devil. They were threatened with torture, taken below to the torture chamber. They were shown the instruments of agony, stripped naked, and prepared for what was to come.*

Soon the screams of the young prisoners pierced the jailhouse walls, resounded through the square, to the church spire, the rooftops lined with onlookers, and the hotel windows where tourists, who'd traveled far for the event, cocked their ears.

The cries of the witches were received well. This, my friends, is what we've come for, to attest to the swift application of justice against the enemies of God.

Is it Veenza's work? Do you think it is he?

Then court officials, noblemen, and various leaders of the church took their reserved places in the grandstand—the moment of truth had arrived.

Having allowed sufficient time for confession and spiritual consolation—the heretics were removed from their cells, manacled, shackled, and placed by local guards on a cart for a procession to the place of execution. A cordoned area enclosed two stakes, fashioned from dead wood, jutting from the ground amid chest-high heaps of straw, twigs, and branches.

A long, slow burn.

Nearby, a kindling fire crackled. Next to it, the executioner's altar displayed an array of odd-looking instruments hinting to the crowd that there were better things to come.

At this point, no space within the entire square was vacant, having been jammed with citizens eager to see an event they would recount for generations, the burning of two local witches.

The procession was a slow, painstaking process whereby the mother of the condemned wailed, prayed, and implored magistrates to spare the souls of her daughters.

45

Jason Wade's motel room in Spokane smelled of stale beer and cigarettes. The green digits of the clock on the night table showed 10:54 p.m. when he tossed his bag on the bed, then called Carl McCormick's home number.

"It's Jason Wade, sorry for the late call, I just got in."

"Hey, there you are," McCormick said. "Where're you staying?"

"Big Sky Suites."

"That's across town from us."

"Sorry I'm so late. My car lost a fan belt in Ellensburg, had to send to Yakima for a replacement. Then my cell phone died. I lost a lot of time."

"No problem. I worked on Cull today, made calls to set things up for us. Get some sleep, I'll come and get you at the motel, say nine a.m. sharp."

After hanging up, Jason put his cell phone on charge, reached for the bag of tacos and refried beans he'd picked up at a drive-through, then flipped through his file on Gideon Cull.

Coming here was a gamble that could cost him more

than a few hundred bucks out of his own pocket. But he couldn't ignore his gut feeling that Cull might be connected to Karen Harding's disappearance and Roxanne Palmer's murder. The Spokane link with the old sex complaint had to be checked out.

He had little experience chasing this kind of serious stuff. He'd likely already missed some important aspect, he thought, getting into bed. But he had nothing to lose. If he was wrong, he'd back off. Then what? The *Times* and the *Post-Intelligencer* weren't options for him.

There was always the brewery.

But what if he was right?

He stared at Cull's picture until exhaustion turned to sleep.

At 9:00 a.m., Carl McCormick's blue Dodge pickup stopped at the motel's entrance. McCormick wore jeans, a polo shirt, and a dark jacket that emphasized his white hair.

"Jason." McCormick shook his hand. "Good to see you."

"Same here." Jason got into the cab. It was littered with newspapers, phone books, and files. "Thanks for helping me."

"No, I owe you. If this Cull is linked to Palmer and Harding, then you've got a big ass-story. Now, given that Palmer's from Spokane, how about we agree to share our data?"

"Sure. What do you think the chances are that he's linked?"

"Too soon to tell. Nothing's ever what it seems. You've got to be careful with these stories. A guy who looks guilty one minute is cleared a minute later."

McCormick had called one of his contacts, Margaret Hipple, a manager in the human resources department of Tumbler River College. She met them at a small restaurant near the school and was nervous at Jason's presence.

"This is all on background," McCormick assured her. "We'll protect sources. We're just interested in the information. As I told you, this man could be tied to some violent crimes."

Hipple hesitated before unfolding a piece of paper with information she'd collected from the college's records on staff and students, archived stuff from the basement, she told them.

"Going back several years, Gideon Cull was a part-time lecturer of religion. He also did a lot of volunteer community work with support groups, addiction groups, the homeless, convicts, people in crisis, that sort of thing. Here and throughout the state. He traveled quite a bit."

"What about complaints against him?" Wade asked.

"Only the one. A student claimed he'd touched her improperly."

"Was it investigated?"

"Yes. Cull was deeply anguished by the allegation. He was held in high esteem, but it was quietly suggested he take a sabbatical while the complaint was dealt with."

"Was it referred to the Spokane PD?" McCormick asked.

"No. The policy on something like that at the time was for the school's Professional Standards Committee to first look into it. If it was credible, they would refer it to the police."

"What was the outcome?" Jason asked.

"The woman who launched the complaint dropped out, then moved away. The committee tried to reach her to follow up on her complaint, but she left no contact information. So it was set aside."

"So no one really knew if it was true or not?" Jason asked.

Hipple nodded. "Correct, but the committee's feeling was that this young woman was somewhat unstable. She'd also said she thought she was being followed on campus by a strange man, which could not be substantiated. She just didn't seem credible. Cull denied her allegation, cooperated fully, and was concerned about her mental state of health."

"How do you know this information?" Jason asked.

McCormick smiled to himself. The kid was learning.

"I chaired the committee at the time."

"So what happened?"

"He resumed teaching at the college. But soon after, he left and eventually went to Seattle."

"With no black mark on his record?"

"We gave him a positive reference."

Jason and McCormick paused to consider the information, and then McCormick asked Hipple to give them the woman's name. She looked away to think about it, then glanced at her page and lowered her voice.

"Bonnie Stillerman."

"Spell that?" McCormick asked. "And do you have her date of birth?"

Hipple gave it to them along with other data, including a lead on finding one of Bonnie Stillerman's old college friends in Spokane. McCormick turned away to make some calls.

"I'm helping because I trust Carl. I don't believe Gideon Cull could be tied to anything like what you've suggested, but I know I'd never live with myself if he was and I didn't help."

Jason nodded.

"That is all I can give you. Now I want your word that this comes from an anonymous source."

"You have it," Jason said, shaking Hipple's hand.

Back in McCormick's pickup heading across Spokane, Wade looked across the city wondering about Cull's case and the complaint.

"It's a puzzler," he said. "I don't know what to make of it."

"It might not be a story yet, but it's information." McCormick's cell phone rang. He answered, listened for a few seconds, then said: "All right, we'll be there in about twenty minutes. Thanks, Dunc."

Next stop: Riverfront Park.

After parking, McCormick and Jason took a path that threaded along a grassy meadow and tall swaying willows that led them to a man alone on a bench overlooking the Spokane River. He was an ex-FBI agent, now a private investigator, who traded data with McCormick. A broad-shouldered man with salt-and-pepper hair and intense dark eyes.

"Dunc, this is Jason Wade, I told you about him."

The man nodded and folded his newspaper.

"What can you tell us about our subject?" McCormick asked.

Dunc grimaced and stared at the river.

"He had assault charges against him. But they were dropped. He was never convicted. Never did time."

Jason pulled out his notebook, prompting Dunc to glare at him as though he'd committed an offense for being so eager, so he put it away.

"He hit his wife with a baseball bat after he caught her cheating on him. He was drunk at the time. She lived. He got a good lawyer."

Dunc glanced at his watch.

"It turns out, the judge liked Gideon and said the situation and circumstances were mitigating. Go figure. Your subject was quite young at the time. A failed philosophy doctoral candidate studying to be a minister. He was remorseful, cooperative, all that crap. Since he was an aspiring clergyman, he offered to counsel convicts so he visited prisoners and he took a lot of courses and also became certified to teach. His wife left him but he started teaching and stayed out of trouble ever since."

"Except for the college complaint," McCormick said.

"Except for that."

"Thanks, Dunc."

He nodded, crossed his arms, and stared at the Spokane River.

McCormick took Jason to a small diner at the fringe of a downtown industrial section. Flies patrolled the grimy corners of the front window. Prices on the menu were updated in ballpoint pen. Jason ordered a BLT on white. McCormick got tuna salad, looked to the street, then summarized what they'd dug up so far on Cull.

"He's been violent against his wife and had an unsubstantiated sex complaint against him from a female college student. Fast-forward a few years and you have a murdered Spokane prostitute. And students at Cull's Seattle college, where he teaches Harding, call him creepy. It's all interesting, but is there a story there?"

Jason didn't think so. Not yet. They finished lunch, then met Bonnie Stillerman's old college friend, Diane Upshaw. She'd shared an apartment with Bonnie at school and was now a real estate agent, an extremely busy one, selling new homes north of the city near the suburb of Mead.

"Bonnie didn't have many friends," Diane told them while leaning against her Lexus outside the model show home as colored banners and builder flags snapped in the breeze. "She was very quiet and shy."

"Did you believe her complaint against Cull?"

"Something happened, because it was a big deal for her to make the complaint. She was so timid."

"Did you know Cull?" Jason asked.

Diane shook her head.

"We understand Bonnie complained that she was being followed on campus."

"Nothing came of it," she said. "She was pretty stressed with school and the Cull complaint. She may have been paranoid. I suggested she take a break. Not long after, she just dropped out and moved away."

"Do you have any contact information on her?"

"No. We lost touch. I think she just left Spokane to start over. Just took off. I still have some boxes of her stuff." Diane opened her bag. "After you called me earlier, I took a quick look through some old pictures. Here." She handed McCormick snapshots of Stillerman. A plain-faced girl who wore large glasses with bright red frames. Diane's cell phone rang. "I think she moved to New Mexico," she said before turning away to take her call.

Jason and McCormick spent the rest of the day unsuccessfully trying to locate old friends of Bonnie Stillerman or Gideon Cull.

In his motel that night, Jason lay on his bed not knowing what to make of what he'd learned about Cull, when he came upon an idea. One he would act on alone. He went to his files, flipping through Carl McCormick's stories on Roxanne Palmer's murder until he'd found what he needed, then glanced at the bedside clock: 11:20 p.m.

Not too late. A good time actually. Jason grabbed his map of Spokane, then a page from his file folder, which he inserted into the glossy outdated visitor's magazine from his motel room's desk drawer.

He headed for his Falcon.

This might work.

46

The last time Roxanne Palmer was seen alive she was working her corner on Spokane's east side, according to one of Carl McCormick's stories in the *Spokesman-Review*.

Beyond that, few other details were known.

No one saw her get into a car. She never called anybody. She was there, then gone, until Hanna Larssen found her.

His idea was a wild one, but worth a try, Jason Wade figured, taking a hit of take-out coffee as he rolled along East Sprague Avenue. He glanced at his passenger seat at the magazine and the page he'd inserted that was peeking from it.

East Sprague was a stretch of fast-food joints, strip malls, neon signs, and run-down warehouses. Long-legged women wearing pumps, micro-miniskirts, and excessive makeup stood at most of the street corners in the area along the avenue known as the Track.

Jason rolled along the strip, coming to the corner where Roxanne had last worked. He turned off

Sprague, parked half a block away, grabbed his magazine, and headed for the corner.

The two women standing on it turned to him as he approached.

"Hi, sugar. Looking for something sweet tonight?" The first was in her early twenties, short black hair, big eyes, and hoop earrings.

"Can we talk?"

"For the right price, we can do anything you like."

The air was heavy with perfume and the smell of strawberry bubblegum being snapped by the second woman, who had long red hair and looked much younger.

"I'm trying to find out some information about somebody."

The brunette's face tightened.

"You a cop?"

"No, I'm a reporter."

"A reporter?" She glanced around. "If you've got a damn cameraman back there, I swear I'll kick your ass."

"No, nothing like that. I'm from Seattle."

"Seattle? Show me some ID."

The redhead stepped away and began pressing numbers on her cell phone. Jason's mind raced. He pulled out his laminated photo-ID from the *Seattle Mirror*, knowing this stunt might come back to haunt him as the hooker seized it, studied it, then gave it back.

"I ain't giving you no damn interview, Slick," she snapped, eyeing her girlfriend, who'd finished her call and nodded. "You know we lost a girl down here. She got murdered down by Kennewick."

"That's why I'm here. I'm researching a story on her case, Roxanne's case. It might have a link to a missing Seattle woman."

"Go talk to the police."

"I'm talking to everybody."

"You're holding us up, driving our dates away. What do you want?"

Jason unfurled his magazine.

"I'm going to show you pictures of a man and ask you if you've ever seen him before. Maybe he's come down here to talk to the women. Maybe he talked to Roxanne?"

The two women looked at each other.

"That's it?"

Jason nodded.

"All right. Show us."

The women pulled closer together as Jason opened the magazine to the color photograph he'd inserted. The one of Gideon Cull.

Gum snapped. Then jewelry jingled as both women shook their heads.

"Never saw him."

When Jason lifted his attention from the picture, he noticed two other women had approached.

"What's up?" a tall one said in a deep voice.

Jason was thinking transvestite when the brunette spoke up.

"Slick here's a reporter from Seattle. Thinks

Roxanne's murder's got something to do with a Seattle woman gone missing. Wants to know if you know the guy in the picture. Show them."

Jason did, to negative results. Word spread along the Track with lightning speed as he walked from one corner to the next along the avenue showing Cull's picture to the women, who soon knew what he was doing before he got to them.

The squeal of brakes and the menacing throb of a car stereo jolted Jason. A polished navy Cadillac pulled alongside him. Inside, a large man with a gold chain, gold watch, and gold-capped teeth gleaming from his scarred face waved him to the passenger door. The music was turned down.

"Yo, Ace, what the fuck you doing stirring shit up?"

"Just showing a picture asking if anyone knows a guy." He stepped closer to the car. "Can I show you?"

"No. You either date a girl, or get the fuck outta here."

Jason saw the grip of a handgun sticking from the pimp's waistband.

"I'm not going to tell you twice, asshole."

"All right. I'm gone. I'm just going to walk back to my car."

The man's eyes bored into Jason's face. The music was cranked, the engine growled, and the Cadillac squealed away. Jason watched for a moment. As he turned to leave, he heard a sound from a back alley.

"You the reporter?" a female voice whispered from the dark.

Jason walked toward it.

"Swear to me you're not a cop, because I don't talk to cops. I'm jammed up with charges, court, my boyfriend, custody for my kid."

Jason pulled out his photo-ID. A frail woman stepped from the shadows. She looked emaciated. Her arms were laced with needle tracks. She studied his ID until she was satisfied.

"OK, show me the picture."

Jason glanced around to be sure he was clear, then opened the magazine, tilting it to catch the ambient light. The woman dragged long and hard on a cigarette as she studied Cull's face. Then began shaking her head.

"No. I never saw him around here."

"Did you know Roxanne?"

She blinked and nodded.

"I worked with her that night. Her last night."

Jason indicated they take their conversation into the shadows.

"So what happened?"

He saw the red glow of her cigarette, then heard her exhale.

"I don't know. She sometimes went off by herself, so at first we thought nothing unusual."

"Did she say anything was wrong, or talk about anything strange in the time before?"

"Nothing."

"Is there anything that you can remember about that time?"

Her cigarette glowed, then was dropped.

"I've gone over it in my mind. She told me about this religious guy who started coming around. I never saw him. No one else remembered him. There's a lot of traffic and a lot of creeps, a lot of religious guys."

"Well, what was it about this guy?"

"She thought he was funny."

"Funny?"

"He wanted to save her. Every other freak wants to save us."

"That's it?"

She didn't answer. She was looking to the street at a car half a block away that was crawling toward them.

"That's it, I have to go," she said, unwrapping a stick of gum from her purse and starting for the car.

"Wait, can you remember anything about the religious guy?"

"I never saw him."

"What did he drive? Don't you guys write down plate numbers?"

She stopped.

"I remember, Rox said he drove an RV. On the back, it had a picture of a duck, or Canada goose. One of the wings was peeled off."

Jason wrote it down, raised his head to thank her, when he heard a car door slam.

She'd disappeared into the night.

47

V ov.

The letters swam into focus on the overhead screen in the boardroom of the Benton County Justice Center in Kennewick.

Then Lieutenant Lloyd Buchanan went around the table making the introductions.

Detective Brad Kintry and Coroner Morris Pitman nodded from their swivel chairs to the others. James Barlow, an FBI profiler from Seattle; Detectives Peter Chase, from the Spokane PD; Hank Stralla from Sawridge; Mike Wicker, Washington State Patrol; and Price Canton, from Klamath County, Oregon, where unidentified female human remains were found along a wooded riverbank nearly a decade ago.

"We've all read the background," Buchanan said. "Price, why don't you start us off with your Jane Doe?"

"What you see on the screen is our key fact evidence from our case. We have nothing on the significance or meaning of the lettering *VOV*," Price said. "A survey crew working in Klamath County near Lost River found the torso and severed head of a white female in a shallow grave some eight years ago. Attempts at identification didn't pan out," Canton said. "After Tony Danko, the original Klamath detective on the case, retired, it was passed to me. I spent a lot of long nights trying to find a fresh way to go at it. Four years ago, I submitted our holdback to ViCAP. Nothing happened until the other day, Quantico called on our key fact match with Benton County. So here we are."

Attention in the room heightened as all eyes returned to the overhead screen, which offered a blowup of Brad Kintry's computer monitor and crime scene autopsy photos of the Benton and Klamath victims. No words were needed. Everyone had locked on the chilling confirmation as Kintry enlarged the chest area over the heart in each picture.

Each victim had been branded with the letters.

VOV.

Kintry clicked to more photos showing that small x's had also been burned into the skin in each case.

Morris Pitman, the coroner, removed his glasses and rubbed his hand over his tired face. "What's your read on this?" he asked the FBI profiler.

"After studying the material of both cases, I'd say you have a serial offender with a clear signature. And I don't think these two women are his only victims."

Barlow paged through his notes.

"Your suspect is very organized, he plans these things, might keep his victim alive and tormented for a period to prolong his sense of control or power, his enjoyment. He's fantasy-driven."

"What types of fantasies?"

"I'm coming to that. The autopsy reports in both cases indicate sexual assault with a so-called Venetian Pear, which could be a substitute for his lack, or failing, or interest, to carry out a sex act himself. His fantasy might arise from vengeance, torture, or humiliation he suffered. He was likely abused horribly as a child. Something involving traumatic torture or physical abuse, something like that, given the brutality and rage in evidence here. And he may have been abused by a female power figure in his life, which would fester and evolve into hatred and degradation of women."

Barlow consulted his notes before continuing.

"I'd say the suspect is a white male, but I'd really be guessing at his age range. It could be the same as his victims, all the way up to sixty, even. The thing I'd say from the body sites is that he knows this region. Moves about it invisibly, so he blends in with the general population. He's likely of above average intelligence, possibly in a position of trust or authority that he can exercise over his victims. Or an unassuming harmless, trustworthy loner, who establishes a comfort level that disarms his targets."

Barlow rustled some pages.

"The Benton victim, Roxanne Palmer, is a single white female aged twenty-four, a known prostitute with a drug addiction, a vulnerable lifestyle. We have no biography on your Klamath victim. She's a Jane Doe, a white female whose age is approximately twenty-two.

With the Benton case we see an escalation of his rage. We see the same dismemberment, but we see display. In Oregon, you have concealment, in Washington, display. I believe that between Benton and Klamath, there are other victims. More important, I think that in the wake of Benton, his cooling-off period is all but vanished. The guy is out of control, given the brutality and display. Taking the risk of being seen by going onto a farmer's property suggests he's bold, daring, brazen, another indication his cooling-off period is growing shorter. Which brings me to the Sawridge County case."

"Karen Harding's disappearance," Stralla said.

"Yes. Her victimology fits his pattern and is consistent with the Benton and Oregon cases. It's troubling how well she fits. Age, race, vulnerable circumstances. Her case also dovetails with his escalation, his brazenness. But on the other hand, her case could be completely unrelated. Unlike Benton and Klamath, you don't have a single shred of physical evidence linking Harding's disappearance to the other two murders, correct?"

"Well, we have the slim comparison of the tire impressions from both scenes. A possibility that a truck, or an RV, is connected to Harding and Palmer."

"I see that."

Privately, Stralla acknowledged that the link was hopelessly weak.

"I'll lay it out for everyone," Barlow said. "You've got to go hard on the victims and the evidence for a connection to the killer. And that'll be tough."

"For now it appears the methodology is the strongest link," Pitman said.

"Right," Barlow said. "If you can come up with a suspect pool of people who would be acquainted with this type of torment, it would help."

"I'm working on trying to determine the precise origin of the branding," Pitman said. "I think it derives from a certain historical case study. I believe if I could confirm that, it might prove to be a guide, might point us to the kind of individual who would have knowledge of it."

"Certainly," Barlow said. "You've got to be philosophical here. You've got a big break in that you've got a link, so that doubles your chances of increasing case information to study. But it won't be easy. You have no bitemarks, no saliva, no DNA. No usable latents or trace. What are the odds of identifying the Oregon Jane Doc?"

"Slim," Canton said. "Her arms and legs were not found. Her severed head was badly decomposed, the lower jaw was detached and missing. We had only a partial upper jaw. We believe the parts were scattered by animals. We were lucky that the torso was not too badly decomposed and we got the details we got."

"Soil analysis? Anything there?" Barlow asked.

Canton shook his head, searching through his notes on the case.

"Oh, we found one thing, which could be related to our Lost River girl."

The others waited as Canton fished a page from his file and passed it around the table. It was a photograph.

"This was taken approximately twenty yards from where the torso was found. Near a hiking trail, so we're not one hundred percent certain it is linked to Jane Doe."

The others took turns glancing at the arm and broken partial frame from a pair of eyeglasses. They were bright red.

48

Heat.

The smell of smoke.

The crackle and rush of burning wood.

All registered with Karen Harding as she regained consciousness and slowly awakened to her nightmare. Fear coursed through her body, blurring her vision, numbing her. Exhaustion had weakened her. Hunger had weakened her. Lack of water and sleep had weakened her. Her ability to form a single thought caused her brain to spasm.

Her will had abandoned her.

Blinking, she tried to concentrate, tried to find the strength to comprehend her circumstances. Chains. She could feel chains. Their metal links were crushing her lower legs, her stomach, her organs, her chest and neck, fusing her to something hard, rough, tall.

A tree.

She was chained to a tree.

Her hands were bound. Her mouth was clear but she dared not speak.

The night was ablaze. An inferno roared before her,

deadwood snapping, hissing, and moaning, spewing sparks to heaven. A breeze sent blankets of smoke toward her, making her eyes sting and tear. She pulled them shut. She had no concept of time.

A memory rippled through her.

She and Julie had escaped only to flee full circle back to the reverend. He'd brought them back to the RV and the campsite. Julie was chained to a tree. Julie? Where was she?

Karen opened her eyes, blinking through her tears. Working to adjust to the firelight and darkness, she scanned the perimeter but saw only black and the outline of the RV. Then she focused and stared through the flames to a vision from hell.

Julie was chained to a tree.

Naked.

Her head had been shorn, all but a few bloodied tufts surviving as a testimony to the rage behind the act.

Julie was half conscious. Not gagged. Moaning.

Karen began working her mouth to call out and comfort her, when she heard a click as the RV's metal door swung open.

Oh God.

Through the hazy smoke-filled night she first saw his black boots, then black pants, a swaying full-length black robe. His head was concealed by a large black hood.

An executioner's hood.

Long metal objects clinked under his arm as he took slow majestic steps toward the fire. They clanked when he dropped them to the ground. He squatted, took his time carefully placing and aligning the long rods in the flames. More wood was tossed on the fire, creating a draught. Karen gazed at the red-orange intensity whirling with sheets of heat at the belly of the blaze. Her skin began to moisten. Her lips became drier.

The black hood turned and he came to Karen, came within inches. He towered over her. Powerful and strong. His hood was the flag of horrors to come.

Behind the slits she met his eyes.

For the first time since her abduction he was staring at her, into her, through her. Her chains began chinking a little and at first Karen could not understand why the tree was vibrating until she realized it was her. In the full force of his gaze, she was trembling uncontrollably. His eyes were clear, bright, and burning with hatred as if she and Julie were guilty of the most egregious affront to him.

A toll would be exacted. A price had to be paid.

He was insane.

Frantically, Karen searched her heart, asked God for strength, then began to plead for their lives.

"Please. I beg you. Please. Let us go."

A large black-gloved hand clamped over her mouth, silencing her. He squeezed hard until she understood her pleading was in vain. Then he began his work. He reached for the first branding iron and began slowly rotating it in the flames.

Karen was sobbing, sending prayers to Julie, sending love to her parents, Marlene, and Luke, as she struggled to make peace with her life and God. She prayed. The reverend stood gripping the iron rod. The letters at its tip glowed red and white in the night. Karen's stomach twisted then she began:

"Hail, Mary, full of grace…"

The reverend stepped toward Julie with the glowing branding iron.

Karen shut her eyes, flinching when Julie screamed.

Once it started it went on forever.

Karen slipped into a surreal state of shock, which took her mind in and out of consciousness as she pleaded to God. To anybody to save them. At times she saw and heard every violation he was inflicting on Julie. At others Karen nearly passed out, engulfed by the horror, by Julie's screams, the sounds of the tools, his branding irons, his saw, his cauterizing plate. *The way it sizzled when he touched it to Julie's flesh.* The screams. The smell. *Oh God.* Karen told herself it was not real, that he'd given her some hallucinogenic drug-induced nightmare. *This can't be real!*

Because a human being was just not capable of doing this.

Karen thrashed against her chains until she passed out. For how long she didn't know. A minute. An hour. She had no idea, but when she came to it was still night. She smelled something pleasant, something that registered immediately with her empty stomach.

Chicken?

Roasting on the fire.

The reverend, dressed in jeans, flannel shirt, and a

fishing hat, was leaning forward from a folding lawn chair, holding a long forked rod with a piece of meat affixed to the end. He was turning it slowly over the flames, looking every bit the part of a benign RV camper cooking dinner.

Karen embraced a small wave of relief.

It had been a nightmare. A bad dream.

The chair creaked and the reverend stepped toward Karen, holding the meat to her mouth. She hadn't eaten in days. She could smell the chicken, saw the tender meat bubbling in its own juices.

As she opened her mouth to take a bite, she glimpsed through the flames the tree opposite hers. Julie was gone. Was she in the RV sleeping? See, it never happened. Karen's eyes adjusted to the base of the tree. Several chains were collared around the trunk. A huge, dark spot glistened in the firelight. A huge *damp* spot, as if a large amount of reddish black liquid had been spilled there. At the edge of the fire she saw the tools.

The saw.

Julie?

Karen began screaming.

Oh God. It's not true. Dear Jesus. It can't be true. She didn't see the things she saw. It's not true, it didn't happen.

But it did happen.

Karen cried out. Her screams echoed above the treetops and rushed into the night.

No one heard them.

49

"A religious guy in an RV?"

The morning after the hooker had told Jason Wade about the man bothering Roxanne Palmer, he was sitting next to Carl McCormick at his desk in the *Spokesman-Review*, telling him about it.

"First time I heard this one." McCormick leaned back in his chair, tapping his pen to his chin. "And she never told the police?"

"Nope."

"Strange, you'd think she'd want that out. For safety, for her friend."

"Seems she was in a bad way with major problems. Hates cops. So I don't know how much weight to give it."

Intrigued, McCormick shrugged, then glanced at the time.

"I'm sorry, I won't be able to help you today. I've got to cover a trial." He tore a page from his notebook with names and numbers for Jason to chase down.

The day and that night were a washout. Jason couldn't flesh out the hooker's RV information. He tried to find her again but failed. And the others working the Track wouldn't talk. No doubt their pimps had warned them to shut up, he reasoned, collapsing on the bed in his room, which carried the foul air of cigarettes and his frustration.

He was done here.

The next morning Jason checked out of the Big Sky Suites, gassed up his Falcon, got on I-90, and headed back to Seattle.

The long drive would give him time to think about his situation at the *Mirror* and his old man. Something good had come out of this trip. His anger toward his father had subsided. He had to help his dad bury his mother's ghost, he thought, as he was visited by a ghost of his own. A sudden memory of Valerie, sitting beside him in the Falcon, her window down, wind teasing her hair. Smiling from behind her sunglasses.

She vanished when his cell phone rang.

"Jason, it's Carl. Where are you?"

"On I-Ninety. About twenty minutes from Sprague."

"Listen. I just heard there was a meeting the other day on Roxanne Palmer's murder in Kennewick. The FBI was there and cops from other jurisdictions."

"You know from where? Sawridge?"

"Don't know. But this could mean they've got something to widen the scope."

"Like what—another body, a suspect maybe?"

"Don't know. It could be major, or it could be an ass-covering exercise. I'll try to find out more.

Anyway, I know it's a detour, but given that you're kinda headed that way—"

"You read my mind," he said.

A few hours later, Jason's Falcon came to a stop at the Benton County Justice Center in Kennewick. He went to the sheriff's office intending to find Lieutenant Buchanan or Detective Kintry. The receptionist was on the phone. He looked at some outdated copies of *Time* magazine, flipping through a story on Middle East tensions while listening to the receptionist's end of her conversation.

"I understand, Mrs. Larssen, but Lloyd's in Richland and Brad's in Benton City. And the others are out doing interviews on the case. Uh-huh. Well, maybe the coroner can help you. He might know if you're clear on doing anything like that on your property. That's right. Morris Pitman, I can transfer you to his office now."

Finished with Mrs. Larssen, the receptionist smiled at Jason.

"I was looking for the coroner."

She called ahead, then pointed the way to Morris Pitman's office.

"Excuse me." He knocked on the open door, pulling Pitman's attention from his desk. "Apologies for not calling ahead. I'm Jason Wade, a reporter from Seattle."

"Oh yes, your name's familiar," Pitman went to a file on his cluttered desk with news clippings. "Ah, here.

You've been writing about the Palmer case for the *Mirror*."

"Yes."

"Move those boxes and have a seat, Jason."

Pitman was a friendly, confident man, who unlike many public officials, didn't fear reporters. Maybe he'd open up a bit.

"I understand there was a meeting here the other day on the case?" Jason asked.

"There was, but I can't disclose what was discussed or who attended."

"Was it about Roxanne Palmer's case?"

"I'd love to help you, Jason, but really, I'm not at liberty to release any details about an ongoing homicide investigation. It's really up to the detectives investigating the case. Perhaps they're going to put out a statement for the press."

"I see." Jason nodded, stalling to think of another way to try to get Pitman to help him. "Is there any aspect you could comment on in general terms?"

While Pitman reviewed reports in a file folder, Jason noticed the stack of textbooks on the credenza behind the coroner. A lot of interesting titles, one or two seemed familiar. He started jotting some of them down for color.

"No, not really." Pitman closed the file and smiled. "If that's all, I have to get to my work."

"It's just that I was in Spokane researching Roxanne Palmer, you know, to see if her case is linked to Karen Harding, the Seattle student, or any others. I was hoping somebody knowledgeable might point me in the right direction."

"Certainly, you're just doing the work of a good reporter."

"I heard of this meeting, so I—well."

Pitman had a warm smile that hinted that he was comfortable with Jason, but that he was not an official who leaked information.

"All I can tell you is that you strike me as a smart journalistic investigator who knows if he's on the right track."

Jason's eyes met Pitman's. Something passed between them. Maybe this was Pitman's way of letting him know something. Jason returned his smile and, standing to leave, nodded at the books.

"Lot of interesting stuff there."

Pitman turned to the books.

"This, oh yes, all part of my homework."

"On the case?"

"As I said, you're a smart journalist." Pitman shook Wade's hand.

50

A few miles west of Kennewick, Jason replayed the coroner's cryptic words.

"You strike me as a smart journalistic investigator who knows if he's on the right track."

Was Pitman trying to tell him that he was on the right track? He looked from the highway toward the Yakima River. He didn't know. Taking in the Horse Heaven Hills to the south and the Rattlesnake Hills to the north, he realized he wasn't far from Hanna Larssen's ranch and his instincts urged him to take advantage of his location.

All right.

He exited the highway for the location where Roxanne Palmer's remains were found.

What the hell?

Standing at her door, Hanna Larssen remembered Jason.

"You're the fella from Seattle who caused a fuss after you talked to me and printed that story."

Larssen's old shepherd, Cody, ambled to the door to greet Jason with the saddest eyes he'd ever seen in a dog.

"But I quoted you accurately. Ritualistic is the word you used."

"I did and it's true. I've got no truck with you. But Buchanan and Kintry didn't like that kind of stuff being known."

"Did they give you a hard time about it?"

"Tried to. But I don't work for them. Last time I checked, they're on the county payroll. So they work for me. And this is a free country. I'll say what I please to whomever I like."

Jason nodded, happy to let Larssen blow off steam since it wasn't directed at him. Then he followed the old woman's mournful stare to the horizon. "I've seen a lot of sickening things in all my years," she said, "but I've never seen anything like what I saw out there that day. Had some bad dreams about it. I've never gone back since and I don't think I'll ever go down there again. Cody tenses up near the path. I want to get flowers planted there, out of respect for that poor girl. Then fence the section off."

Jason said nothing, letting her finish.

"So what brings you by after all the hubbub?"

"Well, I wanted your permission to go out to the scene."

Her eyes narrowed slightly, almost defensively.

"Why?"

"I'm hoping to write a news feature on this case, and how it might be linked to a missing Seattle college student. I need to get a sense of the scene. You know, see it for myself, to be accurate."

Cody yawned as Larssen considered his request.

"There's not a thing down there. The police are all finished. Took everything away."

"I know."

"You still want to go down?"

"Yes."

"Just you by yourself?"

"Just me."

She glanced back to the hills, where she found her answer.

"Drive along the path until it ends at the creek."

"Thank you."

"Just bear one thing in mind. Be respectful. A young woman died out there."

Jason drove at a funereal pace along the soft grassy path that rose, dipped, and twisted as it sliced deep into Larssen's property. The entire Yakima Valley was brooding as massive clouds played with the light, darkening the vast land, concealing the sun, then ushering it back, but only for a moment at a time.

Birds tweeted as they flitted close to the earth where wildflowers nodded in breezes that made the tall grass hiss, like a chorus of whispers. This path and terrain could easily accommodate an RV. Progressing along, he soon understood that he was following the trail of a killer with his victim to the killing ground. What thoughts had gone through Roxanne's mind as she looked upon these very hills with their pretty flowers leading to what must have seemed like the edge of the world? For she must've known why he had taken her so deep into isolation.

No one would hear her screams for help.

If she was able to scream.

Jason crested a hill overlooking a series of small buttes and the creek in an isolated coulee. Here, the path wound down. It was a little rough so he descended slowly, threading his way until it brought him to the flat grassy bank of the creek.

He killed the Falcon's motor, got out, and began inspecting the area. Over the babble of the running water, a crow cawed. Was that a welcome, or a warning? Jason shrugged, spotting something some forty or fifty yards down the way.

The aftermath of forensic work.

Large parts of the area had been identified with bright orange fluorescent paint sprayed into the ground. Large rectangle sections of soil had been meticulously excavated akin to an archeological dig.

Jesus.

A gust lifted dirt into Jason's face and he failed to turn in time. Fine grit found his eyes, making them tear. It took a moment for him to clear his vision and resume taking stock of the site.

One spot appeared to bear the stain of blood-soaked soil still. No, that couldn't be. Had to be wrong about that, Jason thought, blinking away more grit. He walked slowly around the area as more breezes kicked up from the creek bed. He felt a sense of serenity that failed to betray the magnitude of the horror that had taken place here. A murder scene had been transformed into a memorial site.

And soon Hanna Larssen would cover it with flowers.

Jason took his time. There was little to see. Nothing had been left. He sat on a large boulder, pulled out his notebook, and started recording every observation, sensation, and detail about the place, the wind snapping his pages as he wrote.

Jason raised his head from his work and rubbed his eyes for a few moments. That's when he saw it. A small yellow object. Some thirty, forty yards down the bank. He started for it. A small yellow patch wedged among the rocks, flapping in the wind like a frantic finger beckoning him.

Coming to it, he recognized a one-foot section of plastic crime scene tape, which the wind had pushed into some rocks. He stared at it absently, disappointment and frustration nearly crushing him. Why couldn't he get a single break on this story? He'd put everything he had into it.

Shoving his hands into the front pocket of his jeans, he turned to go. Then he noticed something else just as a terrible wind blew, marshaling thick clouds above him, turning the sky to near night.

What was this?

Jason blinked and bent down to something with words printed on it. It was a slim rectangle. About five inches long, one inch in width, shimmed tight into the rocks, as if hurled there. He reached for it.

A bookmark.

Where the hell did this come from?

It was torn, creased and difficult to read. Words were missing. "Twist" and "Books" were the only ones he could make out.

What was this? Probably nothing. Local teens had partied down here. That's what the local paper had reported. He continued examining it. Maybe it was something, a link to something.

Better hang on to it.

Jason put the wrinkled bookmark in his pocket, headed back to his Falcon and the long drive back to Seattle.

51

Marlene Clark dabbed a tissue to her eyes while taking a final walk through Karen's apartment in Seattle. Bill was loading their bags into their car, giving her time alone to face the fact they were returning to Vancouver.

They had spent the last several days here awaiting word, any word, on Karen. Staying in her apartment helped Marlene feel closer to her. Stronger, as they did all they could to find her. They had worked with church organizations, missing persons groups, community associations, and Karen's friends. They helped make calls, posters, update the *Find Karen* Web site, and gave interviews to the press. Marlene's heart had jumped each time a phone rang in the apartment. Her cell. Bill's cell. Karen's home phone or cell.

Please let it be her.

But search efforts and poster campaigns had yielded little as media interest faded.

The hardwood floor creaked as Marlene took a last look at Karen's bedroom. Her landlord had refused to accept several postdated checks from Marlene and Bill to cover Karen's rent.

"This is her apartment and I'm keeping it open for her," she said, insisting Marlene keep a set of keys.

Bill had arranged to pay all of Karen's bills months in advance. Karen's neighbors in the building took in her plants.

"To make sure they don't die," one neighbor said before immediately apologizing for her choice of words. "Forgive me, I'm so sorry."

In the bedroom, Marlene fought her tears as she looked over her sister's belongings. Her dresser, her quilted duvet, and her throw pillow. In the closet she touched Karen's clothes, her shoes, the boxes of cards and treasured keepsakes. When she found a picture of Karen smiling in Luke Terrell's arms, her face tensed.

Marlene wrestled with her anger. Luke's lies, his drugs, his whoring. The fool didn't realize that Karen was the best thing he had going for him and he'd blown it. Didn't he know how sensitive she was? How trusting and loving she was? And she wanted to marry this man! This jerk who'd broken her heart, driven her into a nightmare.

Marlene covered her mouth with her hand.

Detective Stralla had said there was little they could do with Terrell. They could try obstruction charges, but they wouldn't go anywhere. Even though he admitted the cocaine was his, it was a small amount and a first offense. They probably couldn't prove a trafficking charge. But think of the fallout on Karen's case if it were made public. People would write her off as a drug dealer's girlfriend.

All Terrell did was help them establish Karen's true state of mind when she disappeared and fill in some blanks on the evidence. Time and further investigation by the Seattle PD and the DEA would tell if his drug debt led directly to Karen's disappearance.

Marlene went to the living room, to look out the big bay window at downtown Seattle, the Space Needle, and the mountains.

Her cell phone rang.

"Hi, Mommy." It was Rachel, her seven-year-old daughter.

"Hi, honey."

"Did you find Aunt Karen today?"

"No, we're still looking."

"Are you coming home yet?"

Marlene swallowed hard, glancing around the silent apartment, before shutting her eyes.

"Yes, sweetheart, Daddy and I will be home tonight."

"Love you. Oh, wait, Timmy's coming on."

Marlene heard her children sing out I love you in unison.

"Love you too with all my heart."

Marlene's chin crumpled after she hung up. Bill returned and held her. Their children were pulling them back to Vancouver. Over the past few days the kids were not sleeping, their nanny had told Marlene. Then Detective Stralla told them going home, even for a little while, was not a bad idea.

He'd made his suggestion the other day when he came to the apartment after his meeting with other investigators in Benton County. It was confidential, at this point. The Benton meeting was an exchange of information and theories with detectives with similar cases, to confirm any patterns. "So it's just as well you go home and see your children," Stralla said.

Now, as she prepared to leave, Marlene felt defeated. Her body shook as Bill held her. It took several minutes before her tears subsided. She nodded to her husband that she was ready. One last look, then Marlene stepped into the hall, pulling the door to her sister's apartment behind her, and closed it with a soft click.

52

Excerpt from *Reflections on the Ritual*

In the year of Our Lord, A.D. 1557
Somewhere in Europe
The mother's pleas for her daughters en-
thralled the crowd.

It was a spectacle surpassing the theater of the
stage to see the woman wrenching her hair, tugging at the robes of those who could, with the
flick of a wrist, commute a sentence and grant
mercy. But commutation at this late time would
tempt violent revolt. For the magistrates, all wily
politicians, it was wise to maintain a mask of arrogant detachment to the hysterical sobs of a
farmer's ignorant widow, who lived in abject
poverty with her three illiterate daughters.

After all, her condemned children, the elder
sixteen, the other fifteen, had been generously af-
forded lawyers and the patience of the court.

Their crimes were not in dispute. They had
commerce with Lucifer, having been witnessed

*cavorting naked at a woodland pool by a pass-
ing delegation of clergy from the Vatican, en
route to Lisbon on papal business.*

They were practicing witchcraft.

*Exposed while in communion with the Father
of Lies.*

*Of that they were guilty. For such an act there
is no absolution. They had been mercifully pre-
sented with the charity of time to reconcile their
souls before their sentences were carried out.*

*The young women were dressed in white night-
shirts dusted with sulphur. Their heads shorn,
they stared hollow-eyed from their mule-drawn
cart at the large figure trailing behind.*

Their executioner.

*He was wearing black boots, black pants, black
gloves, and a full-length black robe. He also wore
a large black hood concealing his identity. He
embodied the infallibility of the deity. God, and
the holy relic he wore, protected him from forces
dispatched from hell. He was a soldier of light,
charged to destroy any evil that threatened the
Church. Even uneducated, young country girls
who, lacking a tub, bathed in a forest pond.*

*During the procession the executioner ob-
served the anguished mother, gripping the hand
of her third daughter, her youngest.*

She was ten.

*Brilliant white orbs glowed from the girl's head
in testament to her blindness. A defect at birth. She*

was also bereft of speech. Understandably, among simple common people, her strange presence was unsettling. No one had sufficient will to ever look directly upon her, for fear of a curse.

Except the executioner.

From the black holes of his hood, he stared at her vacant white eyes with intense curiosity, until the procession stopped at the appointed place of the final penalty. The heretics were removed from the cart and bound to the poles. Reading from a scroll, the clerk of the court recited with official intonation their crimes and sentence. Priests and their acolytes proceeded with exorcising the young women while crucifixes were waved about. The crowd began taunting the girls to confess.

Command the devil to save you now!

They cried out for mercy, their young voices begging for compassion. They loved God, they rejected Lucifer. The chief magistrate ordered silence, warning all that their pleas were only a sorcerer's tactic to beguile the men of God. In praising God, they were truly swearing allegiance to Satan.

The time had come for the sentence to be carried out, the magistrate extended his hand with its golden rings toward the executioner.

Begin.

The black-clad figure bowed respectfully to the Church, the court and assembled officials.

He crouched at his kindling fire, meticulously stoking it amid spectacular bursts of sparks until he withdrew a long, metal rod, its tip bearing lettering, radiating red and white.

As if gripping the sword of righteousness, he thrust it victoriously to the sky, holding it high, an exhilarating gesture, as he stepped to the first witch where he brought it within an inch of her young, terrified face.

It thrilled the crowd, spectators chanted for a confession.

The girl sobbed. She turned toward her older sister, then searched a sea of bloodlust for her mother's face as the executioner tore her shirt, exposing her pure white skin.

A hush fell over the square as he slowly pressed the hot iron into her flesh over her heart. Those near could hear the sizzle of her flesh while it cooked, as her shrieks rose beyond the square, and the forests beyond the city, startling birds to take flight in fear. The spectators with the sharpest vision could see the lettering left by the executioner:

VOV

The cryptic mark of Xavier Veenza.

The spectators spread the word, speculating as they always did on its meaning, while the executioner re-heated the iron, moved on to the older sister, and repeated the act, branding her. The crowd howled, chanted louder in unison for the girls to confess as the executioner then took up a torch, held it ceremoniously high, then lit the fringe of the pyres surrounding each of the women.

Confess!

Slowly the flames began consuming the edges, smoke rising, swirling carrying ash and sparks. The crowd murmuring with approving pleasure as the fire came to life. As the flames neared, the girls' cries for mercy blended with the rising intensity of the fire. Their mother fell to her knees, her blind daughter clutching at her, mouth agape, her head weaving rhythmically left and right, straining against the death cries of her older sisters.

Soon they were engulfed by roaring walls of flame, and billowing clouds of smoke followed by the liquidy sputter of organs frying, the gurgle of blood boiling, the near-pleasant smell of meat broiling, like a wild boar roasting on the spit during festival time.

In short time, the screams ended.

But the fire raged, accompanied by the hum of satisfied spectators and the soft intonations of the priests.

Broken with sorrow, the mother collapsed to the earth, driving her fingers deep into it while a gentle wind carried a funereal haze toward an indifferent heaven.

53

As his Falcon rolled west along the edge of the Snoqualmie National Forest and the Wenatchee Mountains, Jason was certain that piece by piece something was emerging. But he didn't know if Gideon Cull was part of it.

He'd gone online to pursue the bookmark's angle and had searched the terms "Twist" and "Books." It was futile. All he got, over and over, were discussions, descriptions and reviews about books with plot twists.

He chewed on things until he could no longer think straight. He listened to Hendrix's *Band of Gypsies* and was hungry by the time he'd reached Seattle's outskirts. In Fremont, he stopped at Johnny Pearl's for takeout. Some rice and chicken. Man, it felt as if he'd been gone a week. The only things waiting for him at his apartment were his fish and two messages on his machine. He listened while he ate. The first was from his old man.

"Jay, give me a call when you can. I'd like to see you, Son."

Later, Dad, he thought, biting into an egg roll as the second message started.

"Jason, it's Ron Nestor at the paper. Call me when you get this."

He dialed Nestor's number, then checked the time. Early evening. He was likely gone. Jason left a message on his voice mail, finished eating, then showered. The hot water cleared his head so he could go back to thinking about Cull, his assault against his wife, the old sexual harassment complaint from his college student. Then Roxanne Palmer's ritual killing in the hills. Karen Harding's disappearance. His feeling that Luke Terrell hadn't told him the truth early on, and everything else.

Was it all linked?

Maybe.

Jason toweled off, pulled on fresh jeans, a T-shirt. Fed his fish. Then he fired up his laptop, created a file, opened his notebook, and began entering all of his notes, taking pains not to miss anything.

It had grown dark by the time he began shaping a story, profiling Gideon Cull and how he figured in Karen Harding's disappearance and the other incidents. All of the story's threads came back to Cull.

Cull knew Bonnie Stillerman, knew Karen Harding. Cull knew Spokane, where Roxanne was last seen alive. He had a violent past, was investigated for assaulting his wife. He was a clergyman and a Seattle college teacher of religious history whose street work was once recognized by the governor.

In Olympia, he was a saint. On campus, he was Professor Creepy.

Jason's skin prickled at what he was writing.

This was wild, accusatory stuff. He stopped typing and considered it while he cleaned up his place. He came to Valerie's bracelet, pondering it before returning to his notes and files to make sure he hadn't missed anything. The bookmark fell out, the one he'd found at Hanna Larssen's property. He studied it. Tapped it against his palm. Was this another piece in the puzzle? Was it connected to something else he'd seen? It gnawed at him until his phone rang.

"Hello."

"Jason, it's Nestor at the *Mirror*. I've been trying to reach you."

"I was out of town. I just got in."

"We'd like you back at the paper. Are you ready to come back?"

"Yes."

"Good. Drop by my office early tomorrow."

By 8:30 a.m., Jason was in the *Mirror* newsroom, standing at Nestor's open door.

Nestor was wrapping up a call and waved him in to sit. A minute later, he hung up, then dropped a half-inch stack of paper on the table. An alligator clip held it together. *Wade* was scrawled in pen over the title: *Seattle's Most Dangerous Intersections: Traffic Research Bureau. Confidential Draft Report.*

"I want you back on the night cop desk tonight."

Jason nodded.

"And I want you to start a series on each of the top ten most dangerous traffic spots. Give me five or six hundred words on each one. You've got a couple of weeks. Quote this study, call up traffic experts, community leaders, insurance people. We'll run it as a ten-part series."

Jason's heart sank. This was page-filler. Inside stuff. It was punishment. The paper was reining him in. The silence that passed between them confirmed it. After several moments, Nestor said, "I had trouble reaching you. What did you do when you were off?"

"I poked around on my own on the Harding story and Gideon Cull."

"Her college professor?"

Jason nodded.

"Jesus, Jason. You went right back and did the thing that got you into trouble in the first place."

"I did it as a freelancer. On my own time and my own dime."

"You were enterprising without informing me, your supervisor, as to what you were doing while representing this newspaper. And now you're freelancing in competition with us?"

Jason said nothing.

"What the hell did you do?"

"I went to Spokane. I did some investigating on Cull's background with a guy from the *Review* who owed me a favor. Cull has a connection to Spokane. The Benton County murder is connected to Spokane and Cull is connected to Karen Harding."

"That's a lot of connecting. Did you try to talk to Cull again?"

"No."

"So what were you hoping to accomplish?"

"I'm working on a profile of Cull."

"A profile? What sort of profile?"

"I think he's emerging as a prime suspect in all of this."

"Christ." Nestor dragged his hand across his face, looked through the glass walls of his office at the newsroom, then released a sigh as if deciding what to do with Jason.

"Cull hit his wife with a baseball bat but was never convicted," Jason said. "And he has an unsubstantiated sexual harassment complaint by a student when he taught at a Spokane college. Tumbler River, a few years back."

Nestor's focus snapped back to Jason.

"And did you know," Jason said, "that privately, female students at Cull's college here call him Professor Creepy?"

"You have all of this confirmed? On paper? Named sources? On the record?"

"No. Not yet. But I'm working on it," he said.

"You're working on it. Have police confirmed Cull's a suspect?"

"No, but investigators from several jurisdictions met the other day in Benton County on the Roxanne Palmer case."

"We heard about that. I had Astrid check it out."

"Astrid?"

"She said it was a routine clearinghouse meeting. Nothing significant came out of it."

Jason didn't believe that for a second, because he knew Astrid hated crime stories and would do nothing more than make a cursory check. But he said nothing.

"Look." Nestor folded his arms across his chest, then stroked his moustache. "The fact you enterprise relentlessly is one of your strongest assets. You're a digger. We like that about you."

Jason said nothing.

"We're deeply interested in Karen Harding's story, but you can't go around pointing fingers at people without rock-solid facts to back you up. You can't go out and collect a few pieces of unsubstantiated hearsay, stitch them together into an accusation, and call it journalism. What you have are hunches, the genesis of investigative reporting. But hunches have to be confirmed with documents or people who go on the record."

Nestor paused to ensure that his words were sinking in before continuing.

"Unless something changes, the Benton County murder story is by and large a Spokane story. For us, it's a state story. Karen Harding's disappearance is a Seattle story. Ours. We can do features, updates, we can monitor the investigation with aggressive police checks. Try to get a scoop, that sort of thing. But until something breaks, there's not a heck of a lot more we can do on it at the moment."

Jason thumbed the pages of the traffic study, noticing one of the intersections was near the brewery where his old man worked. How ironic.

"Now, having said that, I don't want to discourage you, Jason. I don't want to dismiss what you may have dug up on Cull. So I'm going to make a proposal."

Jason stopped thumbing the study and looked at Nestor.

"You work on the traffic feature. In your downtime, write up what you have on Cull. But it's for my eyes only. Understand? Just write what you have. *Not for publication.* You do not call Cull without my say-so. I'll go through your draft, then decide how, or if, we'll proceed. If there's nothing to it, well, you will have had your shot. If I think you've hit on something, I give you my word we'll jump all over the story. Fair enough?"

Jason's pulse quickened.

"Fair enough."

54

Wade returned to the *Mirror* early that evening and stopped at the cafeteria for a BLT to eat at his desk before his shift.

"You're back." Ben Randolph joined him at the counter, dropping his voice. "How's your father doing?"

"Better."

"Good. I got an uncle with the same illness." Randolph grabbed a spoon for his take-out soup. "Folded his new Mercedes around a tree in Westchester County. Walked away. Your father's lucky he didn't—"

"Look," Jason said, "I'd rather not talk about it now."

"No problem."

"Jason Wade, investigative reporter, welcome back." Astrid Grant joined them, holding a yogurt tub.

"We heard you drew some heat on the missing college girl story, that you hit the street like a damn Hardy boy trying to nail a villain."

Randolph turned away.

"Astrid," Jason said, "how hard did you push on the Benton County meeting on the Palmer murder?"

"Hard enough. There was nothing to it."

"Was the FBI there? Was Sawridge County there? Could it be they met because they got a lead on evidence, or maybe a link to another murder?"

"I was told it was a routine case status meeting to simply compare notes. Nothing came out of it."

"And you believed it?"

She rolled her eyes. "Give it up, Wade."

"Give what up?"

"You really think that after that scene with your dad, and the fact your rogue research habits pissed off a few people, you're still in the running for a job here?"

Jason said nothing.

"And you're all indignant and possessive over your little Karen Harding story," she said. "Here's a bulletin for you: there are other stories. And if the Harding case ever gets bigger, they'll put their Pulitzer winners on it."

Jason watched the cook assemble his sandwich.

"And another thing," she continued. "Ben and I found out that the editors have a secret point system to select the intern for the full-time job. You get points for the types of stories you do and the play they get. I'm sure you can guess where you're ranked."

He could. Especially with the dangerous intersections story he'd just been assigned.

"Hope your license to drive a forklift at the brewery is still valid." Astrid smiled before walking off with Randolph, their laughter echoing.

At his desk, Jason pushed the traffic study aside and inserted his disk with the Cull feature he was writing.

He read every word, then stared at his phone. He had to know what had come out of the Benton County meeting. He dialed a cell phone number.

"Stralla."

"Detective Stralla, it's Jason Wade at the *Seattle Mirror*."

"Well, well. I understand you've been on the road, doing some digging in Spokane and Benton County."

"That's why I'm calling."

"Hang on, call me back on a landline."

Stralla gave him a number, likely his home number. Jason called back. "Listen, Detective, I know there was a multijurisdictional meeting on the Palmer case in Kennewick. I need to know what transpired."

A moment passed.

"You didn't get any of this from me, understand?"

Jason's grip on the phone tightened.

"Absolutely."

"You're right about the meeting, your timing's good. We've formed a small task force to look for links to the Palmer murder and other cases."

"Who's *we*?"

"Sawridge, Benton, Spokane, WSP, the FBI, and Klamath out of Oregon."

"Oregon? Did you find a link to Oregon?"

Stralla thought about the question. "Let me make some calls. I'll get back to you."

Earlier that day, Stralla had been on a conference call with Buchanan and the others, a follow-up to the meeting. The FBI had urged the investigators to put out a news statement on the new information about the Oregon and Washington cases. The thinking was it would yield a lead. Giving something to Jason Wade now might be the best way to do it, Stralla reasoned.

It took him several minutes to convince Buchanan to release the break to Wade. He was still sore over Wade's use of the term "ritualistic killing" in his first story, but eventually he agreed with Stralla to let some data go. "As long as the guys in Spokane and Oregon were good with it," Buchanan said. Stralla called them and was green-lighted all the way, then he made a note to himself to alert Karen Harding's sister, Marlene, in Vancouver.

On his call back to Wade, Stralla told him that Roxanne Palmer's killer had murdered a woman in Oregon nearly ten years ago.

"What? How do you know?" Jason asked.

"Similar fact evidence found in both cases."

"Can I quote you now?"

"Yes, as a member of this task force. We're looking for any link to Karen Harding's disappearance because it appears to fit a pattern."

"What kind of pattern?"

"We're not releasing that."

"What kind of evidence did you find?"

"We're not releasing that either."

"Are there ritualistic overtones to the murders?"

"I can't confirm that."

"Are you denying it?"

"No."

"Hang on a sec." Jason clamped his hand over the mouthpiece and yelled across the newsroom to the editors on the night desk, "I've got a story coming!"

"Forty-five minutes to first edition."

Jason nodded, then went back on the line to Stralla.

"Have you identified the Oregon woman?"

"No, I'll fax you some details. We're seeking the public's help."

Jason was writing notes fast. He recited his fax number twice. With Stralla still on the line he stared at his computer screen and his draft profile of Gideon Cull. Tapping his pen on his notebook, studying the words on his monitor, he gave it a shot.

"Do you have any suspects?"

"We're looking at everything."

"But any specific suspects?"

"Nothing that we're prepared to discuss publicly."

"Off the record?"

"Can't help you there."

Studying his screen, Jason scrolled through all of the information he had on Cull. It resonated in the wake of what Stralla was telling him.

"Are you going to be around tomorrow?" Jason asked.

"Should be, why?"

"I'm coming up to see you. There's something we should talk about."

"Call me on my cell when you get here."

Jason's story landed on the front page.

That night he walked to his Falcon with a damp copy under his arm, certain he was getting closer to the truth behind Karen Harding's disappearance and the murders of two young women.

55

Karen Harding trembled while listening to the RV's wheels, humming like an ancient chant to the horrors she had seen.

And the horrors still to come.

She was locked in her hidden chamber in the rear.

Her coffin.

The reverend had reinforced the sections she had kicked out, back when she had the will to fight for her life. Now her courage lay dead on the road hundreds of miles behind her. She was weak, tired, and utterly alone.

Julie was gone.

She had watched her die.

Oh, Julie.

Karen swallowed. She was going to die next. Her body quaked, then went numb. She prayed.

Hail, Mary, full of grace, the Lord is with thee…

Karen prayed again and again as the wheels droned and the RV plunged deeper into the high country of the great Rocky Mountain range. She prayed until she lost consciousness and all sense of time.

* * *

The RV's swaying rocked her awake.

They were slowing. Turning. The engine whined. Karen could feel the pull of gravity, heard the click-click of the motor home's four-way lights as they ascended the narrow highways through the mountains.

They came to a town.

Karen was now expert at deciphering sounds, movements, and smells. Stopping at traffic lights, inching their way along a main street, she detected the deep-fried aroma of a fast food restaurant, then a bakery, then the diesel growl of a big truck.

Voices!

She heard voices. People! Salvation was a only few feet beyond the walls that imprisoned her. *Somebody, help me! Please!* Karen tried kicking but couldn't move. She tried calling out but the gag muted her cry. The voices faded. The RV left the community, gathering speed, then resumed traveling on the highway.

Soon they slowed again, leaving the smooth paved highway for a dirt road that twisted and undulated through a dense forest. She could smell the sweet cedar and pine, feel branches brushing against them as they tottered along the rugged terrain. They slowed. Turned again, crawled for miles along a twisting, uneven earthen road before they came to a halt.

How much longer would he let her live?

The reverend killed the engine.

It ticked as it cooled. Karen was overwhelmed with a feeling of finality, that a decision had been made.

Instinct told her this was it. Her time was up. Something was going to happen.

Karen felt the RV dip as the reverend approached her, heard him grunt as he lowered himself, keys jingling, her compartment opening. Blinding bright light hit her eyes. Before her vision adjusted, he thrust a hood over her head, yanked her to her feet, and out of the RV.

The clank of metal, then cold steel on her skin. A chain was secured around her neck. Then the chink of a long leader that jerked, making her cry into her gag, compelling her to walk forward, blind to the terrain.

Blind to what awaited her.

Karen stumbled several times, struggling to find purchase on the earth as tall grass and scrub snagged her legs and arms. Insects pinged on and off of her. She felt their tiny frantic legs on her neck and hands, heard the buzz of large flies, smelled the horrible stink of rotting things.

He yanked at her leash, the chain clinked, the sudden movement lifted her hood slightly, light spilled inside. She could see the ground.

She raised her chin to the sky, catching flash-glimpses of the path they were on and the reverend's back. He was wearing black jeans, a plaid shirt, the chain glinting in the sun. She saw steep foothills, carpeted with forests, rising to the snowcapped mountain peaks.

The leash pulled her farther along the path. It sloped down. And down. Earthen walls canopied by scrub rose like wartime trenches blocking the sun, smelling of damp, foul earth. Light lost to the darkness here.

Jangling as they came to a door. It had three forged steel locks. As he slid a key into the first, Karen felt something furry nudge her feet.

A rat?

She kicked it away but it came back. Then the door opened and the reverend pulled Karen inside. It was too dark for her to see.

Keys jangled again.

Another door.

Karen heard him working the locks, sliding metal bolts. Heard the thud of the weight of the door as he pulled it open. A wave of stomach-churning stench, a mix of feces, urine, and decay, rolled from the interior.

The chain jerked.

Karen was shoved inside, feeling the damp horrid floor after she'd been pushed to her stomach. Her chain and bindings were removed. The door sealed the room, followed by the slamming of steel bolts and the snap-click of locks. A moment later, she heard him locking the second outer door.

Stunned, she collected herself, pressing her hands to the floor, feeling straw and something wet. She cringed, stifled a sob, removed her hood, pulled out her gag, and spat.

Reflex forced her to vomit.

After several moments, Karen stood, her eyes watering. She cupped her hands over her mouth and nose. She dared not move as her eyes adjusted.

She blinked repeatedly to clear her vision.

She was entombed.

A shaft of natural light pierced the ceiling, allowing her to inventory the room. No more than nine feet by nine feet. About six feet in height. It had cinder block walls, sweating and dripping with water. A narrow steel-framed bed with a thin mattress and frayed woolen blanket was pushed to one corner. A manacle and chain was affixed to the bed's head. A shackle with a length of chain, secured to the foot.

Next to the bed, a small case of bottled water and boxes of granola bars and crackers. In the far corner, a plastic bucket. Next to it, several rolls of tissue and a large supply of sanitary items.

Karen coughed.

She touched the ceiling. It had a one-foot-by-one-foot opening. An air shaft. Sunlight flowed through a hole reinforced with steel bars and razor wire. She gripped it and pulled. Rock solid.

No way out.

He must live alone out here. Isolated. There was no one to help her. No one to hear her scream. No way to escape. She stepped to the door, constructed of heavy wooden beams. Hinges on the outside. Lock mechanisms fortified. What was that? Karen drew her face closer.

Scratches.

Fingers had clawed at a crack in the door. It seemed futile. Karen looked to the floor. She spotted a human fingernail, picked it up, and held it under the sunlight. It was glossed, clean, well kept. Karen looked at the door's scratch marks. Fear coiled around her, making her heart beat faster.

She turned.

Holding the nail, she slammed her back to the door and slid to the foul floor as a shaft of light painted a segment of the cinder block wall, illuminating a letter.

Karen concentrated for a few seconds, realizing she was staring at several letters. No, a word. No. Two words. In large letters, scrawled on the wall with something that had dried brown.

Human blood turns brown when it dries.

Karen did all she could not to scream. Her eyes widened at the words:

Help me

56

Jacked up on morning coffee, Jason Wade was in his Falcon northbound to Bellingham on I-5 when Ron Nestor called on his cell phone.

"Nice work on today's front page."

"Thanks."

"I want you to advance the Seattle angle on the story."

"I'm heading to Bellingham as we speak."

"Were you planning on telling me?"

"Sent you an e-mail. I'm going to hook up with Hank Stralla, the detective on Harding's case, push for something on her professor and boyfriend."

"You're going to have to break something new. The Associated Press moved your story on the wire. It means everyone with an interest is going to try to get ahead of us, break the next development on the case. Like your friend in Spokane."

"Right. I tipped him on it last night."

"You did what? Don't do that again. Don't give away our exclusives."

"But I made a deal to share for the help he gave me in Spokane."

"All right, keep your deal with him. But next time tip him *after* his deadline. You can bet he'll do the same. Especially now that he won't be the only one jumping on your scoop today. We've heard that one of the Seattle TV news stations is doing something with its affiliates in Portland and Spokane. The *Times* and the *P-I* will be chasing this. And the *Oregonian*. Find news and keep me posted."

"What about the traffic series?"

"I've passed it to Astrid. At the moment you're the only one I can spare on Harding. It's all yours. I'm getting a sense more could break on this."

This was his shot, he thought, rolling by the Tulalip Indian Reservation, glancing at the file folders he'd tossed on the passenger side. Gideon Cull's photo peeked from them. The guy *was* creepy. If Stralla confirmed he was a suspect, then maybe Nestor would run his profile.

It might break this story wide open.

"Drop me off at the office, Raife," Stralla told Ansboro as they drove through Bellingham.

Stralla was frustrated. Time was hammering against him. A hot lead had fizzled out on them. They'd just finished following up on a fifty-year-old level-three sex offender–kidnapper who lived in a battered RV just outside Bellingham. He'd been registered since the early 1990s after serving his sentence for kidnapping and raping two young women from mall parking lots. The first in Longview, the second in Tacoma.

According to his file he had refused most treatment

and was evaluated as a high risk to reoffend after telling his counselor that he still fantasized about repeating his crimes and often missed taking his medication. He was a trucker, known to frequent the Big Timber Truck Stop. Turned out he was at a motel around the time Karen Harding vanished, but it was a long way off in Portland, Oregon. He was solidly alibied, like the three dozen other offenders on Sawridge County's registry they'd checked out since her disappearance.

Ansboro stopped the four-by-four in front of the sheriff's office and said, "I'll go down to Marysville, see what's new with the lab."

As Stralla got out, his cell phone rang with a call from Jason Wade, saying he'd be arriving soon. Stralla invited him to his office, then looked at the sky, darkening with gathering storm clouds.

At his desk, he scanned the *Seattle Mirror* with Wade's story, then shuffled through his phone messages. Mostly press calls. He cupped his hands to his face and rubbed his eyes.

He hadn't been getting much sleep, or seeing much of his son. He studied his files again. Was he missing something?

He felt like a fool, wrestling self-doubt and pinballing between opposing theories. It was a remote possibility that Karen had staged her own disappearance, hopped a freighter to Central America to find her parents and live there after her blowout with her boyfriend, Luke Terrell.

What a prize he turned out to be. With his drugs and

Rick Mofina

lies. A first-class asshole who'd cost them so much time. He wasn't entirely ruled out as a suspect. This could stem from drug debt. Seattle was working on that.

Still, Stralla's instincts told him that Karen had been abducted and was likely dead. Like Roxanne and Bonnie. Or had she simply run off? Damn. Intentional disappearance, or abduction-homicide? He couldn't get a handle on this. There were so many pieces and possibilities.

Had he missed something obvious?

Concentrate on the evidence.

Her keys, left in her car. No activity on her bank or credit cards. No calls, letters, or e-mails. The State Department had no activity on her passport. Her car could've been disabled. Tire impressions suggested the possible involvement of a truck or an RV, which was consistent with the Benton County case. They'd failed to get any usable footwear impressions here or at Hanna Larssen's farm. No latents, fiber, or DNA.

He examined the file with the inventory of evidence collected from a one-hundred-yard area surrounding the scene along 539 where Karen's Toyota was found. A lot of stuff. Most of it likely insignificant garbage. Stralla scratched the stubble on his chin as he took note of some of the items from the long list.

SWCMP: 231605 HARDING, Karen
WSP CLS CS Exterior Evidence Inventory
Completed by: CRONIN, V. / CSRT

Nine soda cans, see appendix

Six juice boxes, re: appendix

Eleven beer cans, re: appendix

Four beer bottles, re: appendix

Assorted candy bar wrappers, re: appendix

Assorted Newspapers, re: appendix

Place mat map of B.C. from Ida May's Restaurant, re: appendix

One torn work glove

One plastic oil bottle, re: appendix

One torn paperback novel. War and Peace by Tolstoy

Assorted food wrappers, re: appendix

One screwdriver

Nineteen pieces of rubber from shredded tires.

The list went on.

The weather was chaotic that night, rain, strong winds. Unrelated items could've blown into the scene from miles away. How would this stand up in court? Stralla was still wondering if the key was here in the files when his line rang. Jason Wade had arrived.

They got fresh coffee and sat at Stralla's desk.

The sky had turned day to night. Bellingham's offices and stores lit up automatically. Traffic flowed through the core in streams of white and red lights.

"Looks like a big one's brewing," Jason said.

Stralla nodded to the paper on his desk. "Good story."

"Thanks. Anything new on the case?"

"You tell me. You said you needed to talk about something."

Jason reached into his small backpack, pulled out his files and notebook, then glanced around Stralla's small cubicle, as if searching for a way to begin. "Look, let's go off the record," he said. "If we hit on something, we'll reach an agreement on how to use it."

Stralla nodded.

"Do you have any suspects?"

"The investigation crosses into several jurisdictions, so potentially we're looking at a lot of people and a lot of things."

"What about Gideon Cull, Karen Harding's college professor, are you looking at him?"

"His name rings a bell. The Seattle PD, campus police, or the FBI would be the ones who'd interview him. Why do you raise his name?"

"I've been following up leads that came to me from my stories, and his name came up as someone to look at."

For the next half hour, he told Stralla all he'd learned about Gideon Cull, then passed him a folder with photographs of Cull taken from the college Web site, church groups, and snapshots from his charity work Jason had found on the Net.

One of Cull with the governor, one with him helping street people with an RV in the background, one of Bonnie Stillerman, one of him in a group, his hands on Karen Harding's shoulders. Jason noticed Stralla's eyebrows ascend slightly as he studied the pictures.

"Have you ruled out Gideon Cull as a suspect in this case?"

Stralla's face tightened.

"Don't quote me. We're still working on his history. Seattle's looking at him. I know he's on the interview list. We're talking to everyone in Karen's circles. All of her teachers, all of her friends, to get an idea of her patterns, her habits, see how they come into play."

"Can I say Cull has not been ruled out as a suspect?"

"Hold on." Stralla reached for his cell phone and, from what Jason could determine, made a call to a detective in Seattle. Stralla's wooden captain's chair creaked as he walked out of earshot to the far end of the squad room.

Jason doodled in his notebook, aware Stralla could still see him from across the room, yet he was oblivious of what had suddenly transpired. Slowly, Jason's attention shifted to something curious. The open file on Stralla's desk. It was upside down, but it dawned on Jason that before him was the inventory of evidence from the Harding scene.

He stopped doodling.

Subtly and slowly, he wrote every word he could see while Stralla talked to his counterpart. Wade had managed to record most of the list by the time Stralla had hung up and returned.

"All right, I'll tell you this, and you can quote me."

Jason sat up, flipped to a new page, and nodded.

"Gideon Cull is a person we intend to interview."

"Why?"

"It's SOP, we've talked to other college staff who know Karen."

"Your interest in Cull has nothing to do with his past?"

"I'm not certain how much of his past we know. Our

interest stems from the fact he's one of her teachers, all part of a standard investigation."

"Has he been ruled out as a suspect?"

Stralla considered the question as his gaze went to the photographs Jason had showed him.

"At this point, no one's been ruled out or crossed off as a suspect."

"Then he *is* a suspect."

"I didn't say that."

"Fine, but he hasn't been ruled out as one."

"Right."

"But you intend to question him."

"Interview him."

"What's the holdup?"

"Apparently, he travels a lot."

"Do you know his whereabouts the night Karen Harding disappeared?"

"That's one thing we'll want to confirm. It's routine."

"I'm going to offer a story quoting you on the record saying Cull has not been ruled out as a suspect."

"As it stands right now, that's a fact."

Jason thought for several moments before checking the time and nodding. "Thanks." He had nothing more to ask. He collected his files. "You can keep the photographs. I've got copies," he said, shaking hands with Stralla, who then saw him to the elevator.

After Jason left, Stralla stood alone at his desk searching the black sky as thunder pounded over Bellingham. He stared down at the city. What was it

Morris Pitman, the Benton County coroner, had said about the nature of the branding in the cases? It arose from a historical case.

What does VOV mean?

Stralla shuffled through the papers of his files. Pitman had given them a one-page summary of his theory on the branding. Didn't Cull teach religious history? And what about that RV in the photograph Wade had showed him? And Cull with his hands on Karen's shoulders? And Cull with the governor?

Stralla rubbed his temple.

He could feel time ticking away.

57

Hurrying from Stralla's office, Jason lost his race against the rain. Half a block before he reached his Falcon it came down hard, drenching him as he unlocked his door. Inside, he gripped his cell phone and called the *Mirror*.

"Nestor."

"Ron, it's Jason. I'm just leaving Bellingham."

"Get anything?"

"We can say Gideon Cull, Karen Harding's college professor, is a suspect in her disappearance."

"You're certain. You've got confirmation, Jason?"

He flipped through his notebook to the critical quotes he'd flagged with asterisks, then read them to Nestor. "I've got Hank Stralla on the record: "Quote: 'Gideon Cull is a person we intend to interview,' close quote. Then I asked him if Cull was ruled out as a suspect and Stralla said, quote: 'At this point, no one's been ruled out or crossed off as a suspect,' close quote."

Nestor was silent. Lightning strobed, thunder nearly split the sky.

"Did Stralla say why they want to talk to Cull, anything about his past?"

"No. He said it was routine. Did you read my draft profile of Cull? I finished it last night and e-mailed it to you this morning."

"I've read it. It's strong," Nestor said. "Get back here as soon as you can, and find me. Things have been happening. We're looking at going with your Cull story for tomorrow's paper."

Jason was pumped as he got onto I-5. He monitored radio news stations for any breaks. Nothing new was being reported, other than his story in today's paper about the Denton County murder being linked to another, and possibly Karen's case.

Driving back to Seattle in the downpour he thought of her final moments before she'd vanished. Would they find a third corpse? Was Cull involved? Jason searched the darkness for an answer.

In the newsroom he saw his front-page story posted on the bulletin board and smiled to himself.

It acknowledged his work while blaring Astrid Grant's failure. She'd dropped the ball in checking out the Benton County meeting. Maybe he'd get extra points for cleaning up after her. He shrugged it off, then spotted Nestor in his glass-walled office waving him in.

"Sit down."

Nestor's clipboard with the sked of the next day's stories was on the table. Topping it was *Cull-Harding Suspect-Page 1 W/Turn. WADE.*

"We're hearing that our competition in Seattle, and news outlets in Spokane and Portland, are poised to take the lead on your story saying a new serial killer is at work in the Pacific Northwest."

"Just what you figured."

"That puts pressure on us to keep ahead of the pack with a story about a suspect."

Jason's pulse increased.

"I've gone through your Cull draft story. I've sent it back with my notes on everything I want you to check, double-check, and confirm. Lead with the Sawridge detective and suspect stuff. Put a Bellingham dateline on it. Give the photo desk all of your art, or tell them where to find it. Go long with this as a big investigative feature. Exclusive to the *Mirror*."

"How long?"

"Thirty-five, maybe forty inches. I'm selling it to page one, turning to an inside page with pictures. But it doesn't go unless you take care of everything."

Jason nodded.

"You've got a few hours and most of it's done already. I'm pulling you from the police scanners. Find an empty desk in Lifestyles to write."

"Who're you putting on the cop desk?"

Nestor's eyes twinkled. "It's time Astrid took a shift or two."

After grabbing an egg salad sandwich and a large coffee from the cafeteria, Jason worked on the story. Nestor's instructions made it better, and Jason labored to fill in every blank, answer every question, and confirm every point raised.

The news library helped him use public records to try to locate Cull's ex, friends, or relatives. He didn't have much luck. He tried several databases for New Mexico but failed to locate Bonnie Stillerman. He called church and charity groups in Spokane and Seattle and quoted volunteers who offered observations about Reverend Cull.

"A few years back, before he got busier at the college, he liked to drive around in the RV and bring hot meals, blankets, coffee, and counseling to homeless people and people just released from jail," Sister Marie Broward, director of Seattle Street Angels of Mercy, told Jason. "Sometimes he would drive up and down the interstate and help stranded motorists." *There it is. Karen Harding was a stranded motorist. Man, it's looking more like Cull at every turn.* "A while back, the governor's teenaged daughter slipped security after a spat with her mother. Her small car broke down on I-Five and Reverend Cull was there to help, which is why he was recognized by Olympia."

It was early evening when Jason finished his story and sent it to Nestor, who went through it with the night editors, then called Jason into his office. Beale went first.

"I like this story. But it's damning. It pushes things. You're accusing him of being the suspect in the murders of Roxanne Palmer, the Jane Doe from Oregon, and Karen Harding's kidnapper."

"He is a suspect."

"Your cop quotes imply it, but don't state it implicitly. They have deniability. Do you stand by Detective Stralla's comments?"

"Yes."

"Do you have Stralla on tape?"

"No."

"You should've taped him, he could challenge your quotes." Beale sighed. "It's a helluva story. We have the fact that police want to talk to him. And we've got his disturbing history. But you haven't got Cull's response in here. It's not enough to say he was unavailable for comment. I say we don't run the story unless you get Cull."

Mack Pedge, the front page editor, agreed. "The story doesn't go without Cull being given a chance to respond."

The photo editor grunted as he gazed upon the photo-graphs.

"Don't want to piss off Mount Olympus. Man, look at this art. The governor shaking hands with this guy. It's like Gacy with the First Lady."

No one spoke. All in the room knew it was a compelling picture juxtaposed with Jason's story. Every editor wanted to run the story but knew there'd be a price to pay if an intern reporter had screwed up.

"Look," Pedge said, "if this falls through, I've got to juggle front page and the inside page we're holding. You've got about ninety minutes before I pull the plug on it."

Nestor stroked his moustache.

"Try to get Cull, Jason."

"I'm trying. I left messages at his office, his home, his cell."

"Call people at the school or the charities, see if they know where he is. Keep trying."

On his way back to his out-of-the-way desk in Lifestyles, Jason walked by Astrid contending with her first full shift as the *Mirror*'s night cop reporter. She looked bored, flipping through a magazine with the volume turned down on the emergency radios.

"If you keep the radios too low you'll miss something."

She flipped him her middle finger.

"Nice." He ignored her, turned to leave.

"Some guy called for you at this extension when you were in your big meeting."

He stopped in his tracks.

"Who? Did he leave a name, or message?"

"Nope. I think he left a message on your voice mail."

"He didn't say who he was?"

"Nope."

Jason went to the newsroom editorial assistant, a slender red-haired young woman eating microwaved popcorn and proofreading a soft-news page. He asked her to direct his calls to the desk he was using in Lifestyles. By the time he'd returned to it, his line was ringing.

"Jason Wade, *Seattle Mirror*."

"Vern Gibson at the West Sunshine Shelter. I understand a volunteer gave you Reverend Cull's cell phone number."

"Yes, is there a problem?"

"It's outdated. Here's the new one."

Jason wrote it down and dialed immediately.

"Hello?"

"Reverend Cull?"

"Yes, who's calling please?"

"Jason Wade—" He swallowed and searched for his tape recorder, connected it, turned the machine on. Its red light blinked. "Jason Wade, from the *Seattle Mirror*."

"This is a bad time. I don't appreciate your leaving messages everywhere. I'm tied up with something and not in the best position to talk right now."

"Yes, but you should have the chance to respond on the record to what we've learned. It's very important."

"Respond to what? I don't talk to reporters. I don't trust them. I sensed that you weren't being sincere about your intentions when you came to my office. I agreed to see you to help Karen. I didn't like your questions. So I'll refer you to public affairs, Mr. Wade."

"Wait! Sir, you're aware that the police want to talk to you about recent developments surrounding Karen's case?"

The line hummed. It sounded like Cull was driving.

"Hello? Reverend Cull?"

"I'm aware that they've talked to my colleagues about Karen. The police have not yet talked to me because I've been out of town traveling. I really have to go."

"Please, wait, sir, this concerns you directly."

"Me?"

"Your past. You assaulted your wife, your time at Tumbler in Spokane, the sexual harassment complaint from a student. Aspects of Karen's and Roxanne Palmer's cases that you'd be familiar with. I mean you've been known to travel the state in an RV helping stranded motorists, and Karen Harding was—"

"I don't have a clue what you're talking about."

"You haven't been ruled out as a suspect, sir."

"I haven't—what did you say?"

"We're running a profile of you because police haven't ruled you out as a suspect in Karen's disappearance and the murders of Roxanne Palmer and a young woman whose remains were found in Oregon."

"Dear Lord. Why? Why are you doing this to me?"

"Sir, where are you now?"

"I'm trying to help someone at the moment. I have to go."

"Is that your response?"

"Yes, I've made mistakes in the past. I've acknowledged that. I'm only human. But I've paid for my sins and now I help others who've made mistakes find their spiritual way. I don't know what you, or the police, think you know about me, but I'm sure it's all wrong," Cull said. "When I'm not teaching, I travel through the Pacific Northwest helping people find their way. I minister. That's who I am. That's what I do. I've—"

A sudden commotion came from Cull's end. Like a struggle. Then moaning. A woman. Jason pressed the phone to his ear. Cull was trying to comfort her.

Maybe subdue her? Straining to listen, he heard a strange voice pleading.

"No, no, noooooooo." A young woman.

Cull was trying to calm her.

"It's all right, dear. Everything's going to be fine. I'm going to help."

"No! No! Please!"

"No, you have to lie down," Cull said.

Then came screams. A woman's screams.

"Oh God! Please help me! Oh God!"

Cull's line went dead.

Tiny hairs at the back of Jason's neck stood up and his scalp tingled.

58

Minutes after Cull's line went dead, Jason Wade and the night editors tried in vain to reconnect.

They alerted police in Seattle, surrounding counties, the Washington State Patrol, and the FBI, who contacted Cull's service provider. They managed to confirm that Cull was in the state, south-southeast of Seattle. The exact location was unknown and the phone had been turned off.

As his first deadline neared, Jason finished his exclusive. It was lined six columns across the front page under the headline CALL TO MURDER SUSPECT, with the subhead *Line dies with woman's screams*. The story began:

Jason Wade
Seattle Mirror
A woman's screams cut short a cell phone interview last night between the *Mirror* and a Seattle college instructor suspected in the ritual killings of two women and the disappearance of a Seattle college student.

The investigative profile of Gideon Cull ran with huge pictures of Cull shaking hands with the governor, head shots of Roxanne Palmer, Karen Harding, and the blank face of "Jane Doe," the unidentified victim. A graphic locator map pointed to crime scenes in the Rattlesnake Hills, Sawridge County, and the Lost River region of Oregon.

It was a compelling package and it stared back at Jason from his TV the next morning after he had switched on the local news. Making toast and coffee, he was groggy. He unmuted the sound and was jerked awake when he heard, "... as a result, Gideon Cull is being hailed as a hero, which stands in stark contrast to today's *Seattle Mirror*. Mac Thomas, *Live Eye News*, at the Puyallup River near Orting."

Hero? What the hell?

Jason switched channels, catching another local report with footage of a small car being wenched from the Puyallup River. What the hell? Now it cut to a hospital lobby. Cynthia Holmes was being interviewed by *Action First News*. During last night's thunderstorm the young mother of two was driving alone to her Auburn home from a rural church meeting when she had lost control of her car. It rolled into the river, trapping her. Reverend Gideon Cull of Seattle, who also attended the gathering and was following her, jumped into the water and rescued her. "He's my savior," said Cynthia, who suffered shock and a bump to her head. Cull drove her to the hospital as a precaution.

That would account for the screaming during the

phone call, Jason thought. Church meeting. Cull would've gone to that. Jason glanced at Cull's face staring from the front page of the *Mirror*.

He swallowed hard.

His phone rang.

"Jason, it's Ben Randolph at the paper. How you doing?"

"I'm not sure."

"Guess you heard about the shit storm. Look, you got any new numbers for Cull? I can't reach the guy. Your story implies he was killing a woman and here he was saving her life. Neena Swain has gone ape-shit over what's happened. Wants the *Mirror* to talk to him again."

"I don't have any other numbers than what I left. I'm sorry."

"Too bad. Anyway, Neena said to pass you a message."

"What."

"Get your ass in here as soon as possible."

No one spoke to Jason when he arrived in the newsroom.

He walked directly to Neena Swain's vast corner office, overlooking the bay and skyline. She ordered him to sit while she folded her arms and paced around him.

"The bottom line here is your story should never have run. While you reached Cull for comment, your interview was incomplete. You had no grasp of all the facts. It was filled with innuendo and malice, as if you were out to get this man."

She then counted off her orders. Jason couldn't call a damned person, couldn't write a damned word, and for damn sure, couldn't grant any goddamned interviews to other news organizations writing about the "mother of all screwups" caused by the *Mirror*. He was to help other *Mirror* reporters on the Cull follow, until she decided his fate.

By late afternoon, things had worsened.

Several Seattle news stations were saying that Jason, a junior reporter, had been previously suspended for "questionable behavior." One radio station reported "an earlier incident in which Wade's father showed up intoxicated and had threatened the paper's staff." Another suggested the pressure of the newspaper's infamous internship program was to blame.

The governor's office called the *Mirror* to say its reporting was a "shameful character assassination of a man who embodied the virtues of spiritual self-rehabilitation" and "trampled upon the fundamental judicial cornerstone of innocent until proven guilty."

Cull's college said it was aware of his past, stressing that it was long behind him, and the school's administration praised him as an inspiration for turning his life around. Tumbler River College in Spokane faxed a statement saying the ancient sexual harassment complaint against Cull was never substantiated because the complainant, a troubled young woman, had left the school.

"Guess you stepped in it big time, brewery boy,"

Astrid Grant said at Jason's desk. "TV says he's hired an attorney to speak for him. You're so screwed." She strode away.

Jason looked back to Nestor's office.

Neena Swain had been in there having an intense conversation with Nestor, Beale, and Mack. It'd been going on for over an hour. The *Mirror*'s board of directors, many of whom had friends in the capitol, wanted someone's head.

Jason went to the west side of the newsroom to the big windows looking out at Elliott Bay. He loved Seattle. And he loved the *Mirror*. Working at a big metro paper was not easy, but he lived to be part of it. This was his dream. All he ever wanted to be was a news reporter at this paper, writing about this city. The best city in the country. He watched the boats and rush-hour traffic as he tried to make sense of the past few hours, days, weeks. Hell, his entire damned sorry life.

A hand touched his shoulder. He turned to face Nestor. The regret Jason saw in his eyes told him immediately.

"Come into my office."

After closing the door, they both sat at the small, round table. Nestor ran his hands over his tired face.

"Jason, I want you to listen carefully to what I'm telling you. You're the best of the interns. I swear. It's why me, Beale, and Mack got behind you on Cull. You blew us away with what you'd dug up on your own. You're a natural reporter and you have a solid writing style."

Jason's stomach quaked. He knew what was coming.

"We weren't wrong. You did nothing wrong. I swear to God my gut tells me you're not wrong. The facts are there. Cull's past is disturbing, violence against his wife, a reputation for touching women. The RV motorist thing. A connection to Karen Harding. He hasn't been ruled out as a suspect and police investigating two murders and a disappearance want to question him. We have on tape a woman screaming. Those facts were undeniable and we went with them. But circumstances worked against us. Politics have come into play, from the highest office."

Jason nodded.

"Neena is covering her ass. I'm so sorry, Jason. I have to let you go. You're done. Effective immediately."

It felt like a blow to his stomach. Jason closed his eyes for a moment. Opened them and looked out to the newsroom.

"Jason. It's unfair. It's wrong. Beale and I tried to get between you and Neena."

Jason blinked but said nothing.

"Mack, Beale, and I are being suspended for two weeks. Here's my home and personal cell number if you want to call and talk. Take a few days to think things over."

Jason was numb when he walked out of the newsroom. He had a vague memory of shaking Nestor's hand and Astrid Grant wiggled her fingers at him in a little victory wave. What the hell did it matter? What did anything matter? he wondered later, guiding his Falcon along a southbound expressway, taking in the city and trying not to think.

He found himself wheeling into the neighborhood where he grew up. Funny where you go when your heart is broken. His old man wasn't home. And Jason was feeling too shitty to hang around.

He scrawled a note, wedged it into the door, then left.

On the way to his apartment in Fremont, he stopped near the Aurora Avenue Bridge, got out, and walked along its span. Dusk. Lights twinkled everywhere. He looked at the ships in the locks heading for the canal and the Pacific. Then down at Lake Union. The winds lifted his hair and pushed at him, nudging him. For a long, dark moment he contemplated the unthinkable before cursing and walking back to his car.

There was a slower death.

He picked up four six-packs and went to his empty apartment.

He sat alone in the dark, watching his fish glide in the blue-lit water of his tank. As he drank, he went over everything in his mind. *Accept things as they are.*

Resistance is futile.

He was done as a reporter.

There would never be a reporting job for him here, or anywhere. Never. Not after this. Strange, but it kind of completed things. He'd lost his mother. He'd lost Valerie. He'd lost his old man.

And now he'd lost the one thing that kept him going, his dream.

He'd been a fool to think it could ever come true. All along he had been destined to stand alongside his father at the brewery. The failed cop and his son, the failed reporter. He opened another beer and hoisted it to fate.

You win.

He watched his fish, finished his beer, then another. Then another. It was nearly three in the morning when he realized he'd scattered all of his papers, pictures, and research notes from the case around the floor.

Even drunk he couldn't give it up.

It was here. He swore the answer to Karen Harding's disappearance was somewhere in here. It had to be.

Jason believed it until he passed out.

59

Excerpt from *Reflections on the Ritual*

In the year of Our Lord, A.D. 1557
Somewhere in Europe

At dusk, after much of the crowd had departed, the grief-sick mother, her blind child in tow, sifted through the warm feathery ashes collecting what remained of her daughters.

She yelled incoherently, cursing, in a futile attempt to chase off the vulturous relic hunters, who were filling their pockets with bits of charred bone. The scavengers would later emerge at the local tavern, eyes aglow as they recounted the event and solicited offers for their recovered booty. "And what am I offered for a witch's tooth, eh?"

For her part, the mother tenderly gathered all she could find in her apron, tying it into a small sack. When she finished, she held it in her arms as though it where a tiny warm infant.

Watching the scene from a balcony was a som-

ber man who had paused from his work. For a brief moment the mother looked up to him. He may have been a visiting academic, or a theologian sent to record today's undertaking.

Something troubled him as he observed the heartbroken mother's journey from the square carrying the sack of her daughters' charred remains, the blind girl gripping her skirt. Their rummaging drew him deeper into his thoughts, disturbing him until the pair vanished from view.

Night had descended when the mother and her child came to a church some distance from the city's northern edge. They approached a statue of the Holy Mother and prayed at her feet. Then they entered the churchyard and the cemetery where the mother scattered the ashes of her children on consecrated ground. Her face was a tapestry of tear-streaked soot as she lifted it to a three-quarter moon and asked God to watch over her dead daughters.

The woman and her child set out for the long, sorrowful walk to their shack of a cottage, several miles away, unaware that a stranger was following them.

Submerged in her grief, the mother heard nothing of the sounds behind them as she and her child entered the same dense forest where her daughters had bathed.

The stranger came upon them in the moonlight, calling an insult to the woman, compelling her to turn and look up to a solitary dark figure on a horse.

At first, she took him for a wealthy relic-hunter, which angered her.

"What do you want?" She held out her empty apron, charcoal lined with the ashes of her daughters. "I have nothing. They've taken my heart. Have you come for that, too, you cowardly bandit?"

The stranger's mare snorted with spite as he moved it closer, raised his arm, and struck the woman with a single, powerful blow that rendered her unconscious before she hit the ground.

A dream.

Yes, all a horrible dream.

Those were the woman's first thoughts when she awakened, that the executions had been a nightmare. But when her eyes adjusted, she could not find her two oldest daughters.

And the fire blazing before her was real. She could feel its heat. No. She was confused, she was dreaming, it was a nightmare. She called out for her daughters, set out to find them, but was paralyzed, bound to a tree in the woods.

Through the flames she met the wide white eyes of her baby.

Her blind child.

Lashed to a tree.

Displayed before the fire was the same array

of odd-looking metal instruments belonging to the man who'd burned her daughters at the stake.

Then a large black figure emerged from behind the woman, his face hidden by the executioner's black hood.

"I saw you attempt to invoke demons in the churchyard with the ashes of your heretic offspring."

He pointed a black-gloved hand at her only living child.

"She is a sorceress."

He reached down for what appeared to be a surgeon's bone saw used for amputation. He examined its polished blade, then showed it to the mother.

"God's work is incomplete," he said, then approached the blind girl. "This girl is the devil's gangrenous limb and you are the whore-mother of witches."

Feeling his touch, the girl struggled against her bindings as the fire crackled and he calculated where to make his first cut.

In all the years since the difficult birth of her third child, the young mother had begun each day begging God to end her daughter's silence and allow her one small miracle.

The joy of hearing her voice.

A sound, a whisper.

Anything.

It was a prayer unanswered until this final moment.

For before she died that night, the blind girl's agony was so great, it overcame her defect.

Her screams were the first and last sounds her anguished mother heard from her as Xavier Veenza, instrument of God's wrath, completed his work.

60

A soft creaking woke Jason in the morning.

Someone was in his apartment!

He lay in bed listening. His forged steel bike lock was looped around the spindle of his headboard. His phone was within reach. A shadow floated along the wall beyond his door. Jason got up quietly and crept down the hall, his skull throbbing from his hangover. A man was sitting in his swivel rocker reading his files. Jason approached, the lock in a white-knuckled grip, then he froze.

"Dad?"

His father turned to him. "Hello, Jay."

"Jesus Christ."

"Sorry, your note said you needed to see me, the door was unlocked. You OK?"

Jason exhaled, waited a moment.

"I've been better." He opened a cupboard above the sink.

"I know. It's in all the papers, all over TV and radio."

Jason twisted the cap off an aspirin bottle, tapped out three tablets, swallowed them with a large glass of water. He sat on his sofa, massaging his head. He saw the plastic trash bag filled with empty beer cans. His old man had started dealing with the disaster.

A long silence passed as he looked at his father.

"Dad, I know I haven't been around much lately. I know I promised to go with you to meetings, but with this story and all."

"I've gone to meetings already."

Jason stopped rubbing his head.

"I'm the one who should apologize. Embarrassing you the way I did. I see it's in some of the reports. I'm sorry for that night at the *Mirror* and all the others before it."

"Forget it."

His father took stock of him.

"Son, it's safe to say I've learned my facts the hard way. Life isn't fair and there's no point complaining, no point trying to drown your mistakes. Your mother's never coming back, I accept that now, just as you have."

Just as he'd accepted that Valerie wasn't coming back. Just as he'd accepted that the Wade men were cursed to lose every good thing in their lives.

"You need to understand that I'm proud of you, Son."

"Proud? I'm a disgrace. A fuckup. It's in the papers."

"They're wrong."

"You're biased. I'm not a reporter. Never will be. My place is beside you in the brewery. *I accept that now*."

"Bull. The brewery's not the answer for you. There was a time I thought it was, but I was selfish. I wanted you next to me because your mother was gone. And this crap"—he kicked the bag of empty cans—"isn't the answer either."

"What's the answer? Tell me."

"Do what you were born to do. Ever since you started at the *Mirror*, I've read your stories. You're good. I was a cop once, but that dream died before it even got started, a lifetime ago. I'm no detective, no journalist, but for what it's worth, I've read everything you wrote about this Cull and I don't see where you went wrong."

"It's complicated."

"Maybe so, but the way I read things it sounds very political, right?"

"Yeah, maybe. I don't know. Because of me some editors got hurt in this too. Good people I respect. They checked my work, gave it a green light. I don't know what happened." He shook his head. "I don't know."

"Don't give up."

"They fired me."

"Prove them wrong. Rise above it. Get mad. Follow this through to the end. Nobody knows this story like you. Freelance it some place like the *New York Times*, or one of the magazines here."

"Dad."

"I'm serious, you can't quit now. While you were sleeping I read your research. I think you're on to something. I think you just haven't put all the pieces of this puzzle together."

Jason gripped his old man's shoulders warmly.

"I love you for coming to see me. It helps. A lot. And I'm so glad you're going to your meetings, getting better. But I've got to sort this out my way. I need to be alone to think. I'll come see you in a couple of days, OK? And I'll go to a meeting with you. Promise."

In the shower, Jason considered his father's words. As steam clouds rose around him, his fear gave way to anger. He had to pull out of this.

He wasn't wrong.

His mind swirled, pulling him back to what Nestor had said. *"You blew us away with what you'd dug up on your own... I swear my gut tells me you're not wrong. The facts are there."* And Pitman, the Benton County coroner. *"You strike me as a smart journalistic investigator who knows if he's on the right track."*

On the right track.

Whatever happened to Karen Harding, Gideon Cull had to be linked to it. Somehow, in some way he was connected, Jason swore. Forget Cull's halo.

Monsters wore masks.

Jason studied what he knew for the umpteenth time.

Then he made scrambled eggs and a pot of strong coffee. After eating he felt better. His concentration sharpened, he scrutinized his computer and hard-copy data. Every note, every file, every picture, three, four, five, six, a dozen times, refusing to let up.

Damn it.

The key was here.

He spotted something in the plastic trash bag next to the kitchen sink and fished it out. A note stuck to the bottom of a beer can. Something he'd made last night when he was drunk. He squinted at his scrawl. Sawridge scene inventory and Larssen's farm, *BMK*.

BMK?

Bookmark.

He shuffled through his papers until the creased bookmark from Larssen's place fell out. He stared at it, at the only two words he could read, "Twist" and "Books."

He drew a blank.

Then he went to his notes cribbed from Hank Stralla's evidence list. He went over every item as if they were pieces of a puzzle. Soda cans, beer cans, candy wrappers, newspapers, placemat map of B.C. from Ida May's Restaurant.

He stopped at that one.

Pondering it, he looked at the bookmark.

He went online and did an advanced search for Ida May's Restaurant in British Columbia. He got a hit for Ida May's Restaurant. *In Garrison, British Columbia.*

Nothing special.

Dead end.

He searched community and tourism sites for Garrison, scrolled quickly through a few pages, entries blurred by—wait! What was that? Two words leapt from the screen "Twist" and "Books."

TWIST OF FATE
*Rare Occult & Religious Books
Garrison, British Columbia.*

Sweet Jesus.

Garrison, British Columbia.

There was a picture of the store on the community page. It had a sign above the front window. The words matched. The type and font matched the two words on the bookmark he had found at Roxanne Palmer's murder scene.

The Garrison placemat was found at Karen Harding's scene.

Was Garrison the link?

His mind galloped.

A *ritualistic* killing, Hanna Larssen had told him.

He tapped the bookmark in his palm.

Ritualistic. Ritual. Books.

Come on. It was coming. Another piece was surfacing now. The Benton County coroner was studying old books. Part of his homework, he had said. Yes, that was right. Jason had written down the titles. He found his notes. Flipped through the pages. *Here we go.*

One leaped from the page.

Reflections on the Ritual.

Jason looked at the title, repeating it to himself. Yes, it was familiar. He pulled up a college Web photo of Gideon Cull in his office posted online by the college and charities. Books filled the shelves behind him. Jason recalled seeing something. *Reflections.* He enlarged the picture, zooming beyond Cull's face to the books behind him, locking on to one. Bingo.

Reflections on the Ritual.

Ritualistic killing. *Reflections on the Ritual.*

He read the bookstore's telephone number on the card. Cautioning himself to be careful, he dialed it from his cell phone, activating the feature that blocked his number. It rang three times before a soft-spoken man said, "Twist of Fate."

"Hello, I'm calling to track down an old book and was wondering if you might have it."

"What's the title?"

"Reflections on the Ritual."

"One moment."

A silent pause. Then Jason heard a keyboard.

"Just checking for you. It's a dark book. But enlightening."

More keyboard work and a long sigh of exasperation.

"Computer's slow today."

"Do you think you have it?"

"Not certain. But as I recall we've sold it over the last while. Wow, this thing is slow today. You do know the subject matter of this book?"

"Not entirely."

"It was produced in the late 1800s, inspired by the diary of a sixteenth-century torturer. He was a deranged monk who carried out the penalty on heretics, witches. Mostly women. He strived to perfect his methods."

Jason said nothing.

"Here we go. Oh. Bad luck. Don't have it. Sorry."

"Where did your last copy go?"

"One moment. A gentleman in Washington State."

"Can you be more specific?"

"I'm afraid I can't. Store policy. But if you agree to a small commission in the event of a sale, I could relay an inquiry of interest to the purchaser for you."

"Not right now. This is an anonymous query. Thanks," Jason said.

"Okeydoke. But if you change your mind, it would be easy in this case."

"Why's that?"

"The chap who bought it also bought a second copy and sent it to Washington. That customer is local, just outside Garrison."

61

Mist hung over the eternal forest valleys.

It coiled around the foothills like a gargantuan serpent shedding its skin as Jason Wade's Falcon cut deeper into the Canadian Rockies.

Time was working against him.

He was about one hundred miles northeast of Bonner's Ferry, Idaho, where he'd spent the night and fifty bucks for a motel room with a sagging bed. He rose early to push on to Garrison, British Columbia.

The isolated mountain community of two thousand rose from the skeleton of a mining village that had wasted into a ghost town during the Depression. Artists resurrected it and over time Garrison evolved into a sanctuary for bohemians, hermits, misfits, and outcasts. It was also a haven for outlaw bikers, forgotten rock stars, strange sects, and bizarre cults.

Was this his link to the case?

Doubt had seized Jason yesterday when he entered Idaho. His car started making a strange noise and he began questioning if pursuing the bookstore lead was a huge mistake.

Was he on the right track? Or simply desperate?

He needed to check out the local address linked to the book. Because the book could be the link. He needed to lock on to this local address without anyone knowing why, and he needed to move fast.

He was wrestling with his dilemma as he pulled into Garrison.

Its business district was huddled amid a handful of blocks with the assorted amenities of most small towns, a bank, drugstore, bar, restaurants—*there's Ida May's*—a gas station, library, post office, car lot, art and gift boutiques, clothing and appliance stores. Jason found the bookstore at the edge of downtown.

A narrow, two-floor frontier-style building. It had a turn-of-the-last-century storefront facade with ornate wooden spindling framing a large wooden sash window. Hand-lettered on the glass were the words TWIST OF FATE: RARE OCCULT & RELIGIOUS BOOKS.

The transom bell chimed when he entered, the worn planks of the floor squeaked. The shop was darkened, most of its curtains drawn. Even in the overcast morning, it took several seconds for Jason's eyes to adjust. The air smelled of musty old books that choked every inch of space. They were wedged into shelves, stacked floor to ceiling in teetering towers, they spilled from boxes and shot from the floor in island spires.

Jason spotted a cat dozing in a ray of dim light leaking from the half-drawn shade of the front door.

Then he noticed a small counter, and behind it a crown of fluffy white hair belonging to a man sitting near a computer reading a tattered copy of Marlowe's *Faustus*.

"Excuse me. I called yesterday inquiring about a book, *Reflections on the Ritual*."

Soft blue eyes peered over bifocals at Jason.

"Ah yes, I remember you. How may I help?"

"Do you have any more copies?"

"I'm afraid not. I checked after we spoke. However, I can start a search for you. I know there's a copy in Sydney, Australia. I'm quite certain I can locate others through our worldwide network."

"As I recall, you'd mentioned that your last copy was sold to a man in Washington state?"

"Not quite correct." The older man assessed Jason before he turned to his computer and began entering commands. "It went to Washington. The customer who bought it has a place here. And that customer bought a second copy of the book, a different edition."

"You wouldn't happen to have his address, the one here?"

"I believe I told you about our policy on privacy. We cannot release any specific personal details."

"I understand."

"I'd said the customer was local only to let you know that we could expedite contacting him to let him know about interest in a book he'd purchased and if he'd be interested in selling it. We provide that service for a small commission."

"Yes, I know."

The older man considered Jason.

"You're not from around here, are you?"

"No, I'm from Washington."

"I see. Shall I contact the customer on your behalf?"

"No. Hold on that, please. I'd need to think it over."

The older man nodded then, watching Jason leave, grinned to himself. Collectors. An eccentric, eclectic bunch, no matter their age. Forget the oddballs on the Internet. This youngster drove up from Washington and couldn't make up his mind on a book.

Moreover, the bookseller wondered, why the sudden interest in this book, *Reflections on the Ritual*? He did some further checking on the worldwide database for locating rare and antique books. He'd noticed a handful of new queries for it. Maybe he should try to get his hands on a few copies, he thought, before going back to *Faustus*.

All right, forget the bookstore.

Jason started his car. Time for plan B. And he'd better hustle. He didn't trust the bookstore guy to keep quiet about his interest in the book, not with the local aspect.

In a town this small, word would spread fast.

Jason pulled into Garrison Gas, a three-bay garage, grabbed a file folder from his bag, selected a page, and looked for help. This was a long shot. But at this point, everything was.

The busy station reeked of rubber and oil, echoed with compressors and the clink of steel tools dropped in the repair bays. He could hear Shania Twain's voice echoing from a radio.

"Hello," Jason called out.

"Yup." A man in dirty coveralls wiping his hands on a rag waved Jason to the counter. The name patch over his heart said *Gyle.* He was tall, about Jason's age. Hair tied in a ponytail. Forearms sleeved with tattoos. A Harley, death's-head, wings, and flames.

"You guys here work on most of the vehicles from Garrison?"

"We work on all of them. We're the only full-service garage around."

"Ever work on this one?"

Jason showed him the older photos he got from Web sites, of Cull with an RV he used in the background. Jason had made an enlarged copy showing only the RV. Gyle studied it carefully.

"This looks familiar," he said.

"Can you tell me who owns it?"

"Just wait a sec. Deek!"

A moment later a second man in grease-stained overalls joined Gyle. He bent over the counter and studied the picture. Then Deek looked at Jason.

"You a cop or something?"

"I'm a writer. I'm researching some local history, trying to locate the person around here who owns this RV. I need to get permission for some historical research on his property. I need to see the owner."

Deek nodded.

"I worked on this thing." He tapped a knuckle to the

picture. "The owner drives it hard all over the place. Got a V-Eight, moves pretty good for its age and size. Got it used out of Seattle. From a charity, I think, from the paperwork on it. We had to certify it a while back for B.C. plates. Good torque for the mileage."

"You know the owner?"

Deek scratched the stubble on his dirty cheek. "I know engines, I don't know people. I don't know this guy's name, but his place is out by—do you know this area?"

Jason shook his head.

Deek tore a patch of paper from a white take-out bag from Ida's, cursed until he found a ballpoint pen, and began drawing a map.

"Jeez," Gyle said, "is it that place off Gallows Ridge, way out by Scarecrow and Roddy's property?"

"Naw." Deek kept drawing. "Farther than that. The one past Cushing. The last one out there."

Gyle exchanged glances with Deek.

"The property next to McBride's ranch?"

"Yup," Gyle said.

Deek assessed Jason.

"Hell, nobody ever goes out there."

"Why?" Jason asked.

Gyle stared at him.

"Most folks out that way keep to themselves and this guy here"—Gyle tapped a dirty grease-stained finger on the spot where Deek was completing his map—"they just don't bother him at all."

"Why's that?"

"They just don't. What people do out there is their own business. You know, the cops don't even go out there, ain't that right, Deek?"

"That's right."

He folded the makeshift map and handed it to Jason.

62

Bonnie Stillerman stared back at Detective Hank Stralla from the photograph he'd scanned into his computer at his desk in Bellingham.

The picture Jason Wade had given to him.

"This is our linchpin," Stralla said over the phone to Price Canton, the Oregon detective with the unsolved murder tied to Roxanne Palmer's ritual killing in the Rattlesnake Hills. "Look at her glasses."

Canton was at the other end of the line in Klamath Falls studying his monitor.

"Red frames," Stralla said. "Now look at the glass frame from your Jane Doe crime scene in Lost River. Red frame again. What do you think?"

"I'll be damned." Canton clicked repeatedly between the pictures. "Hot damn, I think you're right."

Stralla had e-mailed the photo to Canton and the other task force members, telling them to magnify the frames in both pictures, convincing them that the color, contours, and design were very similar, maybe even identical.

Within an hour the task force had an emergency

conference call to discuss the red-framed glasses, new information on Gideon Cull's past and his connections to Karen Harding and Spokane. Forget the reverend's recent heroics. As far as investigators on the task force were concerned, he hadn't been cleared of anything yet because he was always unavailable for a police interview. Now that they had the glasses angle, Cull was no longer a potential suspect.

He was *the* suspect.

And while the glasses were a critical break, they proved nothing. Investigators had to confirm the whereabouts and welfare of Bonnie Stillerman. And they had to examine Cull's time line and his links to Roxanne Palmer and Karen Harding. And since Harding hadn't been located, they couldn't rule out the possibility she was alive.

And if she was alive, every second counted.

When the call ended, the FBI, along with police in three states and some two dozen cities and counties, had joined the task force in a full-tilt drive on a lead arising from Jason Wade, a disgraced cub reporter at the *Seattle Mirror*.

In Spokane, police executed warrants at Tumbler River College. They obtained Bonnie Stillerman's old complaint against Cull and her reports of being "stalked on campus" by a man. They obtained her private files and medical information to check for next of kin and dental records for comparison with the few teeth found at the Lost River crime scene.

When two Spokane detectives showed up at the

home of Stillerman's former roommate, Diane Upshaw, all the color drained from her face.

"Yes, I still have boxes of her things I kept," Upshaw told the grim-faced detectives who filled her living room. "Bonnie never sent for them." Upshaw led the men to her attic, dabbing a tissue to her glistening eyes. "Call me crazy, but I always thought she'd call me one day. Bonnie was upset and sad in her life during that time. It hurt me that she never called—but what can you do? People have a right to their privacy."

The detectives said little as Upshaw opened dust-covered boxes of her friend's belongings, including a jewelry box. Among the items: a tiny gold rose that Diane recalled had fallen out of an arm of Bonnie's glasses.

A call and photograph sent online to Price Canton in Klamath Falls confirmed it. An arm of the glasses found at the Oregon scene was also missing one of the ornate little roses.

The FBI and investigators in New Mexico could not locate any of Bonnie Stillerman's relatives. Scrutinizing databases of motor vehicles, they found no renewal of her driver's license out of Washington State to any state in the country. Her driver's license had expired.

Banking and credit card activity ceased around the time Upshaw had last seen Stillerman in Spokane. Detectives confirmed that during that period, there was a conference on ancient religions in Klamath Falls, Oregon, which was about an hour's drive from the wooded country near Lost River where Jane Doe's remains were discovered.

Gideon Cull had attended the event.

An urgent, preliminary comparison of dental records indicated the Jane Doe found in Oregon's Lost River region was Bonnie Stillerman. They began the process for DNA testing.

In Seattle, the FBI and the Seattle PD executed search warrants on Gideon Cull's campus office in Seattle. At the college, acting on a heads-up from Morris Pitman, the Benton County coroner who'd autopsied Roxanne Palmer, federal agents gave special attention to Cull's books.

Pitman's research on the historical origins on the branding techniques found in the Palmer and Stillerman murders convinced him that the killer drew his inspiration from an ancient text.

"You're looking for one, a specific title," Pitman was telling the special agent leading the search over his cell phone. "It's a slim volume entitled *Reflections on the Ritual.*"

While agents seized Cull's computer, photos, files, journals, and several personal items, others traced white-gloved fingers along the spines jammed into the shelves of Cull's groaning bookcases.

The lead agent stopped when he hit on *Reflections on the Ritual*, then described it over the phone to Pitman.

"That's it!" Pitman said. "That's the one!"

63

Jason Wade held the map on the steering wheel between his thumbs after he left Garrison and drove deep into the mountain back roads.

The first landmark was the waterfall.

Majestic and breathtaking, he thought, passing it with a curtain of dust in his wake. Next, according to the mechanic's scrawl on the take-out bag, would be, the Dead Forest.

He rolled along immense swaths of charred trees and gnarled stumps, the aftermath of a wildfire. Gradually, stands of dead trees gave way to thick healthy woods as the road ascended the vast slopes before disappearing into forests so dense they obscured the remaining light.

He was uneasy about the region's reputation as the refuge of misfits. Once again, his doubts assailed him. What the hell was he doing here? Did he really believe a screwup rookie reporter was actually on the trail of a killer? Maybe he was reacting to his failures. To this place, which was creeping him out. Maybe he should turn his Falcon around and go home.

And call his old man about going back to the brewery.

Something brown blurred directly in front of him.

Big fear-filled eyes met his.

It happened too fast for his circuits to react. Before his brain issued the order to lift his foot from the gas to stomp the brake, before he could form the cognitive command to swerve, he heard and felt the *thud.*

A thin ribbon of blood streaked over his windshield.

His stomach clenched. He'd hit a deer. Nicked its hindquarter. It trotted down the road and vanished into the trees. He gripped the wheel and took several deep breaths before studying his map and continuing on, telling himself he didn't believe in omens.

This was stupid.

Grow up.

Check out this property, then get the hell back to Seattle.

Less than half an hour and some nineteen miles later, he stopped. The road had dead-ended. Nothing ahead but trees, more trees, and an abandoned logging trail. He was lost. He studied the map as time ticked by. Obviously, he'd gone too far. He turned the Falcon around, made note of the odometer, then examined the shoulder as he retraced his path. He'd gone about two miles before metal captured a sunbeam.

He stopped at a weatherworn gate almost invisible in the scrub and undergrowth. A small sign fastened to it said: KEEP OUT: PRIVATE.

A chain looped several times around the latch and the gatepost. It was secured with two steel locks.

Beyond the gate, a dirt road meandered through the dark forest until it vanished. Nothing else was visible.

He leaned against his car. Other than the birds, all was quiet. He glanced down the road.

Nothing.

His pulse quickened.

You're at the edge of the world. Make the call. Trespass and investigate. Or go back to Seattle with your tail between your legs. Is there a story here? Or only more trouble? Come on, what's the plan?

Locate Cull. Respectfully request an interview to set the record straight. If Cull wasn't here, or if he'd been wrong with his suspicions, apologize, drive home. That was the plan. End of story.

He eased his Falcon away from the entrance, down the road to a soft shoulder and small grassy patch where he could hide it from view. He switched on his cell phone and, as expected, the roaming light indicated service here was erratic. Just the same, he took the phone and walked back to the property where he climbed the gate.

Trespassing was a huge risk. His stomach fluttered as he walked along the dirt road into the property. It went on, meandering for a great distance before he crested a small hill and spotted a structure.

A house.

A ramshackle wooden bungalow with weatherworn clapboard peeling from its crooked walls. Its roof blistered where shingles were missing. Garbage and an eviscerated stove and washer rose like headstones from the ravaged yard. The grass around it was worn and dotted with coils of animal excrement smelling like a backed-up sewer. Then came the buzz of flies as he climbed the rickety steps to the door and knocked.

No sound. No sign of life inside. The door was unlocked. He opened it a crack.

"Hello!" he called.

No response. He turned to the outbuildings near the house, a garage or stable and a couple of small sheds. He rounded the house toward them and froze.

An RV.

Parked at the side of the house.

Oh, Jesus.

On the back was a decal of a Canada goose in flight. One of its wings was broken off.

This is the RV!

Jason's pulse pounded. *Oh, Christ.* He started shaking. *Do something.* He pulled out his notebook, took down the plate, began making notes. *Not here! Get out of sight!* Three paths led from the house in different directions into the forest.

Get out of sight. Find a place to think, maybe make a call. Trotting, he checked his phone. No service. Damn. He hurried down the nearest path, stopping at times to listen, peer through the branches, and make careful notes and sketch a map. He broke branches in strategic places so he could find his way back, his mind racing as he moved on.

This had to be the place.

Then he remembered the mechanics' warning about staying away, how police never came out here.

He stepped into the bush to hide, write more notes, and think. He could go back to the RV and house and try to take pictures with his phone, but he had less than a quarter of battery power. He should've charged the thing before he rushed from Seattle.

Take it easy.

He'd explore the property, get back to Garrison, and tell the police. Get them to call Stralla. That was good. Carefully Jason resumed traveling along the path, his senses heightened for smells, sounds, sights. He eyed something small and white on the ground.

A human tooth.

All of his saliva dried.

He bent down and picked up two more.

Ahead he saw a hill, shaded in a meadow. It looked like some kind of ritual place as he climbed it, noticing a series of large bumps. Anthills. Then he saw objects rising about two feet from the earth.

Small handmade wooden crosses.

He counted nine.

Each at the head of an earthen mound. God Almighty, this was a graveyard. Jason's scalp tingled, his head snapped around. He stepped back into the cover of the forest, and stopped dead in his tracks.

Was that someone's voice? He strained to listen. There it was again. He moved toward it, branches pulling at his shirt as he hurried in the direction, stopping to listen again and sharpen his bearings.

He was getting closer. He heard it again as he came to a moss-covered hill thick with underbrush. It was muffled, weak, but he was closer now. It was a human cry. A woman, pleading.

"Help me. Pleeeaaaase."

Jason hurried faster now until he fell to the soft grass. His leg had caught the edge of a metal pipe jutting a foot from the ground. The voice was echoing from it. *Underground!* The pipe looked like a ventilation tube, the kind for a bathroom.

"Help me."

"I'm here. I can hear you."

"Oh God! Please help me. My name's Karen Harding—"

Karen Harding!

"He's insane. He's murdered people. I saw him! God! Please get me out of here."

Jason's skin numbed. The blood in his ears pounded. She was trapped. He tried to think.

"Karen, I'm going to help you but you must be quiet!"

He heard her struggling to stifle her sobs.

"Are you a police officer?"

"No, I'm Jason Wade, a reporter from Seattle."

"Please help me, Jason, please hurry."

"How did he put you in the ground?"

"There's a door with locks. Two doors. Hurry, God, please! Help me!"

First he had to get help. He reached for his phone. It might've been because he was on the hill, slightly elevated, or that the metal pipe nearby acted like a booster antenna, or that he'd whispered a prayer, but his roam light flickered.

His fingers shook as he punched 911.

His service was good for all of the United States and Canada, but his call didn't connect. *Damn it. Try again.* He tried the very next number that came into his head. His body trembled as static crackled over the air, his heart swelling when the call connected, rang through to—

Voice mail. *Damn it.*

Jason left a frantic message, tried calling 911 again. It didn't work. He hung up just as Karen screamed for help. He scrambled down the hill and worked his way through the choking undergrowth, finding the door; small, fortified, and nearly invisible in the earth and scrub.

It was built from railroad ties, and had triple locks.

He searched the area, grabbing a grapefruit-sized rock, smashing it against the locks. The steel split the rock. He searched in vain for another, then climbed back to the pipe.

"Karen, I have to get my tire iron to work on the locks. It's in my car, I'll be right back."

"No! No! God, please don't leave me! Please, Jason!"

"It's the only way. I've called for help. I'm not leaving you. I'll be back with tools to pry the locks but you have to be quiet."

Her sobs echoing from the pipe abruptly stopped.

His heart hammered against his ribs as he raced along the path, his heavy breathing filling the silence. This couldn't be happening. He was drunk. Or he was dreaming. Branches slapped at his face, snagged his pants and shirt. Heavy scents of pine and cedar mingled with the stench wafting from the main house of the property.

Man, it was all true.

He'd found Karen Harding.

Alive.

He had to get her free. It was a long trip back to his car. He had a tire iron. That would work and— Why were his feet in the air? Why was he choking? Something around his neck. A steel chain solid against his throat jerking him against a human body behind him. Someone strong, grunting, choking him with the steel chain so he couldn't breathe. He was on the hard ground, the sky above him blurring.

The light blocked by a darkness that swallowed him.

64

Ron Nestor was still simmering.

Even now, a few days after the explosion at the *Mirror* over Jason Wade's story. Nestor resented how the paper had sacrificed Wade to the political bull. Portraying Wade as the scapegoat made Nestor sick.

For a moment, he'd considered looking into a standing offer to join the *Chicago Tribune*. But he loved Seattle. This was his town. Hell, it was the only town. He took another sip of beer while the crowd roared at a line drive to second that triggered a Mariners' double play.

He'd come to "the Safe" to see his Ms take on the Toronto Blue Jays. And maybe to sort things out from his seat on the third deck behind first base. It offered views of the skyline, the Needle, and parts of the waterfront while the aroma of garlic fries seasoned the air that cracked with a Mariners' hit. It soared high over center field, but the wind pushed it back, robbing them of a homer, underscoring Nestor's bitterness.

Jason Wade had been robbed. His dream of being a reporter was over. He'd be forever identified with the *Mirror*'s disgrace. It tore Nestor up. For the last few days he'd called Wade's apartment. He couldn't reach him.

And he'd been calling editors he knew at the *Seattle Times*, the *Post-Intelligencer*, the *Associated Press*, papers in Tacoma, Olympia, Spokane, out of state, everywhere, trying to find Jason a job.

"Sorry, pal, your boy's toast. Nobody's going to hire him," the editor of a triweekly told Nestor.

It disgusted him because Jason had promise. Yes, he was rough around the edges, wild even, but he was a powerful digger with a natural instinct for news. He broke the Harding story by enterprising on a slow night. He followed it with brilliant work on Cull. Those arrogant big-school interns were smart, polished, and good. But none could touch Jason's raw talent.

Nestor should've done more for him because now he would most likely end up working at the Pacific Peaks Brewery with his father. Likely risk inheriting his old man's drinking problem too.

What a tragic waste.

Frustrated that several editors had still not returned his calls, Nestor reached for his cell phone, alarmed to learn that he'd forgotten to turn it on. It'd been off all day. He cursed, switched it on, and checked his messages.

Three new ones.

The first was from a friend at the *San Francisco Star*. She apologized but she didn't have any openings for Jason.

The next message was from a crusty old-timer at the *Denver Post*. "Yeah, Ron, we heard about that crap your kid stirred up. Sorry. No dice here."

The third message stopped his breathing.

"It's Jason Wade!—" Static punctuated his words. "I'm outside Garrison! My phone's dying. Garrison, British Columbia! I've found Karen Harding! Alive! I've found her! I'm talking with her now! He's got her locked underground! I think he's killed people here! Call someone! Get the police to come here fast! It's on a property at the end of Gallows Ridge, outside Garrison British, Columbia! My phone's dying! Hurry!"

Nestor's mind raced. Was it a joke? No, it couldn't be. Jason must've chased the story on his own. He'd do that. Nestor left his seat for a quieter location near a section arch, pulled out his small notebook and replayed the call, wrote it down word for word, then went to a public phone.

The stadium quaked with cheering as he dialed 911, a call to the Seattle police, which set off a chain of events.

65

In Seattle, about a mile from the college where Gideon Cull had instructed Karen Harding in ancient religions, several marked and unmarked police cars converged on a large Colonial-style stone house.

The three-story building with the gables, turret, and pitched roof was owned by Jean Sproule, a sixty-nine-year-old, retired high school principal. She rented her third-floor apartment to Reverend Gideon Cull.

Sproule leaned heavily on her cane, her age-creased face turning serious as she spoke to the FBI agents and the army of police officers who'd arrived at her door displaying their warrant to search Cull's residence.

"Well, he's not here," she told them. "Hasn't been for days."

"Do you know where he is?"

"Haven't a clue."

"Could you unlock his unit and let us enter, ma'am?"

Sproule's cat threaded through her legs as she reached for her spare key from the peg, then escorted the police to Cull's door. She eased herself into a cushioned sofa chair, not feeling right, as the agents wearing white latex gloves snooped through Cull's belongings. After watching them for nearly an hour Sproule spoke her mind.

"I know this man and what you're doing is not right. The governor thinks very highly of him."

The agents said nothing as she continued.

"Whatever you think he's done, or what the crazy newspeople are accusing him of, is just plain wrong. He's a man of the cloth, a saint, he helps people. He literally goes out into the night and helps people in trouble."

The senior agent wearing a tailored charcoal suit stood over Cull's desk staring at his corkboard, the pinned notes, calendar, snapshots.

A second agent approached him holding a bundle of letters, handwritten letters, bearing no return address. Faces intense, they shuffled through them, reading their chilling contents.

"Ma'am," the senior agent said, "do you know an individual named Ezra?"

"Who?"

"Ezra." The agent held out a letter.

Sproule slid on her glasses that hung from the chain around her neck, examined the signature, then shook her head.

At that moment, the senior agent's cell phone rang.

"Buckner," he answered.

The senior agent was alerted to a major break coming from a 911 call to a *Seattle Mirror* editor's cell phone at Safeco Field.

"Ma'am," the senior said after hanging up, "do you have any idea where Cull is?"

"I told you I do not. He isn't required to report to me."

A female agent approached Buckner holding a small, hand-drawn map. He showed it to Sproule. "Excuse me, ma'am, but do you know what this is?" His white-gloved finger tapped on the map.

Sproule adjusted her glasses.

"That's how you get to Gideon's place in the mountains."

"Excuse me?"

"His little hideaway retreat. It's far away. He told me he goes there to meditate and prepare his studies. I'm not sure, but I'd say that's probably where he is now."

All the agents stopped their activity, huddled around the map, exchanging glances while the senior agent began pressing numbers on his cell phone, to add their new information to the investigation.

An arrest warrant and a BOLO had already been issued for Gideon Cull.

He was emerging as one of the FBI's Most Wanted fugitives.

In minutes, alerts and updates were rocketing to the FBI's Seattle Field Office, to the FBI's National Headquarters in Washington, D.C., then to the Royal Canadian Mounted Police Headquarters in Ottawa, Canada, and to the RCMP's "E Division" in command of British Columbia, who then, through Telecoms dispatchers in Kelowna for the division's southeast district, alerted the Mounties patrolling the remote mountain region around Garrison.

66

Lisa Roy pulled off the road north of Garrison, British Columbia, to study the alert that had beeped on the mobile computer in her patrol car.

Oh boy.

A multiple 10-35—suspect, possible hostages—on Gallows Ridge originating from a call via the FBI in Seattle. The Emergency Response Team was marshaling to fly out of Kelowna. Air 3, the Bell chopper, was in the Crowsnest Pass. A fixed-wing was lifting off from Golden to do a high and silent aerial. She scrolled through the history. The very first call was now eight minutes old. They were losing light.

The alert advised radio silence.

Typing rapidly, Roy informed her dispatcher of her location. Six or seven minutes from Gallows Ridge. In all, some twenty-two minutes from the property, if she hauled it.

Roy was by herself but by far the closest unit.

Within seconds her computer beeped, advising her to take a traffic point at the location in establishing a perimeter out of sight of the property, out of the line of fire, and await backup.

Ten-four.

Stones and dirt blasted from her marked Crown Victoria, creating a rising curtain of dust as she roared from the shoulder down the road.

Roy was a twenty-six-year-old Royal Canadian Police Constable from Montreal. She was five feet eight inches tall, one hundred twenty-five pounds, and a black belt. She'd graduated top in her troop at the RCMP academy in Regina, Saskatchewan, ten months ago, hoping to one day join Vancouver's Major Crimes Section.

For now, Roy's first posting was here at Garrison where she was assigned to traffic and general detachment duties. She'd assisted on executing warrants on fugitive bikers and helped drug enforcement take down some major hydroponic grow operations. Now this Seattle case. It was a big one. Roy had seen the recent news reports on the Spokane and Seattle stations that broadcast into B.C., never thinking it would reach into her own backyard.

The Crown Vic's engine growled as Roy ate up the road, winding her way closer to that creepy zone with the dead end. The region's lore said the area was the site of some turn-of-the-century pagan cult activity that had attracted worshippers over the decades. If it was true, it was never documented. Some of the locals were a little odd, but there was never any trouble here.

Until now.

Checking her odometer, Roy cut her speed. She was very near and slowed to a crawl. The gated entrance was around the bend, about fifty yards away. This was a good place to stop.

She T-boned her car, popped the trunk, and set to work. She was wearing navy pants with a wide yellow seam stripe, a khaki shirt with shoulder patches bearing the letters *RCMP GRC*. Over her shirt Roy had a blue Kevlar vest. A 9mm Smith & Wesson was holstered in her leather utility belt.

She took her roll of yellow plastic tape and stretched a line across the road, tying it off on cedar trees. She updated her status to her dispatcher.

Roy then loaded her shotgun, found her binoculars, and walked to the bend to surveil the gate. Catching a glint of chrome in the setting sun, she went down the side of the road, using the dense bush for cover until she came upon a car half-hidden in the woods. It had a Washington plate. She took it down and examined the car for any signs of a struggle or violence.

Nothing obvious.

She returned to her car and was transmitting her update with plate information when she froze and listened. Did she hear something? It had ascended from somewhere within the dense forests, riding along the early evening breezes that lifted a few strands of Roy's hair.

A faint cry.

She updated her report, requesting the ETA of the nearest backup.

Her computer beeped. The nearest RCMP members out of Garrison were twenty-five minutes from her.

Roy bit her bottom lip. Decision time. If a life was

at risk and she was too late, she'd never forgive herself. She was going in. It was a judgment call but she was going in now.

Alone.

She updated her dispatcher, tested her portable radio, inserted her earpiece, grabbed her shotgun and extra shells before trotting down the side of the road, using the trees as cover.

Roy hopped the gate, then moved along the dirt road that cut into the property. The sun was plummeting behind the mountains, cooling the air, playing tricks with light and shadow as bird calls echoed from the woods.

She came upon the house, peeked through windows. No sounds or signs of movement. At one side she found the RV. Then, half-concealed in the bush nearby, she noticed another car with Washington plates.

She examined it, took down the plate.

Light winds hissed through the trees, beckoning Roy to choose one of the paths twisting from the main house area. She chose the nearest, feeling a sense of dread as she moved through the dark woods with its surreal light play. And the silence.

Something was wrong. She could sense it in the air.

She tightened her grip on her shotgun and swallowed. Her blood pumped in her ears against the earpiece of her radio. As she came to the top of a rise her heart stopped. She swung her gun down to a man lying on his stomach.

She scanned the area for a weapon and saw none.

Adrenaline jetted to every corner of her body, her nostrils flared with her hard breathing. Shafts of dying light stabbed the treetops, her eyes adjusted, then it hit her.

The man's head was gone.

67

Karen Harding was upright, spread-eagled, and trembling under the ropes binding her to the twelve-foot cedar beams that formed an X.

All of her hair had been shorn, she had been stripped of all her clothing and dressed in a long nightshirt saturated with sulfur. The reverend turned to her from the fire and began the ritual by pronouncing her sentence.

"The court has found you guilty of communion with devils and condemns you to renounce your allegiance." He stepped forward, drawing his hooded head to within inches of her face. "Do you wish to confess?"

The fire hissed. Karen's soft sobbing joined the rush of the blaze and the shrieks of night creatures.

"Please." Her voice barely reached above a whisper. "I don't know what I've done wrong but I'm sorry. Please let me go. Please."

He did not move. A long moment passed before he spoke.

"Reconcile your soul, witch."

He turned back to his work at the heavy wooden table—his altar. It displayed an array of branding irons, knives, pliers, scissors, hooks, surgical saws, and a Venetian Pear that had survived several centuries, like the malice burning in his eyes as he proceeded to the next act.

He blessed his instruments to thwart any sorcery that might render the prisoner's sentence painless. After praying over each item, he pulled on his long leather gloves studded with silver rivets. They sparkled when he went to the fire to withdraw the steel rod he had been heating in the flames.

The small X on its tip glowed red as he turned to Karen, holding it in front of her eyes as he moved the glowing iron closer.

She felt its awful heat.

Please. Somebody help me.

Turning her head in terror, she glimpsed the other tall Xs' standing far off like specters in the distant darkness.

Hanging from them were the rotting remains of corpses.

68

Lisa Roy forced herself to squat down and take long, deep breaths to slow her heart. She dragged the back of her hand across her moist brow. *All right. Let's go.* She tightened her grip on her shotgun as she moved along the path. She went about a hundred paces, froze, and looked up to a man's head spiked on a stick.

It stood before her, matching her height. Open-eyed. A grinning obscenity, dripping like an ancient talisman endowed to ward off transgressors. Roy whitened, steadied herself against a tree, and dry-heaved. Then she let her training kick in. She was smart, still in control.

But alone.

She reached for the radio, checked the connection to ensure that her earpiece had not come loose, keyed her mike.

"This is Eighty-three," she whispered.

"Ten-four, Eighty-three."

"I'm on-site with one confirmed ten-thirty-five. A white male. No weapons. No suspects sighted. Requesting ETA on backup."

Trying to subdue her breathing, she glanced skyward as she waited for a response. The treetops formed a natural canopy over the forest. They'd lost the light. Whoever was out there in the dark had the home field advantage.

"That you, Lisa? It's Rob. How bad is it?"

"It's a nightmare, Robbie."

"Hold on. I'm almost there." She could hear the roar of his SUV. "Starchuk's right behind me. We're coming, hold on."

"Ten-four."

A blood-chilling scream shattered the night. *Oh, Jesus.* Roy couldn't wait for her backup and let another person die. She continued down the path.

69

Karen rolled her head from side to side, imploring the reverend to stop, but he moved closer. She could hear his breathing against the black fabric of his hood. She searched his eyes for mercy, but found nothing but darkness.

"Cleanse your soul," he said. "Confess now so that you may be converted."

"I love God," she said. "I love my family. My mother—"

"Liar!"

"I love my father. I love my sister. And, and, and I— I forgive you."

"Stop the lies, witch!"

"Hail, Mary, full of grace, the Lord is with thee..."

"Stop! Blasphemer! When you speak of Mary, you intend Lucifer! *You love Lucifer!*"

Karen continued, "...now and at the hour of our death."

"Confess your guilt now! You've had commerce with the Lord of the Flies! *Look!* Lucifer has endeavored to rescue you, but to no avail!"

The reverend whirled from her, seized a knife from his altar, and marched to the large X standing opposite and held the blade to the throat of the man bound to it: Jason Wade.

His eyes fluttered opened, to the flames, to Karen bound to the X across from him, to the reverend's ranting.

It wasn't real.

Jason was dreaming. He was falling from heaven, arms and legs flung outward, descending to hell. Seeing the fires, hearing the agonies of the tormented. No, he was floating in a nightmare.

Time to end it. Time to wake up. *Wake up.* Why couldn't he awake? Then it all came thundering back, crushing him. Finding Karen, running for help, being choked into semiconsciousness. Being tied to beams, his body hoisted upright. This was no fantasy.

Karen was praying.

Why?

There was no God here. No hope. Only fear. Jason stared into the eyeholes of the executioner's hood—grotesque windows to something dead inside.

"You." He pressed the blade into Jason's neck until it punctured his skin. Blood webbed from the wound. "You're a soldier serving Lucifer!" the reverend rasped. "You will know the soul-purifying pain of the ritual!"

Jason summoned every molecule of his strength to battle against the bindings. The ropes bit into his wrists, creaked against the wooden beam, loosened but not enough.

He strained again.

The heat of the fire, his fear, his struggle made him sweat, lubricating his skin against the coarse rope, slipping on his flesh as he persisted.

The reverend went to the fire, returned to Jason, his gloved hand overflowing with glowing red embers.

"Satan is present."

His other hand blurred under Jason's T-shirt. A knife blade stretched the fabric before slitting the center from his waist to his neck, exposing his chest. It rose and sank with his breathing as the reverend chose a large piece of charcoal from the smoldering heap in his palm and used it to circle Jason's heart, then filled it in until it looked like a hole in his chest.

Jason writhed as it scorched his flesh.

The reverend returned to the fire as Jason fought against his bindings. Blood slicked over his raw-flesh wounds, but he felt no pain. He was in shock, struggling for his life as Karen's screams echoed to the mountains.

The reverend selected the handle of a large serrated knife that he'd set in the fire, its blade blazing pink in the night as he held it to Jason's eyes.

"Demons dwell in your heart! You require *the Transformation.* I will remove your beating heart and consume it before your eyes, devouring the demons, giving you solace that your soul has been purified."

Fire gleamed on the knife's blade as the reverend positioned its tip a quarter inch from Jason's heart, then inhaled for the strength to plunge it into his chest. Later he'd use the saw for the ribs.

"Freeze! RCMP!"

Roy crouched at the edge of the darkness, arms extended, hands gripping her 9mm Smith & Wesson. She fired, but the reverend had turned and in a quick, fluid motion, positioned himself to put Jason in front of him.

"Drop the knife! Step away! Get on your knees!"

The reverend tensed, flung his knife at Roy, hitting her vest. She flinched, sidestepped, slipped as the reverend lunged at her, sending both of them to the ground, fighting for her weapon.

Karen screamed.

Jason twisted wildly against his bindings, pulling one wrist free, strips of his skin slapping like torn rags as he released his other arm. Pain shot to his ankles, which took his full weight for they remained restrained to the X as he pivoted hard to the earth.

Roy drew upon all she'd learned from her self-defense training. She shifted her weight, anticipating the reverend's moves, attacked vulnerable spots, kicking and kneeing where she could. But he was big, fast, strong, and Roy was hampered by her Kevlar vest.

She could feel him winning, slowly prying her gun from her hands.

One of her kicks sent the knife to Jason, who seized it and cut himself loose. Bleeding, he limped to the edge of the light, found Roy's shotgun, and trained it on the reverend.

But he was too late.

The reverend now had control of Roy's handgun and stood over her, drilling it against her temple, wedging her head to the ground. The air exploded with six shots, hoisting the reverend from his feet, hurling him into the darkness.

RCMP Constables Rob Talon and Paul Starchuk, Roy's backup, stepped into the light. They signaled quickly for Jason to drop the shotgun. He did. Then they approached the reverend with their guns drawn and handcuffed him.

There was no need.

He was dead.

Roy sat up, drew her knees to her chin, and buried her face in her hands.

Karen had fainted, her head hanging down like a Christ figure on the cross. The Mounties moved to free her from her bindings, as the fire dispatched sparks to the stars.

It was over.

70

As Jason helped the Mounties free Karen Harding from her bindings she came to and locked her arms around his neck and cried.

Her body shook against his and he stayed with her, adrenaline still rippling through him as they stared into the fire.

Starchuk and Talon tended to Roy.

Soon their radios sizzled with transmissions and the world began learning of the nightmare at Garrison.

The RCMP's Emergency Response Team arrived. Through the trees, Jason saw their laser sites raking the property as heavily armed members conducted a building-by-building, room-by-room check of the compound. Air 3, the Bell 206h out of Kelowna, thundered overhead, using its infrared and "Night Sun" to scour the terrain.

No other suspects or living victims were located.

After ERT secured the scene, the RCMP's homicide people moved in. Medical crews were led to Karen, Roy, and Jason near the altar in "the killing zone." The helicopter's intense light swept the area. As a female paramedic bandaged Jason's wounds, his attention followed the jagged line of large standing Xs, stretching to a hilltop in the forest like a surreal perversion of Golgotha, the hill were Christ was crucified. Then, under the blazing light, he noticed tiny half-buried metal objects glittering on the ground around him.

Gold chains, rings, watches, necklaces, jewelry of the victims.

His concentration narrowed on something.

"Sir, please don't move," the paramedic said.

Jason turned to alert someone, but the investigators were huddled, comparing notes, shouting in each other's ears over the rotor wash. Ignoring the paramedic, he got down on his hands and knees and inspected the items until he came to a piece that jarred him.

A bracelet.

A familiar beaded bracelet. Gooseflesh rose on his skin as something cleaved in his heart and a new fear consumed him with one thought.

Valerie.

He reached for it but did not to touch it. His breathing grew deep and ragged. Blood pummeled his eardrums, making him deaf to reason, deaf to anything but the new horror swirling in him as he lifted his head to the light.

Valerie.

The bracelet was identical to the set she'd bought for them in Pike Place Market, to the one in his apartment, on his bedpost.

Had she been—*oh, Christ, no.*

He glanced around. Helpless. Had she somehow been among the victims? *No, this can't be.* Tears stood in his eyes. Something caved inside. Something collapsed. A shadow fell over him, and then a latex-covered hand grasped his shoulder.

A detective bent down beside him, seeing what he was seeing.

"I think this belongs to someone I know," Jason said.

Concerned, the detective stared at him, then flipped to a clear page in his notebook.

"Who?"

"Valerie Hewitt of Seattle."

"And your relationship to her?"

"We used to be together."

"You're her boyfriend?"

Jason nodded, struggling with his anguish.

According to his card, the detective was RCMP Sergeant Warren Taylor.

"We've found wallets, purses in an underground safe he kept behind the house," Taylor said. "Is this item unique?"

"I—I don't." Jason stared. It was unique to him. "I don't know."

"Listen, unless this piece is one of a kind, it could belong to anyone. We're going to need time to confirm things."

Jason took a long, hard look around at the images he would carry forever.

"Sir, we have to go," the paramedic said.

They put Karen and Jason on stretchers. Medical crews and Mounties carried them to the ambulances parked with the emergency vehicles that jammed the clearing in front of the house. Their strobing lights painted the trees and buildings red. Radios scored the chaos as the two ambulances inched to the gate.

Their release from hell.

Jason saw more cars there, including an SUV with the call letters of a Cranbrook radio news station. A reporter, a young woman, was holding a microphone and trotting alongside a grim-faced cop.

The story was going to break worldwide.

Jason's ambulance gathered speed, its siren wailing. Behind them the pulsating lights of the scene faded like a dying heartbeat.

He thought of the bracelet.

Of Valerie.

And he struggled not to scream out her name.

71

In the immediate aftermath it didn't take long to tentatively identify the headless corpse Roy had come upon along the path.

It was Gideon Cull.

Investigators had checked his driver's license against his severed head, then run his fingerprints at the scene using a mobile scanner.

Then they set out to process the reverend. They removed his hood and saw a bearded white male in his late forties, about six feet tall, one hundred eighty pounds. He matched Cull's body type.

Lawrence Allan Haines of Seattle, according to his Washington State driver's license. But closer inspection and computer checks proved his license was fake, as were the two dozen others discovered in the house.

He had manipulated and deformed most of his prints.

His true identity was a mystery.

The investigators would run him through FBI and RCMP databases. Once they confirmed his identity, they could begin sorting out the case. How Cull came to be at the property and his links to the suspect were key starting points.

The expanded international task force now involved the Royal Canadian Mounted Police, the FBI, the Seattle PD, and police agencies in Washington and Oregon whose officers were en route, or in contact.

Early estimates put the total number of dead women at the site at eleven.

So far.

72

It took fourteen stitches to close the gash the reverend had made under Jason's jaw. He had first-degree burns on his chest, abrasions on his ankles and wrists. Time would diminish his scars, the doctor at the Cranbrook hospital told him.

A sedative put him out for a long time.

When he woke a nurse took him to a large meeting room where detectives were waiting to take his statement. Jason told them all he could and they shared a little of what they'd pieced together.

They'd confirmed the suspect's ID: Ezra Skeel, a U.S. citizen of no fixed address. A convicted felon for assaults against women. Skeel was finishing his time at Coyote Ridge in Connell, Washington, when he met Gideon. Cull was his spiritual adviser. It appeared that was where the two hooked up. The detectives had their theories, but the exact role Cull and Ezra played in the killings had yet to be substantiated. They still had plenty of work to do.

Hank Stralla from Sawridge County glanced around the table.

"One thing we're sure of, Jason," Stralla said, "is you connected a lot of the dots. Your reporting was critical. It helped end the killing. And you helped save Karen Harding's life."

Jason said nothing.

"The victim count on the property is now fifteen. We expect it will rise," Taylor said.

"How many have you identified?" Jason asked.

"Eight. Six women from the U.S., two from Canada."

Jason exhaled and his eyes stung as Taylor read the question in them.

"Nothing on a Valerie Hewitt. I'm sorry, Jason," Taylor said.

That evening, down the hall from Jason's hospital room, Karen Harding's sister had arrived with their parents. After long hugs and teary kisses, Marlene wiped Karen's cheeks.

"I just never gave up on you, kid," Marlene said.

Karen's mother and father were haggard and tanned. They brought balloons, flowers, and Karen's favorite treat, chocolate-covered almonds. They held her hands for much of the time.

"I prayed and prayed," Karen told them. "I made my peace because I believed I was going to die."

Her mother stroked Karen's hair. "God had other plans, sweetheart."

Later Karen went alone to Jason's room where he was sitting in a chair looking at the mountains. He turned to her and she smiled.

"I wanted to thank you for what you did. The police told me everything when I gave them my statement."

"I was just chasing a news story."

"You risked your life to save mine."

"So did Lisa Roy."

"Yes, I talked to her."

"Did Luke come with your family to see you?"

She shook her head.

"He wanted to." She touched her fingertips to the corners of her eyes. "I asked him to stay in Seattle. Marlene and Detective Stralla told me everything. I'm going to need time....To think about my life, you know."

Sure, he knew, he told her.

She kissed his cheek.

After Karen left, Jason resumed searching the mountains. It was pretty here. As the sun sank, he tried hard not to think of Valerie. But it was futile knowing what he knew. Every time his fingers brushed his bandages, it reminded him.

Did she suffer?

Ezra Skeel was demented. He made certain they all suffered.

Jason ran his hands over his face when the phone next to him rang. The nurses had said the hospital was screening calls from reporters. They were coming in from all over the world. He hesitated before he answered.

"Jason, is that you?"

"Yes."

"It's Ron Nestor."

"Ron." Jason's face brightened. "Man, I'm so glad you got that message. You were my only hope."

"I was at Safeco watching the game. Are you all right?"

"I think so."

"The wires have been moving updates. That's a helluva thing you did. A helluva thing. CNN and the others have gone live. We've sent an army up there. All hell's breaking on this. Are you sure you're all right?"

"I think I'm OK."

"It's really hit the fan here. Neena Swain has agreed to take an indefinite leave of absence. Largely because she let her politics interfere with her news judgment. I'm the new assistant managing editor and I'm offering you a full-time job with the *Mirror*, if you want it."

Jason said nothing.

"You've got every right to tell this paper to shove it. But Beale and I are hoping you'll say yes."

"I don't know. I've got a lot to think over in the next few days."

"Absolutely. Take your time."

Before hanging up, Jason agreed to give Nestor an interview over the phone, recounting his pursuit of Cull's link to Garrison, his doubts, his fears, and all that followed. Jason ended the call without telling him about the bracelet and Valerie.

73

Two boys on skateboards counted seventeen TV satellite trucks among the sixty news vehicles that overflowed the hospital parking lot for the press conference that took place there the next morning.

It was held outdoors in a corner of the lot where nets of cables snaked to humming generators. Karen and Jason were flanked by Canadian and U.S. police officials at a folding table that was heaped with microphones and cassette recorders as they faced TV lights and a shower of flashes from still news cameras.

Karen and Jason answered a few questions.

"I believe in my heart…" Karen paused. "I believe that in the wake of this evil thing that has happened, we cannot accept that these women died in vain."

As Jason summarized his pursuit of Cull, he saw Phil Tucker and Nate Hodge from the *Mirror*, then Carl McCormick from Spokane, and nodded subtly, signaling that he would talk privately to them later. Then the investigators read prepared statements that revealed little.

The body count had climbed to eighteen.

The conference wound down with the TV networks demanding that police allow news pools to tour the property and lift the restriction on the air above it so they could get aerial news footage.

Mounties were escorting Karen and Jason back into the hospital to be discharged when Jason stopped. He'd spotted his red Falcon in the lot, then his father. The two men embraced each other as cameras jostled to capture the moment.

"Hank Stralla called me," Jason's old man said. "I flew up so I could drive you home, Son."

Jason nodded, then hugged his dad again.

Very tight this time.

As they drove west along I-90, Jason thought his father looked better and stronger than he had in years. They said little during the drive, letting the vistas, the farmland, the rivers, and the rolling countryside serve as balm for Jason as he struggled to understand it all.

At one point, he turned to his old man, looked at him for a long moment, realizing so many parts of his father's life remained unknown to him.

"What happened to you when you were a rookie cop? Why did you leave the force?"

His old man considered the question for nearly a mile.

"Someday I'll tell you, but not now."

Jason turned to the window. Memories of Spokane, Kennewick, and Hanna Larssen's farm in the Rattlesnake Hills rushed by him before they were eclipsed by images of Garrison, and he revealed his fear about the bracelet and Valerie.

"They still can't confirm if she was there. I may never know."

His father listened thoughtfully, offering no opinion until they ascended the Cascade Range and Jason asked for his advice.

"You have to let it go, or it'll eat you up for years," he said. "Don't make the same mistakes I did, Son. Let it go and let time do the rest."

Jason looked off to the vast forest, thinking maybe he could bury his memories of Valerie and his mother there. He worked on it until they came to Seattle's outskirts and his mind shot back to when he'd first heard Karen Harding's name from Hank Stralla. How that night on the cop beat had led to this.

And how he had nearly given up.

It was time for the news. He switched on the radio.

The body count had risen to twenty.

74

The day after he returned to Seattle, Jason Wade decided that the only way he could cope with everything was to keep busy.

It would be therapeutic.

He drove his Falcon to the *Mirror* and accepted Ron Nestor's job offer. He was welcomed back to the newsroom with attaboys, backslapping, and handshakes from reporters and editors. But he sensed an uneasy reverence beneath their smiles in the way their eyes were drawn to his scars, satisfying their ingrained skepticism to confirm that his ordeal was true.

"There are no words." Ben Randolph shook his hand. "You're now an immortal in the business."

Astrid Grant's eyes were glistening when she handed him a single red rose.

"Thank God you're okay, Jason." She smiled. "My father knows some agents. So, if you're thinking of writing a book, I could make some calls."

Jason's new desk was among those along the glass wall of the newsroom's west side, overlooking Elliott Bay. The spot where he had dreamed of landing a job with the *Mirror.* Settling in, he was seized with memories of bracelets and the killing ground before letting them go.

"How you holding up?" Nestor asked.

"I think I'll be all right."

"Just concentrate on telling me your story. Go as long as you want. Leave nothing out."

The drone of the newsroom slipped away as Jason summoned up the images and emotions of his experience and for the next several days he worked on what would be a sixteen-thousand-word first-person exclusive.

The story of how a rookie reporter overcame the odds to track a monster who nearly killed him.

Investigators who found letters, diaries, and notebooks told Jason that Ezra Skeel and Gideon Cull were like brothers, two parts of a unified psychological force. They looked alike, thought alike, and shared a pathological hatred of women.

Ezra's resentment arose from his horrific upbringing. As Ezra's visiting spiritual adviser at Coyote Ridge, Cull, the intellectual, gave him articles with passages from the old book, *Reflections on the Ritual*. The small text was based on the diary of Xavier Veenza, a deranged monk and notorious executioner during the Inquisition.

Ezra loved it, using it as a how-to-guide to justify his vengeance against women.

Early in their relationship, Cull confided his problem with Bonnie Stillerman to Ezra. Cull had come close to going to prison himself because of a woman: his sinful, cheating ex-wife. He would not risk prison because a young witch named Bonnie Stillerman had failed to understand his sanctified sexual desires.

Upon his release from prison, Ezra conspired with Cull to emulate Veenza's work by first sentencing Bonnie Stillerman to death for her crime. But after their first kill, Cull grew uneasy and parted ways with Ezra Skeel.

Gideon Cull kept his past hidden behind his mask of respectability. But Ezra's rampage continued in the years that followed, escalating until it threatened to expose and destroy Cull, who rushed to Garrison to confront him.

Ezra was off the scale, out of control. He'd assumed the role of a reverend while believing he was Xavier Veenza, reincarnated from the days of the Inquisition. He was inspired by the book. It was where he took the mark Veenza burned into his victims: VOV.

Vincit Omnia Veritas.

Latin for Truth Conquers All Things.

For Ezra Skeel, women were in league with the devil and it was his duty to kill them. When he found copies of *Reflections on the Ritual*, he sent one to Cull, hoping he would rekindle "his righteous fire."

Ezra would at times imitate Cull's charity work to the point of buying an old RV from one of Cull's groups and using it to hunt prey. In his journal he wrote that Karen Harding happened to drift into his radar at the Big Timber Truck Stop the night of the storm. He'd noticed her *ichthus* bumper sticker, the fish symbol for Jesus. Ezra decided it was a deception and that Karen Harding was a witch.

Forensic experts probing the Garrison site for human remains now estimated that the body count would exceed thirty. Nine had not yet been identified. No confirmation that Valerie Hewitt was among them, the investigators told Jason.

But a growing fear writhed in his stomach.

His hands froze at the keyboard.

There was one secret about Valerie he could never reveal; could never tell a soul.

Jason hesitated, pushed it away, then moved from Valerie to the other difficult aspects of his article, concentrating on it until he was done.

His feature was syndicated in a six-part series and published in newspapers across the U.S. and around the world. A few days after the series ran, Nestor showed him congratulatory e-mails from friends at the *Washington Post* and the *New York Times*, urging the *Mirror* to submit the story for a Pulitzer Prize.

75

The horror at Garrison remained huge news in Seattle for weeks. From time to time Jason had called Stralla, Karen, and his father to talk. But he never unburdened his conscience.

Instead, he withdrew.

One night as he left the newsroom for his Falcon he heard the gulls on the waterfront. This time their cries floated along the bay breezes like an accusatory chorus. He drove off, taking Denny Way, glancing at the Needle and the skyline, rolling north until he came to the Aurora Avenue Bridge.

He couldn't take it anymore.

He parked and walked along the bridge. Stopping somewhere in the middle, he stared at the lights of Gas Works Park and the boats navigating the locks. There he confronted his demon, the secret he could never share with anyone. Like his father, he had driven away the woman he had loved.

Valerie.

They had fought because of him.

She had left because of him. He'd forced her out of

his life and though he tried to find her, tried to reach her to say he was sorry, he'd always failed. Not knowing where she was had eaten him up inside.

Now he knew and it haunted him.

He looked into the night.

Because of him, Valerie had somehow ended up in the Canadian Rockies like all of those other women.

He felt responsible for what had happened to her.

He struggled to hang on to his sanity as he battled the truth beckoning from the black water below. How could he live with himself? He searched long and hard for an answer that refused to emerge. He didn't know how much time had passed before he somehow found the will to get back into his Falcon and make his way to his apartment.

The stairs creaked as he trudged to the third floor, unlocked his door, and stepped into his living room. He went to his fridge, reached for the lone beer he kept there, then sat in the dark before his fish tank.

Fate was a cruel mother.

She had given him exactly what he'd wanted. He had ached for a job at the *Mirror*. He got it. He had dreamed of nailing the big story. He got it. He demanded to know what had happened to Valerie.

Now he knew.

And now he was condemned to live alone with his ghosts.

He sat in the dark pondering his beer and the bracelet Valerie had given him. Be careful what you wish for, he warned his fish. The images of his life consumed him and he raised his hand to his face.

Oh, Christ.

He struggled to force them from his mind until he was exhausted. His eyes grew heavy and he let whatever remaining thoughts he had carry him. He stayed that way for as long as he could until he sank into unconsciousness.

Then he heard ringing.

He worked through the awkward process of waking, realizing he had fallen asleep in his living room chair; that his phone was ringing and it was the middle of the goddamned night and who the hell was calling at this hour? He snapped up the receiver.

"What is it?"

"Jason? Jason, is that you?"

Her voice stunned him and he held his breath as long-distance static cracked in the silence. His eyes went around his empty apartment and he squeezed the phone so hard. So happily hard. He was not drunk. He was not dreaming. He knew this voice and the sound of it heaved a great weight from him.

"Valerie?"

"Yes! I read about what happened and oh, Jason, there's so much I need to tell you. I was so stupid and I miss you so much."

"Me too, I'm so sorry."

"I've thought about you every day. I'm in Paris, but I'm coming home. I want to come home and…"

They talked through the night as Jason watched his fish swim in the serene blue water.

AUTHOR'S NOTE
AND ACKNOWLEDGEMENTS

My thanks to my editor, Audrey LaFehr, for her work on this manuscript and bringing Jason Wade to life. My thanks to her colleagues at Kensington, my US publisher: Laurie Parkin, Steve Zacharius, Doug Mendini, Michaela Hamilton, Joan Schulhafer and so many others who played a role in the production and distribution of *The Dying Hour*.

My thanks for the help and support I've received from Mildred Marmur, Jeff Aghassi, John and Jeannine Rosenberg, Shannon Whyte, Donna Riddell, Beth Tindall, Therese Greenwood, the staff of *CrimeSpree* magazine and the Florida gang, who always save me a seat at Bouchercon. Thanks to Barbara, Laura, and Michael.

Thanks to John Helfers and Michael Connelly for including my short story in the Las Vegas anthology.

I would also like to thank my British publisher, MIRA UK, for their fantastic work. And I tip my hat to the crew at www.shotsmag.co.uk. As well, my thanks to my Toronto agent, Amy Moore-Benson, and my London agent, Lorella Belli.

To those of you whose expertise of sixteenth-century history exceeds mine, the texts referred to in *The Dying Hour* are all products of my imagination. Particularly, the fragments from the fictional title, *Reflections on the Ritual*. While I strived to remain true to the period and methods used around the time of the Inquisition, I hope you'll forgive any inaccuracies from the creative liberties I took.

I would like to offer a very special thanks to sales representatives, bookstore managers and booksellers I've gotten to know during recent years, who play a critical part in putting my work in your hands.

Which brings me to you, the reader. Thank you for your time. I hope you enjoyed the ride and that you'll be back for the next one.

Don't miss the next Jason Wade novel,

EVERY FEAR

Read on for an exclusive look at the first chapter.

CHAPTER 1

In the hour before sunrise, a blackbird slammed into Maria Colson's bedroom window, jolting her awake, its wings flapping in panic against the glass before it vanished.

She reached for Lee's side of the bed. He wasn't there. He'd gone out on a call around midnight. Something about a rig on I-5, up near Jackson Park. His whiskers had brushed her skin when he'd kissed her good-bye.

Maria considered the bird. It was crazy to worry Everything's fine, she assured herself, nestling in the middle of the bed. By the light of the dying moon she saw Dylan's crib across the hall. Maybe she should check on him. A bird hitting the house was an omen her grandmother had always feared. But Maria was so exhausted. She had been up every hour with Dylan and all night last night. She was too tired to be superstitious. Unease prodded her until at last she heard him stir and sighed with relief.

Everything was fine, just a crazy bird and a silly old wives' tale. Maria floated back to sleep but it was troubled. Her dreams were haunted by the anguish she and Lee had endured over the last few years, grotesque flashes of the painful times and her irrational fears of something bad lurking out there.

Stop. Never again. Please.

Mercifully, her subconscious guided her to her sanctuary. A Caribbean beach, the warm azure water caressing her toes, palm fronds swaying in the breeze. The sounds of a baby crying. A *baby*? Dylan was pulling her back to reality. She groaned awake.

"Oh honey. Just a few more minutes."

His crying intensified.

"All right, sweetie, I'm coming."

Stiff and tired, she dragged herself first to the bathroom, then downstairs to the kitchen, then back upstairs to Dylan's room. She took him into her arms. He was wet. She changed him, settled into her rocker, and fed him.

She kissed his fingers and his head.

Dylan was her miracle.

Because she'd injured her pelvis in her teens, the doctors had told her she would never be able to have children. But she had refused to believe them, refused to give up hope. She had begged God to let her have a baby, pleaded that if heaven allowed it, she would ask for nothing more.

And it happened.

After years of trying. Everyone was surprised.

Everyone but Maria.

She smiled at Dylan and rocked him gently, her heart aching with love for him, for Lee, for their life together. It was not perfect. The dark times had stained their marriage. The hard times had strained their bank account. But things were better now.

Lee was earning a little more at the shop. It had been a struggle, but with his overtime and bonus they were adjusting to the reduced income while she stayed home with Dylan. Deep down Maria knew that as long as they had each other, everything would work out.

The sun had risen.

Dylan had fallen asleep. She put him back in his crib, showered, dressed in faded jeans, a Mariners T-shirt, and white sneakers. The kitchen was a mess in the wake of the last few hectic days with Dylan. Lee had done his best to clean up. She'd take care of it today, she thought, getting herself orange juice, a banana muffin, and the morning paper.

She unfolded the *Seattle Mirror* and gasped.

The large, front-page photo showed a fireball from a series of delayed explosions after a tanker had rolled on I-5 at the city's northern edge.

Lee's tow truck was in the chaos.

The phone rang and her heart skipped a beat.

Upstairs, Dylan began to cry. She stared at the news picture, then at the ringing phone. Lee's truck glowed. She couldn't see him.

Oh no.

Her mind raced and she forced herself to answer.

"Hey babe, it's me," her husband said over the chaos of compressors and steel striking steel.

"Lee! Thank God, you're okay!"

"Why wouldn't I be?"

"I just saw the picture in the *Mirror*."

"Oh, that. Wild, huh? I had just pulled up. The driver thought his pup trailer was empty, but there was some sort of vapor lock. Nobody got hurt."

"I'm so glad."

"Yeah, not a scratch on my truck. I went right to the shop after we finished up at the scene. How's it going at the homestead?"

"It's been a strange night. A bird hit our window."

"What? Did it break the glass?"

"No. It was just odd."

"How's Dylan?"

"Cranky. Cried all night and he's crying again. We're out of milk and bread. I'll take him over to the store."

"Listen, Lou told me this morning that he's serious about selling the towing business. I figure that when you go back full-time at the supermarket we might be able to swing a small loan. This could be our chance. What do you think?"

A few seconds of silence passed.

"Maria?"

"We should talk about it later. I've got to get Dylan."

"Sure, give him a kiss for me. I love you."

"Love you too. Be careful."

After dressing Dylan, Maria said, "Let's go, kid, we're taking this show on the road."

A few minutes later, Dylan was murmuring softly in his stroller.

The Colson's small, two-story frame house was in Ballard, a sedate older neighborhood in northwest Seattle. Located near Salmon Bay and the Ballard Locks, its history reached back to the late 1800s as a community of shipbuilders, most of whom had come from Scandinavia.

It was safe here.

Maria loved the tranquility. Birdsong and breezes swept off Puget Sound through the maple, sycamore and willow trees. Two doors down, the

Stars and Stripes fluttered from the flagpole over the retired colonel's porch. He kept it so pretty, Maria thought, admiring the overflowing flower boxes.

Not much happened in the sleepy part of Ballard, except at the end of the street at the Lincoln place. The estate was renovating the big colonial house and there was an influx of strangers. A lot of contractors' trucks coming and going. They were doing a beautiful job.

At the corner, while crossing the street, Maria thought how weird it was with the bird, Lee at the wreck, the picture in the *Mirror*. Lee would tease her about her omen of doom.

Then he'd want to talk about buying Lou out.

And what was she going to tell him? While he dreamed of owning his towing shop, she dreamed of staying home and trying to have another baby. They would have to talk it over. "Take stock of our situation," Lee would say. Maria looked at Dylan. The motion was making him drowsy.

Several blocks later, by the time they had arrived at Kim's Corner Store, Dylan was sound asleep. Great, Maria thought.

Kim's had a narrow, pioneer-style storefront with large windows and a small, two-stair, step-up entrance.

Shannon, the teenage clerk with the captive-bead ring in her pierced eyebrow, was out front sweeping the sidewalk. Music leaked from the headset of her CD player as she bent over to coo at Dylan.

"Ahh. He's such a little angel."

"He's been a little devil keeping me up these last few nights," Maria said as she began maneuvering the stroller through the doorway. Dylan started to cry. "All right. All right."

She stopped, parked the stroller on the sidewalk next to the store window and picked him up. He cried harder, squirming in protest until she put him back down. Exhaustion rolled over her as she surrendered to the fact that Dylan wanted to sleep.

"You're killing me, kid."

Maria exhaled and Shannon slipped off her headset.

"You could leave him out here with me and let him sleep."

"That's so kind. Would you mind?"

"No problem."

"I just need to grab a few things, thanks so much."

Maria glanced up and down the street. Dylan would be fine outside with Shannon, just like the other times she'd left him with her. Maria was so tired and he'd been so demanding these past few days, she would relish these few moments of peace. The transom bells chimed.

Behind the counter Mrs. Kim smiled over the bifocals, her strong wrinkled fingers not losing a stitch of her needlepoint.

"Hello, Maria."

"Good morning, Mrs. Kim."

The worn wooden floorboards creaked as Maria headed to the back and the cooler. She heard a distant cell phone ringing. No other customers were in the store, it had to be Shannon's.

After selecting a carton of milk with the freshest date, Maria went to the bread shelf, glancing through the shoulder-high aisles to the front window. She could see the top of the stroller and Shannon talking outside on the phone. She looked upset.

Maria went to Mrs. Kim at the front counter to

pay. She set the milk and bread down, snapped open her wallet and checked the sidewalk.

"Baby's sleeping?" Mrs. Kim nodded pleasantly.

"Yes, he's been a fusspot for the last two days."

The transom bells jingled. Shannon strode to the rear of the store, phone pressed to her head, submerged in conversation. "That's *so not true* and I've got her letter in my bag. I'm getting it – "

Maria checked on Dylan's stroller, so close to her on the other side of the glass she could practically touch him. He was fine and she'd be finished in a few seconds.

As the register clicked, Maria noticed the revolving rack of the latest paperbacks near the counter, unaware of the large shadow that floated by out front. She needed a new book to read. A suspense thriller. Maybe she'd take Dylan to the park. The rack squeaked as she inventoried the titles. Catching something in her periphery, she looked up at Mrs. Kim, who was looking outside. The woman's face was all wrong, contorted as her jaw worked but formed no words. Maria followed her attention to the street. Her heart slammed in her ribs.

Dylan's stroller had vanished.

In less than a second, part of Maria's brain screamed at her circuits to form the cognitive command to react. Her body spasmed and a deafening roar split her ears.

Adrenaline propelled her to the street. All of her senses were pushed to superhuman levels as she saw Dylan's stroller, rolling, toppling over the curb; saw the flash of his soft cotton blanket; heard the thud of a strange van's door, the growl of its engine; felt her hand on metal, felt her fingers grip a handle, a mirror, as the van began pulling away.

Maria threw herself onto the hood of the moving van and pounded on its windshield. She glimpsed fingers clenching Dylan's blanket, glimpsed his tiny arm, his hand, heard his screams blend with hers as she tried in vain to claw through the glass.

The van lurched, bucked, its motor snarling, brakes screeching until the world jerked to its side and the street flew up with a flash of brilliant light and pulled Maria to the ground. Through a galaxy of shooting stars she saw the van disappearing, Dylan's stroller on its side, its wheels spinning as warm blood webbed over her flickering eyes.

The last things Maria remembered were Dylan's sweet breath, Lee's whiskered kiss good-bye and the blackbird that hit her window.

© Rick Mofina 2006

EVERY FEAR *by Rick Mofina*
Available April 2010